THE SEA BREAK

When Lt. Commander Widmark, D.S.C., R.N.V.R., seizes a German motor vessel from the neutral port of Lourenço Marques, he is flouting not only Admiralty orders but the Geneva convention.

But Widmark is a man with an obsession—a vicious hatred of the enemy. In his view, the rough and bloody business of war is a game which only the ruthless can win . . .

D1334669

ANTONY TREW

The Sea Break

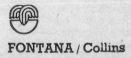

FONTANA / Collins

First published by Wm. Collins 1966
First issued in Fontana Books 1971
Second Impression August 1973

© Antony Trew, 1966

Printed in Great Britain
Collins Clear-Type Press London and Glasgow

'Sir Francis Drake to Sir Francis Walsingham, after Cadiz 17th May, 1587:

There must be a beginning to any great matter, but the continuing of the same unto the end until it be thoroughly finished yields the true glory.'

The last entry in the diary of Lieutenant-Commander Stephen Widmark, D.S.C. and Bar.

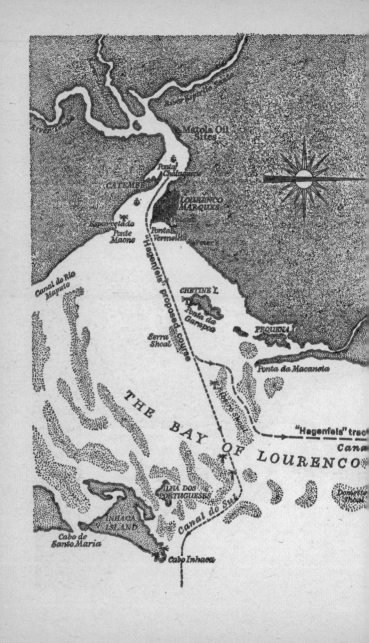

River Espirito Santo

Matola Oil Sites

Ponta Chaluquene

CATEMBE

LOURENÇO MARQUES

Reparcelado
Ponte Maone

Ponta Vermelha

"Hagenfels", proposed course

Canal do Rio Maputo

CHETINE I.

Ponta da Ciampos

Serra Shoal

PEQUENA

Ponta da Macaneta

THE BAY OF LOURENÇO

"Hagenfels" track

Canal

ILHA DOS PORTUGUESES

Domestic Shoal

INHACA ISLAND

Canal do Sul

Cabo de Santo Maria

Cabo Inhaca

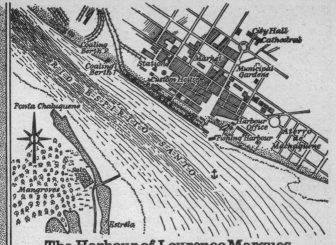

Coaling Berth 2
Coaling Berth 1
Ponta Chaluquene
Station
Custom House
Market
City Hall
Cathedral
Municipal
Gardens
Harbour
Office
Fishing Harbour
Aterro
de
Mahalguene
Mangroves
Salt
Estrèla

RED ESPIRITO SANTO

The Harbour of Lourenco Marques

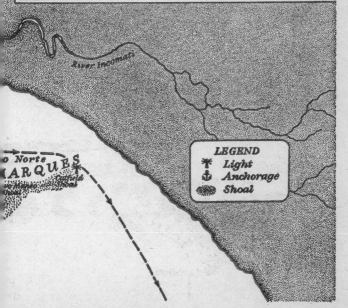

River Incomati

o Norte
MARQUES
o Manlo
Catfield
Shoal

LEGEND
* Light
⚓ Anchorage
🐚 Shoal

There were German ships in Lourenço Marques during the Second World War and one of them, the *Uhenfels*, did break out in 1939; but this ship and her crew should under no circumstances be confused with the *Hagenfels* and her crew which are entirely figments of the author's imagination, as are all the incidents in the book and all its characters whether they be German, Portuguese, Greek, British, South African or any other nationality. The entire story of the break out of the *Hagenfels*, what led up to it and its sequel, are pure fiction. If there is the slightest resemblance between any person dead or living and the characters in the book, that is entirely due to the long arm of coincidence.

The Background to the Hagenfels Affair

World War II had few better kept naval secrets than the circumstances surrounding the break out from Lourenço Marques in November, 1942, of the German freighter *Hagenfels*. To this day no official account of the incident has been published, nor was there any reference to it at the time other than a brief naval communiqué. Constituting as it did a flagrant breach of Portuguese neutrality by armed forces of the British, the *Hagenfels* affair created a delicate situation between Britain and Portugal although it was carried out as a private venture without the authority of the Admiralty.

For some time, the Wilhelmstrasse's denials notwithstanding, the Portuguese Government believed that the break out was a German operation, but as time went on and evidence accumulated it became clear that the ship had been under British command.

It was fortunate for British diplomacy that the affair ended as it did and that the principal witnesses were not, while the war lasted, available to the Portuguese. Although the operation was well conceived and skilfully executed the Navy claimed no credit for it, maintaining an uncompromising silence which no amount of inquiry has been able to break. But all this happened a long time ago since when some of those concerned on both sides have talked, and with the aid of Lieutenant-Commander Widmark's diary it has been possible to piece together the story. In particular David Rohrbach, now working on a kibbutz in Palestine, and Johan le Roux, a farmer in the Western Transvaal, have provided useful information. On the German side Captain Kurt Lindemann, living in retirement in Westphalia, has been equally helpful.

In considering the conduct of Lieutenant-Commander Widmark, the prime mover in this unusual affair, it is as well to have some knowledge of his background. The only child of a wealthy Cape family, he read law at Cambridge and on his return to South Africa entered his father's legal practice in Cape Town. He showed little enthusiasm for the law, however, his real interests being yachting and the RNVR. He collected naval books, built up a useful naval library, and became a minor authority on Nelson, whose tactics and strategy he had closely studied.

In 1937, with two friends, he sailed the ketch *Albatross* from Cape Town to the West Indies and thence through the Panama Canal to San Francisco, where he sold her, he and his crew returning to the Cape by way of England. This voyage established Widmark as a man of considerable determination and a resourceful seaman. Reserved, with a dry sense of humour, his close friends knew him to be both responsive and sensitive.

When war broke out he was a lieutenant in the Cape Town Division of the RNVR (SA) and was soon in command of a mine-sweeping trawler based on Simonstown. Later he graduated to an anti-submarine trawler. At the end of 1940 he was given command of the Antarctic whaler *Nordhval*, then fitting out in Durban as an anti-submarine escort vessel. He took her to the Eastern Mediterranean, arriving in Alexandria in April, 1941.

A month later she was ordered to Suda Bay to assist in the evacuation of the army from Crete, that operation having reached a critical phase.

Three days after her arrival in Crete, *Nordhval* was dive-bombed and sunk in the Kasos Strait in the early hours of the morning while escorting a small merchant vessel. The destroyer *Vibrant* was soon on the scene and although burdened with some six hundred Australian troops, she picked up the *Nordhval*'s survivors.

Later in the morning she herself was attacked by dive-bombers, sinking shortly before 11 a.m. Widmark then found himself on a Carley float with fifteen other men, one of whom was his first lieutenant, Richard Olafsen, an old friend from RNVR Cape Town days. Towards noon a number of low flying Messerschmitts made systematic runs over the area, machine-gunning the men in the water. Widmark saw most of the men on his float killed or wounded, including Olafsen, who died in his arms. At nightfall the destroyer *Whiteside* arrived and picked up those who had survived, among them Widmark.

On his return to Alexandria he was sent to Cairo on survivor's leave. This over he was given command of the A/S whaler *Southern Berg*, a more modern vessel than the

Nordhval, attached to the Inshore Squadron for escort duties on the Libyan coast.

Early in July he arrived back in Alexandria in *Southern Berg* to learn that his mother had been lost when the ship in which she was returning to South Africa had been torpedoed in a gale by a U-boat south of Madeira. There were no survivors.

Those close to him saw a marked change in Stephen Widmark at this time. He became cold and withdrawn and it was evident that his mother's death, and the manner of it, following so closely on the incident in the Kasos Strait, had affected him profoundly.

On 7th August, soon after dawn, *Southern Berg*, bound from Alexandria to Tobruk escorting the water-carrier *Tidewater*, obtained a promising asdic contact off Mersa Matruh. The contact was classified as 'submarine' and Widmark took his ship into the attack. After a thirty-five minute hunt during which he dropped five patterns of depth charges, he forced a U-boat to the surface and there attacked it with gunfire. The U-boat's crew abandoned ship and there were many men, including wounded, in the water when the submarine sank. It was a fine day with a calm sea but Widmark made no attempt to pick up survivors, leaving the scene at high speed and later rejoining *Tidewater*.

On his return to Alexandria he was criticised for failing to pick up survivors, but defended his action on the grounds that he had sighted the periscope of another U-boat and had at once proceeded to the north-west to attack it. Failing to make asdic contact, he said he had felt it his duty to return to *Tidewater*. It is significant that he did not make a sighting report at the time, nor did he mention the periscope to anyone on the bridge of *Southern Berg*. For his action in destroying the U-boat he received a bar to the DSC which he had earned at Suda Bay for taking off survivors from an Admiralty tanker while under enemy air attack.

A month later he was again in the news. The convoy he was escorting was attacked by enemy aircraft off Ras Azzaz and an old ship, *The Maid of Kilkenny*, carrying some seven hundred German prisoners of war, was hit and sunk. *Southern Berg*, steaming at full speed and zigzagging, engaged the enemy aircraft and while doing so twice steamed

11

through clusters of German POW in the water, killing and drowning many of them.

The Senior Officer of the escort in the AA sloop *Peregrine* signalled *Southern Berg*: *Keep clear of men in water.* Somewhat ambiguously, Widmark replied: *I am engaging the enemy more closely in defence of the convoy.*

On his return to Alexandria he was sent for by the Chief of Staff. What took place at their interview is not known, but a few days later Widmark was relieved of his command and returned to South Africa five months before the completion of his normal tour of duty. It was these incidents which earned him the nickname 'The Butcher.' It was known to his associates that he resented the nickname and felt he had been the victim of a grave injustice. On reaching Cape Town he was promoted to lieutenant-commander and was placed on the staff of the Director of the SA Naval Forces, whom he later represented in the Combined Operations Room at Naval Headquarters. He made no secret of his resentment at being assigned to what he regarded as a non-combatant rôle. It was while engaged on these duties that he conceived and planned the capture of the *Hagenfels*.

So much for the background. To what extent its events played a part in shaping Widmark's determination to embark upon the operation remains a matter for conjecture, but it seems likely that they had disturbed the balance of his mind and that his dislike for Germans had become psychopathic. It is evident from his diary that he brooded long and deeply over the decision he had made, for he foresaw it would endanger many lives and the cause to which he was devoted.

A final word in his defence. He has been much criticised among other things for involving women in the *Hagenfels* affair, only one of whom had any complicity in it. It is clear, however, that once the operation had been launched he could not have put any of the women ashore without hazarding its outcome and, perhaps more important, without destroying the impression he had so carefully created that the break out was a German venture.

During World War II the Polana enjoyed an international and somewhat raffish reputation because with Portugal neutral, secret agents of both the Allies and the Axis Powers were able to indulge in espionage and counter-espionage in Lourenço Marques just as they did in Lisbon. The spies of both sides naturally made the seaport's luxury hotel their stamping ground.

South African, British, American, German and Italian intelligence officers used to bow gravely to each other in the lush public rooms and in the bar of the Polana.

The Sunday Times of Johannesburg
5th January, 1964

Chapter One

The grey Buick drew away from the shade of the jacarandas
in front of the Union frontier post at Komatipoort, went
out through the gates opened by an African policeman and
moved slowly over the small no-man's-land to the Portuguese post at Ressano Garcia; there it stopped outside a
brick building with a red-tiled roof which shimmered in
the midday sun.

Stephen Widmark got out and stretched. 'God! I'm stiff
and hot!' He took a linen jacket from the back seat and
slung it over his arm, then, methodically, he gathered up
the camera, binoculars and sunglasses. McFadden came
from the far side of the car carrying the brief-case with the
passports and other travel documents. Their faces were
streaked with dust and perspiration and they looked as if
they'd come a long way, but McFadden's eyes were still
bright.

'What I cuid do to a beer is nobody's business, Steve
boy!'

'There's a roadhouse at the Matola Bridge. Won't be
long now, Chiefy.'

As they walked up the steps to the screen door, a car
came in from the Mozambique road and parked on the
far side of the building.

There was nobody but an immigration official in the
room they entered.

Widmark put the camera and the binoculars on the
counter. 'Pretty quiet,' he said. 'When I came through here
last, there were about ten cars waiting.'

'No petrol rationing then, laddie.'

They showed their passports to the Portuguese official
and filled in his forms and then went out along the veranda
to the customs room. When they had finished with the
clerk there and were turning to leave, the screen-door
opened and a man came in, as dusty as they were. Tall and
sunburnt, he had blond hair and, unexpectedly because he
was so fair, brown eyes. On his left cheek-bone, neat and
symmetrical, were two small scars. He stood aside as the

15

others passed and, speaking Portuguese, greeted the clerk, who seemed to know him. For a moment Widmark's eyes met the tall man's and he was aware of a flicker of recognition. Then he and McFadden had left the room and were walking back to the Buick. On the other side of the driveway they saw a beige Chevrolet with Lourenço Marques number-plates.

They drove through the far gates, handed the customs clearance slip to the African policeman and accelerated down the gravel road which led through bushveld and over the Lebombos to Lourenço Marques.

'See that chap who came into the customs office as we left, Chiefy?'

'The tall man?'

'Yes. Notice anything odd about him?'

'Can't say I did, really.'

'Didn't you see the duelling scars? Left cheek?'

'Aye. I saw them. Could've been from an accident, Steve.'

Widmark shook his head emphatically. 'Not those scars. That was a Hun, Chiefy, even if he can speak Portuguese.'

'Ah, weel. There's plenty of Jerries in Lourenço Marques by all accounts.'

'Tell you something else. Whoever he is, we've met before. There's something unpleasantly familiar about him. Can't place him, but I'm pretty certain he recognised me. Saw it in his eyes as we passed.'

'Well,' said McFadden philosophically, 'there's no law against you and me taking a wee journey to LM. I wouldn't fash myself about a stranger.'

Widmark frowned. 'If he is a stranger.'

They drove on in silence, Widmark trying to place the tall man, wondering where he'd seen him before. If he were a German he couldn't enter the Union. What was he doing at the frontier post? His thoughts were interrupted by McFadden's chuckle. 'I could'a wet maself when that African policeman looked behind the back seat.'

'I never had a moment's worry about *that*, Chiefy. After this ruddy war's over we're going into the smuggling business. McFadden and Widmark—proprietary limited. Smugglers and Over-the-Border Requisites.'

For a long time after that Widmark was silent, and McFadden knew him too well to try and force the pace.

Many miles on Widmark said, apropos of nothing. 'I suppose you realise what this means, Chiefy?'

'What's that, Steve boy?' McFadden looked sideways at the sombre face, the eyes staring ahead, the emphatically shut mouth.

'This job. You realise it means we meet these bastards face to face.' He said it with an intensity of feeling the Scot couldn't understand. The enemy was something abstract. It was *the other side*. Something he thought of as dangerous, unpleasant, to be respected, feared, and in those brief moments of combat which were war, something he tried indirectly, by doing his particular job, to destroy.

Widmark went on. 'Face to face. I've been wanting that for a long time.'

At the Matola Bridge they sat on the veranda of the road-house and ate bread rolls with goat's milk cheese and olives, and drank a glass of white wine. When they reached Lourenço Marques, Widmark dropped the Scot and his suitcase near the railway station on the Praça McMahon, where McFadden took a taxi to the Cardoso Hotel. He knew that Rohrbach and Johan le Roux were already there but he would not recognise them, nor they him, for they were to be complete strangers. Widmark drove on to the Polana. The Newt would be there but they, too, would be strangers. There were many advantages in concentrating their force in small groups in three hotels, and that was why Michael Kent and Hans le Roux, when they arrived by train that day, had booked in at the Hotel Clube near the Vasco da Gama gardens on the Avenida Aquiar. To the hotel staff and its residents, these were two young South Africans holidaying in Lourenço Marques: very welcome at that time of year, outside the normal tourist season, because visitors from the Union were by no means plentiful after three years of the Second World War.

Widmark dined late that night, at a table in the shadows on the veranda, alone, remote, absorbed in his thoughts. They took him back to the ante-room outside the Chief of Staff's office in Cape Town—it had really begun there. He sighed. They had come a long way since.

Chapter Two

Although the third-officer Wren appeared to be busy she was watching the man in the wicker chair, and he was aware of it. She thought, so this is him. Saturnine, high cheekbones, dark hair. She'd liked his voice when he came in and announced himself. But so serious? No smile in the cold, withdrawn eyes, his manner quite impersonal as if he were talking to a machine? She'd heard a good deal about him. Who hadn't? Thirty, lots of money . . . with cool, feminine, calculation she awarded that a high priority . . . a bachelor, unattached; there was plenty of gossip about him but none involving women. It was the other business.

But he didn't look like that.

She remembered the stories she'd heard, looked at him again and tried to imagine him doing those things. Were they true? She watched the delicate hands, the long tapering fingers holding the *Naval Review*, the well-proportioned head and aesthetic face. He's like somebody I know, she thought and worried about that, trying to place him. Laurence Olivier! That was it! Rather harder, not so good-looking, but Laurence Olivier, nevertheless. I wonder if he's noticed me, she thought. I'm not bad looking. The others all do. Is it an act? Concentrating on that magazine?

She said: 'Lovely day, sir, isn't it?'

'Is it?' He turned a page without looking up.

Loves himself, she thought, and realised he'd made it difficult for her to go on.

He put the magazine down. 'I said, "is it?" '

'I heard you.'

'Well, *is it*?'

'Oh, for heaven's sake! What sort of game is this?'

'I'm curious, that's all. Haven't seen the day. Just come up from the ops room. Been there since four this morning.'

Blast it! she thought. Now I've been rude. The buzzer sounded and she picked up the phone.

'Aye, aye, sir.'

'He'll see you now.' She smiled as she put the phone

down, trying to make amends.

They went down a passage to a door labelled 'Chief of Staff.' She knocked and led him in.

'Lieutenant-Commander Widmark, sir.'

The Commodore was tall, angular and red-bearded, with friendly eyes. 'Thank you.' He waved her away. He was a new arrival on the station, and hadn't in his five days in Cape Town yet met his visitor. He was surprised at what he saw. Somehow he'd not expected him to look like this; he should have been bigger, older, coarser. Not this slight young man of medium height looking at him with dark uncertain eyes.

Somewhere in the Commodore a conditioned reflex registered approval of the blue and white ribbon with its silver rosette, and through long habit one part of his mind signalled to another: *DSC and bar. Good man.* He held out his hand and smiled. 'I've heard a lot about you.'

As soon as he'd said it he was sorry, because the younger man flushed and looked away, and the Commodore felt his embarrassment as if it were his own.

'Sit down, Widmark.' He pushed a silver cigarette box towards him.

Widmark shook his head. 'No thank you, sir.' Since he smoked heavily he didn't really know why he'd refused. Probably to put the Commodore at some sort of disadvantage, but if so it didn't succeed for that officer lit his cigarette with a flourish. 'Sensible chap! Now tell me, Widmark, why've you come to see me?'

'About an operation, sir. Something I've been working on privately and unofficially with some brother officers.'

'What is it?'

'A proposal to take a German merchantman as prize.'

'There aren't any at sea, Widmark. Only a few raiders and supply vessels and we're hunting them hard.'

Widmark leant forward, his hands clasped together on the desk. 'This one's not at sea, sir. She's in harbour.'

The Commodore leant back in his chair. 'I'm not with you, I'm afraid. Which harbour?'

'Lourenço Marques, sir.'

'You don't mean one of those German merchant ships which've been there since the show started?'

Widmark nodded. 'Yes, sir.'

'My dear chap, we can't stage a naval operation in a

19

neutral port. Good heavens! We'd breach half a dozen Geneva Conventions. Lose the privileges of Portgual's neutrality. Offend our oldest allies. The very thought would give Their Lordships the twitch.' He quickly amended that; one didn't joke with subordinates about Their Lordships. 'I mean the Admiralty just wouldn't wear it, and quite right too.'

Widmark had expected this. Now he waited, timing his pause, the Commodore watching him, puzzled at his silence. At last he said: 'The way we've got it planned it won't do all those things, sir.'

'What d'you mean?'

'Well, it won't be a British naval operation. At least not *officially*. It won't be a naval operation at all. As far as the Portuguese are concerned it will be a German effort. A break out by a German freighter under orders from the German Admiralty to make a run for it. Like the *Uhenfels*'s bolt from Lourenço Marques in October '39.'

'That was early on. We weren't properly organised.' The Commodore was on the defensive.

Widmark's dark eyes never wavered. This was what he'd wanted. Now he'd press home his point. 'Like the *Tannenfels*'s break out from Kismayu last year, sir.'

That registered. The Commodore looked at the ceiling and then out of the window. This young man was being difficult.

'That *was* a bad show. We should've got her. She's one of their most successful raider supply vessels now. In fact she's a first-class headache.' He lifted his shoulders in a small shrug of disapproval.

'I know, sir. And it can happen again. Naval Intelligence's latest reports from Lourenço Marques mention rumours that the *Hagenfels* is standing by for a break out.'

The Commodore tapped his teeth with his fingers but Widmark was not to know that this was a sign of irritation. 'We're ready for that. She won't get far. *If* they're foolish enough to try.'

'Of course, sir. We'll intercept, Jerry'll scuttle, and seven or eight thousand tons of seventeen knot freighter which we badly need will go to the bottom. Under my plan we'll *get the ship*. There won't be any scuttle. But we'll get a lot more than that.'

The Commodore sat back. This young man was being

tiresome but he'd have to listen to his story. 'Right! I'll buy it. Go ahead!'

Carefully, precisely, pausing for effect at times, Widmark explained 'Operation Break Out.' When he'd finished, the Commodore's smile was somewhere between admiration and annoyance.

'It's a clever scheme. If nothing went wrong it would be a winner. But in war there are too many imponderables, Widmark. It's certain that something will go wrong. It always does. And when it did with this one, the fat'd be in the fire. The last thing we want is an infringement of Portuguese neutrality. We've got enough problems already. Why manufacture a teaser like this for the sake of one German freighter?'

Widmark realised that the interview was all but over. This was the usual blank wall of officialdom. He began to withdraw behind a cloak of frustration and disappointment. 'It's much more than that,' but he said it without conviction and the knowledge that he was capitulating made him tired and dispirited. The plan *wouldn't* go wrong. The detail had been too carefully worked out. It was bound to work. The Chief of Staff was hide-bound. It was this 'play the game, you chaps' attitude which could lose the war. The other side didn't bother about playing the game; technical infringements of somebody or other's neutrality, Geneva Conventions, didn't worry them. They did what they could get away with, ruthlessly and efficiently. You couldn't win wars if you insisted on keeping to rules. There were no rules in this one. It was the tooth and claw of the jungle. You killed or were killed. It was as simple as that. The Commodore and those he represented didn't seem to understand that.

'Is that all, sir?' He had become cold and remote, anxious now to be gone, to end this discussion which was leading nowhere.

The Commodore opened a drawer and shuffled some papers. His head came up and he looked blankly in Widmark's direction.

'What's that? H'm, yes. I'll put it up to C-in-C. He's away in Freetown just now. Don't think it has a hope of his approval, but we'll try. With luck there'll be a reply within twenty-four hours.'

Widmark was careful not to show surprise, and he didn't

smile; indeed he rarely did, but the bleak look left his eyes. 'Thank you, sir. It's very good of you.' He meant that.

He got up to go.

'One moment, Widmark. What's the security like on this? These brother pirates of yours? Will they keep their mouths shut?'

'I can assure you,' said Widmark, cold and withdrawn again because he felt the remark was unnecessary, 'that they will, sir.'

'Good. It wouldn't help us if the Portuguese ever got to know.' He thought for a moment. 'Have you discussed this with your boss—Director, SA Naval Forces?'

'No, sir. It's outside his authority. I knew it would need C-in-C's approval. No point in worrying the Director at this stage.'

'I see. One other thing. How many men would be necessary and who would lead the party?'

'Seven, sir. And I would.'

This time the Commodore's smile was uncomplicated. 'Never really had any doubt about that last part, but thought I better ask. C-in-C would want to know.'

There wasn't a reply within twenty-four hours. It came two days later, chilly and unequivocal. The Commander-in-Chief rejected 'Operation Break Out' and ordered that any record of the proposal be destroyed and the matter never again discussed. The signal bristled with displeasure, and so did the Commodore who felt that he'd been caught in the line of fire. All this he made clear to Widmark. He was to tell his brother officers, said the Commodore, that if they so much as uttered a whimper about 'Operation Break Out' they'd be in trouble.

Widmark left in a misery of disappointment and frustration. As he went through the anteroom the third officer Wren thought she'd try again.

'Lovely day, isn't it, sir?'

'I think it *stinks*!' he said.

As the door swung to behind him she made a face.

'Love yourself, don't you?'

Back in his flat in Orangezicht, Widmark slammed doors, threw his uniform cap into the corner, and with rough, exaggerated gestures of annoyance changed into a dressing-gown.

His mind clouded by anger, he lay on the studio couch looking through the open windows to the slopes reaching up to Lion's Head: to the fresh green of the oaks, the blue-grey of the pines, tall and leaning to the north-west in old protest against the south-easter. Lower down the trees gave way to heath and the brown scars of quarries; below that the fringes of the Malay quarter, yellow ochres, burnt pinks and browns, the houses clustered about steep streets. High above, flanks of basalt rock gleamed in the sunlight, the primordial ramparts of Lion's Head. Huge agglomerations of cloud, pluvial and forbidding, rolled in across the Cape Flats, their shadows preceding them, dark blankets spreading across the town, up the slopes of Signal Hill and beyond, reaching into the sea, turning its blues to metallic greys.

Widmark's mind was a dark storm, the wind of frustration fanning seas of rebellion, and that reckless mood he knew so well, always feared but could never control, was taking charge. What right had the C-in-C, three thousand miles away in Freetown, to scotch this plan so carefully thought out, so meticulously built up over the last two months? When the Commodore said, 'I'll put it up to C-in-C,' it seemed as if things were really on the move, that all the hard work was to be rewarded. Unless he'd felt there was something in the plan, that it had a reasonable chance of success, the Commodore would never have said that. So he *had* seen that it had more than a chance of success. Why then had it been turned down? Because it meant taking a chance? Not if it were just a naval chance: the Navy had always taken those. Was it the political chance? It had taken the C-in-C forty-eight hours to answer the signal. Why? Because it had been put to Downing Street, to the War Cabinet? The politicians? They'd turned it down! He became certain of that. And why? Because there was just the slightest chance that something might go wrong. That Portuguese neutrality might be infringed. So what! To blazes with Portuguese neutrality. Britain was at war. The whole bloody world was at war. Fighting for what? Not for any high-fangled ideals. Not for the freedom of Poland. Not for 'our way of life,' whatever that meant. Just for plain bloody survival, that was all. And they turned down a first-class operation and the offer of an eight thousand ton, seventeen knot freighter handed to them on a plate and more than that. *Much more!* The opportunity of hitting the Hun where he thought he was safe. Giving his morale the kick in the backside it so badly needed. That was the real thing. The main object of the exercise. If his ships weren't safe in Lourenço Marques, then they weren't safe in Rio, or Montevideo or Buenos Aires or in a dozen other neutral ports. So they'd have to make a run for it. Some might get through the blockade, but most wouldn't. Even politicians ought to be able to see that.

Slowly Widmark's thoughts changed and he got up and stood at the window looking out towards Robben Island. The clouds were building up, seven tenths now, and most of the sea was dark and forbidding. But it drew him. It was the element on which the best and worst moments of his life had been spent, and there was not a day on which he didn't long for a ship again. But they'd put him on the staff. It was their idea of humour. We can't prove anything against Widmark but we've got to teach him a lesson. He's got to learn to play the game according to the rules. So what'll we do with him? We'll put him on the staff. In the Combined Operations Room at Cape Town. That's pretty far from the struggle.

Let him sweat it out there, and when he sees signals coming in from ships that have been torpedoed, from hunting and escort groups that are groping for their attackers, and from cruisers that are playing hide-and-seek with surface raiders, it'll remind him that he's not there, and he'll have to make do with watching pretty girls in uniform push coloured pins into a plot. That's as near to the fight as he'll get.

And when signals come in reporting lost contacts, and fruitless searches and sweeps, and waterlogged lifeboats without survivors, and his nerves jangle with the iron of frustration, then he'll have time to reflect that it pays to play the game.

Now he was back on the couch, staring at the wall, his fists so tightly clenched that the fingernails bit into his palms. He knew where his thoughts were shifting to, the Kasos Strait, and he tried to stop them but couldn't. He saw once again the green froth, flecked with blood, oozing from Dickie Olafsen's mouth, the protruding tongue, dry and swollen, the glazed grey eyes frightened.

'Jesus! My guts!' Dickie had mumbled, knowing that he

was dying, his blood-spattered hands clawing at his entrails, trying to push them back into his stomach. And there had been the smell of fæces and blood, warm and sickening.

Widmark sat up on the edge of the couch, his face in his hands. 'God!' he muttered. 'Why did he have to die like that?' Then he lay back on the couch and curled up against the wall, and for a long time he struggled with his thoughts. When he got up he took a bottle of whisky from the cupboard under the desk, poured a stiff tot, added some water and drank it. Feeling better he changed into grey flannels and a sports coat and went down to the car.

He drove fast out over Kloof Nek, keeping to the high road at first, then dropping down to the sea and following the coastline, the mountains on his left and below him the rocks, beaches and surf of the South Atlantic. He could never do this drive often enough. Like the Grande Corniche, but fresher, less sophisticated. Camps Bay, Bakoven, Llandudno, passed quickly and now he was clear of the built-up area.

The roar of the wind in his ears, the power and thrust of the car, were sedatives and his mind cleared and he forgot the dull pain in his head. Up over Hout Bay Nek the proteas were blooming and the heath glistened after the rain. As the car passed over the Nek he made his decision, deliberately and with a clear appreciation of the consequences. And having done so, he knew, knowing himself, that it was final and that for better or worse he was committed. But now all doubt was gone and he felt better. Not only had he made the decision, but he had justified it to himself. That made him feel much better.

They arrived at the flat soon after nine, coming in out of the dark of a wet gusty night. Andrew McFadden first, and that was right because he was closest of them all to Stephen Widmark. He was a small high-complexioned Scot with narrow eyes that glinted fiercely or merrily according to his mood, and tousled sandy hair. He had been with Widmark since the war started and had been his engineer officer in *Southern Berg*. Now an engineer lieutenant on the staff at the Minesweeping Depot in Cape Town, a job he found boring and irksome, he longed for some break in the monotony of his daily routine. It was to him that Widmark had first confided the plans for 'Operation Break Out,' and no one more ardently supported them than McFadden. Early on Widmark had cautioned him: 'I don't think this is for you, Chiefy. You're a bit long in the tooth, and you've a wife and three children.'

McFadden's eyes had glinted. 'She'll be glad to see the last of me. Hangin' around the house. It's no place for a fightin' mon.' But Widmark had always counted on him. He needed a marine engineer with good diesel experience, a man he could trust absolutely. McFadden had done twelve years in diesel tankers before settling down in Durban as an industrial salesman on the staff of an oil company; he was tough, determined, and reticent—made for the task Widmark had in mind.

Soon afterwards the door opened and a slight sallow young man with sad, spaniel's eyes and a dark beard came in. He wore the uniform of a lieutenant, with the red patch of the South African Navy over the executive curl.

'Hallo, David!' Widmark pointed to a chair. 'Take a pew.'

The young man looked round nervously. 'Johan not here?' David Rohrbach's clever sensitive face gave a misleading impression of apprehension. He and Widmark had first met in Haifa in 1941 when Rohrbach was in magnetic mine-sweepers, and the friendship had grown when they re-met in Cape Town. Rohrbach had taken electrical engineering at Munich, where his family had a cable factory. But the Rohrbachs were Jews and in 1938 he had left the university and with his mother fled to South Africa. His father, two sisters and a brother, if they survived, were still in Germany. It was due to these circumstances among others that Widmark had chosen him. Rohrbach's intense anti-German feeling, his intelligence, eagerness for action and absolute dependability were important factors. But there was another, more vital: German was his mother tongue.

Widmark was pouring them a drink when there was a knock on the door, and a large bearded young man came in. Johan le Roux looked what he was: good natured and enormously athletic. He had taken an undistinguished BA at the Witwatersrand University where his real interest had been locking together the front rank of the university's scrum. He had crow's feet at the corners of his eyes, a square jaw, broken nose and cauliflower ears. Three weeks earlier he had been promoted to lieutenant at the age of twenty-four and was still rather self-conscious of the two gold stripes on his sleeves. He, too, had served with Widmark in *Southern Berg*.

Widmark passed him a glass of beer. 'You're late!'

'My self-starter jammed.'

McFadden made a rude noise.

Widmark lifted his glass and said 'Cheers!' and then his face tightened and he became serious.

'I've news for you.' He paused, watching the eager, intent faces, as always timing the moment. 'It's on.'

There was a moment of silence, an unseen ripple of shock, until McFadden said: 'Tell us more, laddie.'

'Are you serious?' The doubt in Rohrbach's dark eyes emphasised his question.

Widmark looked at the window against which the rain was flattening itself into quivering lines of reflected light. 'Saw the Chief of Staff this afternoon. He showed me the *official* signal from C-in-C. That one turned it down in the plainest terms. Clever little security touch. Must have a good naval intelligence officer in Freetown.'

'There was another signal then?'

Widmark nodded. 'I didn't see it, David, but for reasons you'll understand. *Officially*, the operation was turned down because of the political risks. Infringement of Portuguese neutrality and all that cock. *Unofficially* it's on, but we are,' he mimicked the Commodore's voice, 'to maintain the strictest secrecy.' There was a brief, cold smile. 'As if we wouldn't. We're to organise it privately, without the assistance of naval authority, entirely on our own initiative and responsibility. If things go wrong the Navy will repudiate us.'

'I'm sure they will,' said Rohrbach.

'*Magtig*,' said le Roux in Afrikaans. '*Daar's 'n ding*—there's a thing.' McFadden held out his glass. 'A wee drop, if you don't mind Steve. It's first-class, I'll be saying, because we'll be having a free hand. No senior officers to push us around. Please ourselves.'

'No you won't,' said Widmark. 'You'll do what I tell you, when I tell you. If this operation is going to succeed . . . and it *is* . . . we need strict discipline. I don't mean spit-and-polish and yes-sir-no-sir-three-bags-full, but the real thing. Absolute obedience to orders however bloody silly they seem. Got that?'

27

'*Goed, meneer,*' said Johan. 'When do we start?'

'Tomorrow,' said Widmark. 'There's a lot of preliminary work to be done and we must get cracking. The operation must be launched within the next few weeks, but first things first. Tomorrow we'll set about building up our party from four to seven. I'll approach the Newt. David must get hold of Mike Kent. And Johan—you contact that brother of yours, but tell him to keep his ugly mug shut.'

'Rude, aren't you? We're identical twins.'

Widmark ignored him. 'Security is top priority in this job. If there's any leak, the whole thing's off. The Chief of Staff is emphatic on that. And remember, if there's the smallest buzz they'll be waiting for us at the Mozambique border and we'll spend the rest of the war in a Portuguese gaol. They're not very comfortable.'

When the party broke up at two that morning it was still raining and the northwester was coming in over the sea.

Chapter Three

The next week was one of purposeful but discreet activity.
No two members of Widmark's party served in the same
ship or shore unit so their preoccupations passed unnoticed
and their applications for leave occasioned neither surprise
nor interest. It had been arranged that they would all apply
for three weeks' leave, but not from a common date since
the advance party was to start a few days ahead of the
others. David Rohrbach was on the staff of the Deputy-
Director (Technical) where he was responsible for fitting
out and maintenance duties, and there had been some
doubt about his leave at first because he'd taken some
four months earlier. The difficulty was ironed out when he
applied on compassionate grounds: a mother in Johannesburg who was ill, which was true though not the reason.
   The le Roux brothers served in the Mine Clearance
Flotilla but in different ships and their leave applications,
handled by their respective commanding officers, caused
no eyebrows to lift. It was all quite normal.
   Widmark had undertaken to approach Newton who,
though he did not know it, was to be a key man in 'Operation Break Out' for the good reason that he spoke fluent
Portuguese. He was the only member of the party not in
the SA Naval Forces. A lieutenant RNVR (London Division) he had spent most of the war afloat as a watch-keeper
in the cruiser *Dorsetshire* hunting surface raiders in the
South Atlantic and Indian Oceans, until an attack of jaun-
dice landed him in the Royal Naval Hospital at Simonstown. It was in the course of a long convalescence that he
met Widmark at a party and the two men quickly became
friends. Both were keen yachtsmen and Newton was soon
crewing in the twenty-eight-footer Widmark kept in the
yacht basin in Table Bay. Newton was married to a girl
in England; after a brief wartime honeymoon he had gone
off to sea and not seen her in the two years since. Life
ashore at the Cape had been fun at first after the monotony
of long stretches of sea time, but he longed for a ship
again; preferably one which would take him to England.

He longed, too, for the end of the war so that he could take Betty to Oporto where he worked in his father's wine firm when he wasn't sailing.

Widmark met Newton by appointment at the Yacht Club. They sat on the small veranda looking out over the moored yachts and across the Duncan Basin to the sea beyond where the south-easter was kicking up white horses.

Widmark watched the Newt from the corner of his eye. This fair young man of medium height with quizzical grey eyes, neat beard and languid manner, was very important to their plans.

'Think you could raise three weeks' leave, Newt?' Widmark started guardedly.

The Englishman pulled at his beard, tidied his moustache with the side of his forefinger, and then tasted the pink gin which the doctors had forbidden him. 'Life for me is one long leave. I'm still officially on sick leave. Why?'

'Good show. Now I've got to swear you to secrecy, Newt.'

'About what?'

'Something top secret and operational.'

The Newt's eyebrows lifted. 'Should you tell me? Isn't it "Hush—most secret. Not to be read"?'

'I'm going to tell you because I want you for this party. *If* you're interested. *If* you're looking for something unusual. That's what the leave's for.'

Newton sat up in his chair. 'Steve! You're talking in parables. Come off it. Of course I'd like something unusual. Who wouldn't after sitting on his arse for three months. What's the form?'

'It's a cloak and dagger job.'

'What? Here in Cape Town? There isn't any war here, old boy. Only parties and pretty girls trying to seduce you.'

'They don't have to try very hard in your case.'

'Let's scrub round my private life and get on with the secret.'

Widmark told him the whole story ending with: 'If you're not game, Newt, I can't imagine what we'll do. I don't know of another NO on the station who speaks Portuguese.'

'You know,' the Newt held up his glass, squinting at it with one eye shut. 'It's not very flattering. I mean asking a chap to join a cloak and dagger job just because he speaks the lingo. I hoped it was my seamanlike bearing, my courage and determination, that marked me down.'

'Well, of course, I wouldn't have asked you if you'd been an absolute moron.'

But he got his man and when they parted that evening James Fellowes Newton had joined 'Operation Break Out.'

David Rohrbach in due course sought out Michael Kent, who was a leading telegraphist in the W/T office at the Naval Base in Cape Town Docks. Kent had graduated from Cape Town University in 1940, majoring in politics, philosophy and economics.

A serious young man who read philosophy most of his time off duty, he felt keenly, as if it were a personal burden, the state into which mankind had fallen. The war when it came shattered his belief that in its broad onward sweep humanity was triumphing over the forces of evil. Indeed, all that was happening suggested to him that the forces of evil were in the ascendancy. Hating the idea of war, he had felt impelled towards it. In the moment of historical crisis he couldn't stand aside. Sure in his young mind of the moral issues involved and the righteousness of the cause, he presented himself at the naval recruiting office. But poor eyesight and an academic background conspired to keep him away from the battle, and though he soon mastered wireless telegraphy and was promoted to leading telegraphist he was kept in Cape Town: first as an instructor and later when he complained and asked to be sent to sea, as a watch-keeper in the W/T office at the docks. It was there that Rohrbach had met him and learnt to respect his keen mind and singleness of purpose. When Widmark said that a really good telegraphist was essential to the operation, Rohrbach had suggested Mike Kent.

Slight, with spectacled eyes which looked out on what they saw with a mixture of scepticism and youthful curiosity, he had brief flashes of cheerfulness, almost of exuberance. Then, as if his inner self had caught him doing something he shouldn't, he would draw back, a little ashamed, into the shell where he spent so much time contemplating mankind.

When, after careful sounding, David Rohrbach invited him to join 'Operation Break Out,' Mike Kent smiled with embarrassment: he couldn't imagine why he had been chosen for such an honour. Rather hesitantly, he said:

'Thank you very much, sir.'

'It could be dangerous. You realise that?'

'Yes, I suppose so. I mean I do.'

The last man to join the party was Hans le Roux, Johan's twin brother. There had never really been any doubt about him. Both McFadden and Johan had pressed his claims, because he was so much what was wanted. A diesel mechanic by training, he had joined the Navy when war started and soon became a stoker petty officer. He now served in a mine-sweeper looking after the diesel generators which energised the sweep used against magnetic mines. But it was dull work, for there were no magnetic mines in Cape waters and Hans very much doubted if there ever would be.

Like Mike Kent, he at once accepted the proposal put to him by McFadden. The promise of action at last seemed almost too good to be true, and that his brother was to be in the party made it all the more attractive. Hans, too, was a rugby player and kept himself fit. But there were other likenesses. But for his unbroken nose and the absence of a beard, he would have been difficult to distinguish from Johan.

During that week they got together the necessary equipment. It was comparatively simple but since it could not be drawn from Naval Stores, it had to be bought in and around Cape Town.

This was done diffusely, each member of the party getting the items assigned to him by Widmark. The Newt, on his own initiative, devoted much energy to procuring a small bottle of capsules, sodium seconal, from the RN Hospital at Simonstown. Nurse Wilson, who adored him, got them for him from the young surgeon-lieutenant who adored her. The Newt kissed her devotedly and scratched 'Love Potion' from his list.

Rail warrants were exchanged for railway tickets, those who hadn't passports got them, money for travelling and subsistence expenses was handed out, petrol vouchers obtained—strings had to be pulled here, and the Widmark and Rohrbach business connections were invaluable—and the accounting side generally had to be seen to. Widmark had meant to bear the cost of the operation but the Newt, a man of means, had insisted on sharing them. 'Won't cost me a sausage,' he pulled at his beard. 'Comes out of Newton Ltd's coffers. The old boys who hog the port and sherry in St James's really pay for it.'

Ten days after Widmark had told them the operation was on, the party met together for the first time. At his flat they arrived in ones and twos, in plain clothes in order to avoid arousing curiosity.

Widmark sat on a reversed chair in the centre of the living-room, the others gathered round him.

'Well, let's recap.' His dark restless eyes took in the room. 'Today's the fifth of November.'

'Appropriate day, sir,' Mike Kent blinked, surprised at his own daring.

Widmark went on: 'The two British ships sail from Lourenço Marques on or about the twenty-third/twenty-fourth. The period of no moon is the twenty-third, twenty-fourth and twenty-fifth. During those three days we'll have to launch the operation.'

There was a pause, and unspoken excitement spread through the room like ripples on a pond.

'Everybody's leave all right?'

There was general assent.

'Got the signal and W/T drill taped, Kent? Know the procedures for challenging Allied merchant ships, and the replies?'

'Yes, sir.'

Widmark got up and poured himself a whisky and soda, and then pointed at the silver tray with his chin. 'Help yourselves if you're ready for the other half.' He perched on the edge of the table.

McFadden and Hans were the only takers.

'I've checked the plot,' he went on, 'and I'll do so up to the last moment. I've a pretty good picture of the Indian Ocean situation, the raiders and U-boats operating, and the disposition of our own forces. I've got the charts and the Admiralty sailing directions. Three charts.'

The restless brown eyes settled on McFadden. 'How's the equipment coming along, Chiefy?'

'Got it all, sir, but for the shoulder-holsters.'

'They'll arrive tomorrow,' said Rohrbach. 'We can buy the hammer, punch and hacksaw in Lourenço Marques.'

'Good.' Widmark's hands gripped the edge of the table

on which he sat and he swung his legs. 'Now for the order
of battle. David and Johan will be the advance party. You
because of your German, David. And you, Johan, because
you can do the rebel Afrikaner bursting with anti-British
sentiment.'

Johan made a face, 'Sure I can. Can't stand the *rooineks*.'

The Newt smoothed his moustache. 'Why are so many
bods here anti-British actually?'

'*Actually*,' mimicked Rohrbach, 'I wouldn't know.'

Widmark frowned. 'Let's concentrate on this, shall we.
Once in LM, David and Johan will go to the Cardoso.
You've got our Johannesburg address and the private code.
Okay?'

'Okay!'

'Soon as you've completed your recce, wire me. Then the
Newt will come down . . . by train . . . and we'll follow by
car two days later. If any snags crop up between the time
of your signal and our ETD you let us know pronto. Got
that?'

Rohrbach nodded.

Widmark went on. 'I'll fix you up with Johannesburg
addresses in the next few days. One in the Western Transvaal for Johan and Hans. They'll be from telephone direc-
tories. Genuine enough, but none of you'll be known there
so you can't be traced once the balloon's gone up.'

Again they checked the plan from beginning to end to
make sure that everyone knew the part he had to play. On
the table Widmark had laid out a leaflet he'd got from
Naval Intelligence who, on the outbreak of war, had found
it in the Cape Town offices of the agents for the Rudolph
Heissner Lines of Bremen, owners of the *Hagenfels*. The
ship was designed to take twelve passengers in six large
cabins and the leaflet advertised the attractions of travel in
a modern freighter, and gave a detailed plan of the accommodation.

Widmark reminded them that they were, in the few days
left, to visit freighters in Table Bay docks.

'Say you're keen to look over the ship, being a naval type
who's never served in a merchantman. Get to know your
way around. Seven to eight thousand ton freighters have a
lot in common. Don't forget the bridges and engine-rooms,
and go for motor ships. They've no boiler rooms and the
layout's rather different from the steam jobs.'

Before they left he reminded them of an essential detail. 'When you go into Mozambique be sure you haven't got a single stitch of uniform with you or any naval papers. And keep your mouths shut. The less you say, the better it'll be for all of us.'

When they'd gone, Widmark sat at his desk writing up his diary.

There were other last-minute details to be attended to, including the fitting of false compartments in Rohrbach's and Widmark's cars. This was done by McFadden in the garage at his house in Rondesbosch, with the assistance of Hans le Roux, some fine gauge sheet-steel and a welding outfit. The compartments were built in behind the backs to the rear seats, and into them fitted snugly the equipment they needed.

Rohrbach and Johan le Roux drove to Lourenço Marques by way of Johannesburg. There Johan got one barber to remove his beard and another to dye his hair and eyebrows dark brown. The change in appearance was remarkable. and but for the broken nose Rohrbach would have had difficulty in recognising him. A telegram was sent off to Widmark: *Aunt Mabel leaves for the farm to-morrow morning at eight*; and the next day they drove across the Transvaal highveld to the Drakensberg escarpment dropping down through Schoeman's Kloof to the lowveld, ablaze with flamboyants and jacaranda, and orchards of orange, avocado and paw-paw. The road was hot, there was dust everywhere, musky and penetrating, and the sun beat down on the steel roof of the car. They were silent, Johan's thoughts on the farm at Swartruggens far away to the west; a small sense of guilt in his mind because he was not spending his leave there with his parents and would not be seeing Anna Marie . . . but mostly he felt excitement at what lay ahead. David Rohrbach was thinking about other things: first, worrying as he so often did about his family in Germany, then recalling Lawrence's description of the weather as they waited in a ship off Jedda: . . . *the heat of Arabia came out like a drawn sword and struck us speechless*. That had happened as they reached the foot of Schoeman's Kloof and started along the valley towards Montrose Falls, the heat of the lowveld encompassing

35

them like a fog, humid and clinging. Rohrbach felt other things, too: a deep satisfaction, for example, at the course of events. At last there was to be something tangible; identifiable; direct action, and for a worthwhile objective. He was too sensitive and intelligent to imagine that their plans would be easy to execute, that nothing could go wrong. Unlike Widmark, he envisaged the possibility of failure and wondered in what way it might come and what its consequences might be. But these gloomy thoughts soon gave way to optimism, for it was not easy to contemplate failure with the Butcher. Rohrbach thought about him. His enormous self-sufficiency, his determination and—Rohrbach jibbed at the thought—his ruthlessness, inspired unusual confidence. He remembered when Johan le Roux had told him about Widmark at Suda Bay: 'We were oiling at the time, alongside *Fleetol*, and about thirty Stukas piled in. All hell broke loose and we couldn't do a thing except poop off an occasional burst of Lewis-gun fire which was about as much use as a catapult. It was our first experience of air attack. *Fleetol* was hit and a bloody great fire started and there was the Butcher on the bridge with smoke and flames all round him acting as cool as a cucumber while the *Fleetol*'s survivors tumbled aboard. Then it was "Let go bow line! . . . let go aft! . . . hold on to that spring! . . . starboard twenty! . . . slow ahead!" All in the same dry voice. If it hadn't been for the noise of the air attack and the flames you'd have thought we were getting under weigh from the Alfred Basin on a quiet Sunday morning. As we got clear, some low-flying Messerschmitts buzzed us and the coxswain caught a burst of machine-gun fire in the face and bits of him got plastered all over the bridge, and the Butcher takes the wheel and looks at what's left and says quietly, "Poor old Cox. He's got hurt." You'd have thought the coxswain'd been laid out in a rugger match, the way the Butcher said it. *Hy's 'n snaakse kêrel*—He's an odd bloke. I don't think he feels things the way other people do. Unemotional type.'

'I wonder,' Rohrbach had said. Beneath the cold exterior he had seen marks of strain, of bottled-up emotion. It showed through unexpectedly: the restless brooding eyes, the long fingers clenching his fists into a ball until the knuckles were white. Once Widmark was telling him about the sinking of a liner eighty miles south of Cape Point:

'There were a lot of women and children on board. Service families coming back from the Middle East. It was blowing hard. Some of the boats capsized as they were lowered.' There was a pause and he could see the veins standing out on Widmark's temple. 'Women and children in them. Can you imagine it? What it must have been like? In the dark, I mean. So many helpless people. Those children.'

Rohrbach saw that he was tormenting himself. 'No good thinking about it, Steve. Doesn't help, you know.'

Widmark turned on him, white faced and shocked. 'For Christ's sake! What d'you want me to do? Pretend it didn't happen? Look the other way?'

Johan and Rohrbach experienced no difficulties at the border posts at Komatipoort and Ressano Garcia. They produced their passports and the documents for the car, and were identified and accepted as South African civilians visiting Lourenço Marques on holiday. They declared their cameras, testified that they had no firearms, and filled in the customs and immigration forms. The luggage and the car were cursorily examined, and they set out on the last lap of the journey; some eighty miles across the Lebombos, abundant with acacia thorn, wild fig and the tangle of African bush, and then on through the fever trees of the lowlands to Moamba and Lourenço Marques. At six o'clock that evening, they reached the Cardoso Hotel, tired and dust streaked. After a bath they changed and went down to a dinner throughout which, covertly, they searched the room for familiar faces. There weren't any and they sighed with relief and decided to make an early night of it. But they were more effectively disguised than they knew, because Rohrbach had started growing his beard only two months before, and Johan had just lost his.

That night they slept soundly.

Chapter Four

Next morning, in shorts and open-necked shirts, sandals and sunglasses, they took their bathing bags and drove down to the beach at Polana. They had a camera with them, and binoculars in one of the bags. They changed in the kiosk, swam in the shark-netted enclosure, lay on the sand in the sun, photographed each other and, for good measure, played leap-frog. It was a hot day, the sun burning down from an empty, quivering sky. Rohrbach wiped the sweat from his forehead with the back of his hand and shook his head. 'No weather for a beard.'

Johan said: 'If we don't look like a couple of tourists, man, then I don't know.'

Rohrbach looked at his watch. 'Now for the job. It's after ten o'clock.'

'What's next?'

'Let's drive into town and park somewhere near the City Hall. Then wander down to the harbour.'

'What's that road with the name like a gun? The one passing the Cardoso. From that park next to the hotel we can see over the harbour.'

'Avenida Miguel Bombarda?' Rohrbach stumbled over the words.

'That's it.'

'We can see the harbour from the terrace in front of the hotel.'

'Yes. But we can't use binoculars there without attracting attention.'

'Okay! Let's go.'

They changed, got into the car and followed the steep winding road up the cliff, then through the Avenida do Duque de Connaught to Bartolomeu Dias and along it to Miguel Bombarda where Rohrbach stopped the car. But for a few Africans, sweeping and cleaning, the park was deserted when they got out and walked across to the edge of the cliff. Below them lay the casuarinas and blue gums of the Aterro do Machaquene; on the right the reds, yellows and greys of the town buildings, on the left the older buildings: the Port Captain's office and its precincts, the Old

Fort, the dry dock and boat harbour, a cluster of tugs, two Portuguese sloops, and then the sheds and warehouses along the Gorjao Quay where the bent heads of the cargo cranes looked like monstrous birds feeding from the ships alongside. Beyond them the Espirito Santo, a mosaic of blues, browns and greys, shimmered in the sunlight, stretching across to the sandy beaches and scrub of the far bank where barges lay offshore. Small boats and lighters were moving among the ships at anchor.

They'd been there for a few minutes when Rohrbach said: 'Don't turn round but there's a policeman watching the car.'

Slowly Johan put the binoculars back into their case. 'Not to panic,' said Rohrbach quietly. 'We're in a parking *prohibido* zone. It'll take him two or three minutes to reach the car.'

'Which are the Jerries, David?' Johan was looking down the river to the oil sites where, beyond a three-masted barque, her bare poles high and tapering, four merchant ships lay at anchor.

'Those over there. Down towards Matola.'

'They look pretty harmless. Third from the right must be the *Hagenfels*. No boiler-room ventilators. Low, thick funnel.'

'Did you see her name with the glasses?'

'No. Too far.'

Rohrbach looked back towards the street again. 'The Portuguese cop's coming this way. Let's shove off.'

They drove into the town, parked the car and walked across to the fishing harbour where they mixed with the tourists, hangers-on and fishermen. There was something restful about the place, reflected Rohrbach. The boats with their atmosphere of hiatus between a task completed and one about to begin. Some fishermen, leather faced, were squatting on the quayside repairing nets, talking in monosyllables; near them a man lowered a bucket over the side of a boat, slowly recovered it and sluiced the deck, steam rising from the sun-hot planks. Beyond him a youngster in blue denims, a black cigarette drooping from his mouth, gutted a fish while he talked to an old man who was working on an engine, his hands and face smeared with grease. On the far side of the harbour, the motor ferry for Catembe was filling with Africans who chattered gaily under

39

their load of babies and bundles.

Rohrbach beckoned to Johan and they moved on, making their way across to the Gorjao Quay, past the tugs and sloops and the sheds beside the big ships where the bustle of cargo work, the shouting of stevedores, the whirr of electric cranes and the puffing of shunting engines, shut out other sounds. They went down the line of ships, walking between the railway trucks, the heavy lift cranes and the cupola, past the coaling berths and cold store. The quay was clear here and they could see up river towards Matola. The German merchantmen were within half a mile. The ships looked bigger, darker, more menacing, thought Rohrbach, probably because they were the enemy. Men could be seen moving about their decks.

There were four steamships and beyond them a sailing ship. The steamers' names had been painted out, but they knew from the list Widmark had given them that one would be the Italian ship, the *Gerusalemme*, and the others the Germans. The old four-masted steamship was the *Aller*, the newer vessel with two masts and a single funnel the *Dortmund*, and the largest of the three, the only motor ship, was the *Hagenfels*. They watched her with curious unbelief. They'd talked about the ship so often, conjured up endless mental pictures of her and here she was at last.

'Lucky they don't know what's cooking,' said Johan.

'Come on,' Rohrbach started across the quay, 'let's see what these blokes know.'

Some handline fishermen sat on the quayside, their legs reaching down towards the water. Rohrbach and le Roux made for them, walking at a leisurely pace, and once among them asked about the fishing.

At the first three they drew blanks; either dumb stares or head shakes and '*Não falo inglés*'; but number four paid off. Eyeing them mournfully, spitting into the water with slow deliberation, he shook his head: 'Bastards no bite.'

Johan was sympathetic. 'Must have plenty patience, hey?'

'Have got. Have got.' The Portuguese lifted his shoulder in a gesture of hopelessness. 'Bastards no bite.'

'Too bad!' said Johan.

They sat down next to the Portuguese and found that he was friendly, his dismal appearance notwithstanding.

40

Cautiously they chatted about this and that: the weather, the prospects of rain, the beauties of Lourenço Marques, its excellent food and wine, its fine buildings, shops and *avenidas*, and the charm of the Roman Catholic cathedral.

They exchanged first names—his was Fernando—and worked the conversation towards their subject, via the futility of war and the hardships of those who went down to the sea in ships. Fernando had been a sailor. Spitting for emphasis, he said: 'Sea no good. Worka lika sheet. For what?' His eyes rolled. 'For what?'

'Couldn't agree more,' said Johan. 'Sea no good.'

Fernando nodded gloomily, resigned to this shared truth.

Slowly but purposefully they steered the conversation to what they wanted. Rohrbach pointed to the German ships. 'Lucky, those ships. No war. Stay here all the time. No torpedo. O.K., hey?'

Fernando looked out over the Espirito Santo. Once again he shrugged his shoulders. 'For heem, all right. Plenty food. Plenty wine. Plenty women. No sea. For heem verra good.'

Diffusely, they led him on. Were there many sailors on board? Did they go ashore often? What were their habits generally? Did people from the shore go off to the ships? If so why, and how, and who were they?

Colourfully, and with appropriate gestures, Fernando answered them. No! Not plenty men on board. Yes. Come ashore three times a week. No spik Portuguese. The launches which took them to and fro belonged to the Catembe ferry service and were manned by Africans. Sometimes the agents went off to the ships. Sometimes boats took them food and stores.

Visitors? Yes. Sometimes. Ladies? Of course! Fernando squinted, the tired eyes a mixture of browns and reds. Holding up his hand, he pressed the thumb against the second finger. 'Sailor like women too much. Must have.' Soberly he repeated his belief. '*Must* have.'

From him they learnt that the launches berthed in the boat harbour and worked to a simple timetable. With expressions of mutual esteem and a promise to look him up again before long, they went on their way.

'This afternoon,' said Rohrbach as they walked back towards the dock gates, 'we'll visit the boat harbour and check on Fernando's timetable.'

Johan spat on the road. 'Worka lika sheet! For what?'

Otto Stauch was a middle-aged man of generous proportions due to an appetite for food and beer which he had indulged without restraint for thirty of his forty-five years. A pink face above a thick neck on rounded shoulders led down to the balloon of his stomach. Towards the ground he tapered off, ending with feet which seemed too small for their load.

Small deepset eyes and a low hairline gave him a dull, peasant-like expression which was misleading, for he was quick witted and observant. Working at the desk he breathed heavily, mopping at the perspiration which ran down his face in spite of the electric fans. With stolid concentration he deciphered the message, writing with one hand and turning the leaves of the cipher book with the other. A thin angular woman with steel-rimmed glasses came in from the outer office.

'Will you be needing me again this evening, Otto?' she asked in German.

Without raising his head he replied: 'No. That is all, Paula. I've nearly finished.'

She stood looking at what he was doing. Undecided.

'Is it good news, Otto?'

'It is not bad news.' He was guarded. 'They say we must put the ship on twenty-four hours' notice from Tuesday. That she must be fully oiled, watered and provisioned, which she already is as I have twice told them.'

'Is it still the *Hagenfels*?'

'Of course! She is the only motor ship.' His speech was laboured, as if the heat and his exertions were too much.

'When does the Freiherr arrive?'

'I am not sure. In a few days, perhaps.'

'Nothing can happen until he arrives?'

'Nothing, Paula. He is in charge of the operation. Though why it falls under the Abwehr and not the Wilhelmstrasse I cannot understand.'

'Probably because both Intelligence and the Navy are concerned. The Freiherr is a naval officer, but he reports to the Abwehr because his duties until now have been Intelligence. The Chancellery, the Wilhelmstrasse, the Abwehr, the High Command—they are all mixed up in these things.'

'Possibly. But here the brunt of the organisation, the responsibility, the risks, fall upon me.' Stauch sighed. 'I hope the Wilhelmstrasse will give credit.'

She knew this was his Achilles heel. The fear that others might get the kudos. 'Of course, Otto. Of that you may be sure.'

'I hope so.' With a podgy forefinger he loosened his collar. 'Don't wait for me, Paula. Kleinschmidt will give me a lift.'

'Where is he?'

'In the transmitting room.'

Frau Stauch bent over the fat man and kissed him on his moist forehead. '*Auf wiedersehen*, Otto.'

'*Auf wiedersehen,* Paula.' It was not necessary within the family, but from long habit he raised his right hand. '*Heil* Hitler!'

She replied '*Heil* Hitler!' but didn't trouble to raise her hand.

Downstairs she locked the door of the shipping agency her husband had managed for so many years.

Frau Stauch was thoughtful as she drove home. She hated the British, the Jews, the Portuguese and the Africans; but above all she hated Lourenço Marques and its humid heat. She longed for Munich and the Walchensee. Yet once Germany won the war, she must stay here for Herr Stauch was high in the party hierarchy and though not *Landes-kreisleiter* designate of Mozambique, an office he coveted but had no hope of getting, his knowledge of the territory was such that, come the victory, he would certainly be needed here.

Two days later the Newt arrived by train and booked in at the Polana. The pointed beard had gone, but not the moustache, which was of such elegance that he might have been RAF. In the hotel register he wrote the address of his family's house in Oporto and to the receptionist he made it known in fluent Portuguese that he was an English wine merchant from Portugal who had been in South Africa when the war started and had decided to stay. Now he was in Lourenço Marques on business but intended taking things easy. In the afternoon, he went down to the beach and sipped iced tea in the kiosk. It was a Sunday and there were many people about; mostly Portuguese because the

43

weather was too hot for tourists. Near him, two girls with dark eyes and scarlet lips ate sticky cakes and whispered and giggled. Talking about men, thought the Newt, looking at them wistfully. The bathing enclosure was full of swimmers and the Newt watched a youth make a high dive, arching into the sea, then coming up, white teeth flashing as he shook the salt water from his face. The Newt heard the scrape of chairs behind him and familiar voices.

There was no recognition but he looked at his watch. Four-thirty, exactly. They were punctual.

When they got up and walked downstairs, the Newt followed, keeping his distance, first into the roadway and then along the promenade, past the grey walls and green roof of the Yacht Club. Beyond the club they sat on a bench, the sea lapping the wall below them.

The Newt stopped a few feet away, his back to them, looking out to sea, leaning on the concrete balustrade.

Congratulations on changed appearances were exchanged, and then Rohrbach reported progress. Where the ships lay, the habits of their crews, the launches' timetable, and much else. The two British ships, due to sail about the twenty-third, had been located: the *Tactician* and the *Clan McPhilly*. Both were discharging at the Gorjao Quay, and had not yet started loading. They gave him the position of the *Hagenfels*: about five cables to the south-west of the far end of the Gorjao Quay.

The Newt fidgeted with his moustache. 'I'll knock around the docks to-morrow. Try and make friends with some Portuguese. Been out in the harbour yet?'

'No. Johan and I are hiring a boat to-morrow morning. We've got some fishing tackle and we've chummed up with a bloke who lets out boats. Domingos Parao. He wasn't too keen on letting us go solo. Wanted to send his man with us. We talked him out of it.'

'To-day's the tenth,' said the Newt. 'We must aim at finishing the recce by the twentieth. Main thing is to establish the number of men on board and how many go ashore at one time.'

Out towards Chefine Island banks of cumulo-nimbus were building up and a breeze came in from the sea and ruffled the surface of the water; the scattered clouds cast dark shadows and the fairway buoys glistened white in the sunlight. The sea-birds were flying south to Cabo da Inhaca, away from the gathering storm. At the mouth of the river, almost lost in the heat haze, a tanker rode high in the water, her hull rust-streaked, a white gush of condenser water discharging from her side.

Another two days passed and then they met the Newt in a dark lane near the Cardoso. He had spent the afternoon in a tug where he'd made friends with the mate who was from Lisbon. In the evening they'd done a pub-crawl before dinner and he'd learnt a good deal. The mate had heard the rumour that the *Hagenfels* was standing by to break out, but there were always such rumours, he said; the Germans started them, their security was excellent. He'd agreed that if any ship broke out it would be the *Hagenfels* because she was a motor ship; if a steamship raised steam it would be seen in the harbour and British Intelligence would at once know.

Johan frowned. 'Wasn't he suspicious?'

'No. My questions were pretty mildly put, and at long intervals. We talked of much besides. Both old Lisboans, you know. Towards the end, Artur was pretty high. A great thirst, that man.'

Johan and Rohrbach gave him their news. That afternoon two women had come ashore in the 5.30 launch which brought off crewmen from the German ships. There were eighteen Germans in the launch, and the women had taken a taxi into the town with the ship's Captain and one of his officers.

'How did you know it was the Captain?'

'The women spoke English. One called him "Captain Lindemann," the other "Kurt." He's Kurt Lindemann, master of the *Hagenfels*.'

'How do you know that, David?'

'*Iche spreche Deutsch*. The launch's coxswain asked what time the *Herr Kapitän* would like to be taken off to the *Hagenfels*. Lindemann said midnight.'

Johan le Roux rubbed his hands. 'Tell him about the lovelies, David.'

'One of them lives with us. She's staying at the Cardoso. We're like that.' Rohrbach held up two fingers. 'Two nights ago she drank with us and swopped news. She's single, lives with Pa and Ma on a sisal estate in northern Mozambique. Down here on holiday. She was at school on the Reef. A convent where many Portuguese girls go. Speaks good English.'

The Newt whistled. 'Blimey. You're a fast lot. She talk about Lindemann?'

'No.'

'Funny.'

'Not really. Why should she tell us her private life. We'd just met.'

'Did she see you two at the launch?'

'Sure. Smiled sweetly. Didn't she, Johan?'

'Might be useful,' said the Newt. 'I take it you'll follow up?'

'Sure. Sure. Seeing her tomorrow. Nice girl, isn't she, Johan?'

'Fabulous! Our Mariotta Pereira.'

The Newt plugged on. 'The other bloke in the taxi with them. Who was he?'

'One of Lindemann's officers.' Rohrbach made a rude noise. 'Didn't like his looks. Brooding type. Nasty young man, I'd say.'

Johan nodded. 'Sombre character. Shaggy eyebrows.'

After they'd parted, the Newt took the cliff road to the Polana. It was past ten when he got there and there were people about. The lounge was unpleasantly hot, so he went out on to the veranda. It was a dark night with a waning moon, the southern sky shimmering with stars. Over the water across the bay the light at Ponta Garapao flashed every five seconds.

Below him the terraced garden led to the edge of the cliff. Somewhere a dance band was playing. The Newt thought of his wife in London and felt lonely.

From the shadows behind him came a woman's voice: 'Beautiful, isn't it?'

Chapter Five

It was an oppressive morning and the *Hagenfels*'s crew sniffed the wind coming up from Matola and smelt the mudflats and crude oil and knew that a hot day was coming. In the officers' dining saloon, Kapitän Lindemann sat at the head of the table, his grey streaked hair moist with perspiration. His eyes, set wide apart in a weather-beaten face, had the uncomplicated directness of the seaman. To his right was Siegfried Kuhn, the chief engineer; small, bespectacled, alert, his thoughts were in Deugswald, the village outside Frankfurt where his wife and child had been billeted by the authorities. It was no longer possible to receive letters and his only news of her was in the form of messages from the German Consulate which came at long intervals.

On Lindemann's left was the second officer, Günther Moewe, a sullen, sallow man of medium build. Next to him was a big man with the flattened nose and receding eyes of a boxer. This was Heinrich Schäffer, the second engineer. These were all the officers in the skeleton crew left on board while the ship sheltered in Lourenço Marques enjoying the sanctuary of a neutral port and safe from enemy interference as long as she remained there and observed the regulations laid down by the port authorities.

In addition to these officers she had on board a bosun, a carpenter, six sailors, three mechanicians, three greasers, a cook and an officers' steward. Müller, the steward, waited on the officers, did their cabins and looked after them generally, and though the busiest man on board he never complained. Young and cheerful, he knew that life in Lourenço Marques was a lot easier than in a U-boat which would have been his lot had the *Hagenfels* got back to Germany.

At breakfast the tension between Lindemann and his second officer was much in the air. Moewe disapproved of the Captain, who was not a member of the National Socialist Party, and who was unenthusiastic about Hitler. Not that he'd ever said anything against the Führer, but he'd never said anything *for* him. In Moewe's opinion the Captain drank too much, went to too many parties ashore, and too often brought women on board. Where was the dedication to the cause, the fervour, the zeal, so proper to a German patriot?

The Captain disliked Moewe for his lack of humour and fanatical Nazism. Lindemann knew he was not important in the Nazi hierarchy—a section leader in the *Hitler Jugend* before the war—but Moewe took himself seriously. He'd been at the Nürnberg Rally in 1938, a member of the guard of honour inspected by the Führer. The great man had stopped and asked him his name. Moewe stammered a reply and Hitler had given him an enigmatic stare before moving on. This was epochal for Moewe and ever since he'd preached National Socialism with messianic fervour. He was a good ship's officer and a useful navigator, but intellectually a lightweight.

The officers were waiting for Lindemann to leave the table, but he showed no sign of moving. Instead he said to the steward: 'Müller! You can go now. Close the pantry door.'

Müller disappeared. Lindemann turned to the expectant faces of his officers, and said: 'There is important news. We are to stand by—twenty-four hours' notice.' He paused. 'This won't involve much change in our routine. But in future all leave will end at midnight.'

He nodded to Siegfried Kuhn. 'Turning your engines regularly, Kuhn? Fuel and water tanks full?'

'Ninety per cent full, Herr Kapitän. Tomorrow they will be topped up.'

'Good!' Lindemann turned to Günther Moewe. 'Let me have the times of moonrise and moonset and of high and low water each week in advance, please.'

The second officer's eyes shone with patriotic fervour. 'Very good, Herr Kapitän!'

'The strictest secrecy, please. The men are not to be told. The change in leave will apply to all German ships here. It will be said to be in response to new orders from Germany arising out of complaints ashore. Is that understood?'

It was.

'There are new radio frequencies, Moewe. Come to my cabin for them.'

'Very good, Herr Kapitän.' As well as navigating officer, Moewe was now doing radio duties, the original radio officer having been repatriated to Germany via Portugal with the other half of the crew. When the signal to break out was received, the skeleton crew would be augmented by men from the other German ships; at the last moment before sailing and under cover of darkness.

The chief engineer asked the question which was in all their minds. 'Herr Kapitän, do we return to Germany or shall we act as supply vessel?'

'We shall not know until we are at sea. Bad security to tell us now. We do not need the information.'

The effect of the news on Lindemann's officers was electric. For more than three years they'd been bottled up in Lourenço Marques, holding themselves always in readiness for a break out. Twice they'd been at forty-eight hours' notice, but nothing had come of it. Now for the first time twenty-four hours' notice had been ordered. A situation must be developing.

The monotony of life on board an anchored ship in a sub-tropical port far from home might soon end. There would be action. Return to Germany or the dangers and excitement of supplying German raiders and U-boats in the Indian Ocean and South Atlantic. All were moved by these prospects. Günther Moewe glowed with pride. To strike at last a blow for the Führer, to get away from this God-forsaken place. His only regret would be Hester.

The feminine voice from the shadows sounded an alarm bell somewhere in the Newt, but when he saw its owner he felt better. She got up from the easy-chair behind him and moved into the light from the lounge window.

She was good to look at: chestnut hair and firm regular features, but her eyes were the thing. Laughing and friendly, cornflower blue, with crow's feet at the corners. The Newt had some experience of these things and he was impressed.

'*Very* beautiful.' He was deliberately ambiguous, looking at her and then at the sea. 'Hot this afternoon but cool now.'

'Always so at this time of year.'

'You know the climate well?'

'Fairly well. I live here.'

He offered her a cigarette. She shook her head. 'Not now, thank you.'

'Mind if I do?'

'Not in the least.'

'Care for a drink?'

'Love one.'

In the lounge they sat where they could see over the bay, sipping the drinks the waiter brought them.

He soon knew her story: Di Brett, a widow—late twenties, he judged—obviously well off; she'd spent the first year of the war in Cape Town, the next between Durban and Salisbury, then Johannesburg, and in Lourenço Marques for the last eight months. She'd married an Englishman, lived in England most of her life, though born near Grenoble, which accounted for the slight French accent.

'I love this place,' she watched him over the rim of her glass. 'So cosmopolitan. Like a breath of the Continent after the stodginess of the Union. The food, the wine, the way people live—oh, so sophisticated. And I *adore* hot weather.'

She soon knew a good deal about him. An Englishman from Portugal, in the family port and sherry business, in South Africa for the firm when war broke out, stayed on and now visiting Lourenço Marques on business.

'Why aren't you in the war, if you're an Englishman?' Her eyebrows arched.

'Well,' he frowned in his embarrassment. 'Would have been if I'd gone back to England. To be honest, I've lived in Portugal too long to feel any emotional involvement. I think it's an unnecessary war.'

She seemed shocked and looked at him sideways, evidently not quite sure about him.

'War's a hateful thing.' She said it with much feeling, and he thought she must have lost her husband.

'Let's forget it,' he said and there was a long silence. Then they walked down the veranda to where the band was playing. It was dark and musky and rather good fun, he thought. He found a table, ordered a bottle of wine, and they danced under subdued lights. A little distantly at first, but not for long, for the Newt felt time floating away on the wings of soft music, and held her close and she seemed to like it.

Next day Rohrbach and Johan worked together, the Newt operating on his own.

That night they met on an empty building site down a

dark lane opposite Gigi's restaurant and swopped news. The Newt had learnt from the mate of the tug that there were about twenty men in the *Hagenfels*'s skeleton crew, and that half of them went ashore on three days of the week. He also confirmed that the *Hagenfels* was lying to two bower anchors. In the afternoon Rohrbach and Johan had hired a small fishing boat and travelled down the Espirito Santo into the bay beyond.

'We caught some fish,' said Johan. 'And David was sick.'

Rohrbach made a clicking noise. 'Didn't bring up, but I felt lousy. Small boats, you know.'

'You and Nelson!' the Newt said coldly.

They'd also checked that the *Clan McPhilly* and *Tactician* had finished discharging and begun loading.

'To-night,' Johan made a circle with his thumb and forefinger, 'is the night.'

'What's on?'

'We've a date with Mariotta and her girl friend.'

'Who's that?'

'Cleo. The other doll in the launch.'

'Well, enjoy yourselves but watch your libidos.' He thought of Di Brett and his appointment to dine and dance with her that night. 'There's a time for everything,' he added in his chilliest manner.

Johan said: 'Yes. We feel it's to-night.'

The breeze came to them cool and laden with frangipani. A car passed at the top of the lane, gramophone music sounded somewhere and in the distance a dog barked.

Mariotta was a dark, lively Portuguese beauty, with hair and eyes that were almost black. The Greek girl, Cleo Melanides, had that special quality of femininity which makes a woman so attractive to men. Possibly it had to do with her high cheekbones and slanted hazel eyes, which were a curious mixture of interrogation and surprise. She and Mariotta spoke good English.

From the Cardoso they drove in Rohrbach's Studebaker to Peter's, a beach roadhouse beyond the Polana. After a meal of prawns, washed down with *Serradayres*, they danced to a piano, saxophone and drums. Before midnight they drove back into town where the bars, bistros and honky-tonks of the Araújo were doing business with the crews from the ships on the Espirito Santo.

Along the street there was a confused jumble of sound: the deep voices of men, the higher ones of women, the occasional shouts of sailors and the excited shrieks of girls. Taxis hooted, and from somewhere came the steady thump of jazz.

Johan insisted on the Pinguin. He had drunk a good deal and drifted into a euphoria which seemed likely to last the night.

Mariotta complained. 'It ees for sailors, Johan. Not for us.' Cleo agreed, but Johan swept their objections aside. The Pinguin was filled with so much smoke that it seemed to be on fire, and the orchestration of many voices, rising and falling like a heavy sea, fought with the band.

They danced, drank Portuguese beer, talked, argued, flirted and enjoyed themselves with the ardour of youth. Rohrbach heard Germans at the next table. There were four men there and he knew from what they said that they were seamen. One of them, the big one who looked like a prize-fighter, had been in the launch with the two girls in the boat harbour. Rohrbach nudged Mariotta. 'Those chaps at the table—next to that mirror—aren't they my countrymen?'

Puzzled at first, she smiled. 'Of course! You're German. I keep forgetting. You speak such good English. Yes, they are Germans. From the ships. I know one. Do you wish to meet him?'

He shook his head. 'Not here. I can't hob-nob with Germans ashore. Make things difficult for me in South Africa.' He pulled at his beard; he was determined not to let this chance pass. 'When you and Cleo came ashore in the launch the other day, who was the bloke who helped you ashore—middle-aged? Then you two went off in a taxi with him and another type?'

Cleo wagged a finger at him. 'You are like a spy.'

'Ha! Ha!' Rohrbach knew his laugh was feeble and hated himself for it.

'That was Captain Kurt Lindemann of the *Hagenfels*. The other was his second officer, Günther Moewe.'

Rohrbach yawned, looking round the room. 'How come you were in the launch?' It really did sound casual: much better than his guffaw.

'We'd had tea on the *Hagenfels* with Kurt.'

'You *are* lucky! I'd love to go on a German ship again. Feel myself on German soil. Speak my language.'

'Me, too,' said Johan. 'I'm not German, but I admire them. Like to meet them. They're terrific fighters.'

'They are very brave people,' said Mariotta. 'Wonderful soldiers.'

Johan said: '*And* sailors. Wonderful sailors!'

Blast him, thought Rohrbach. He's so bloody obvious.

'You're a great admirer of theirs, aren't you, Johan?' said Mariotta.

'Terrific!' The beer made a drain-like noise as he up-ended the tankard. 'One day I hope to fight with them.'

'Is that possible?' Mariotta was puzzled.

'We shall see,' said Johan. 'We shall see.'

Rohrbach kicked him under the table, hard.

Mariotta was staring at the German who looked like a bruiser. He bowed and she smiled. 'He is the one I know,' she said to Rohrbach. 'Heinrich Schäffer. Second engineer of the *Hagenfels*.'

'Pouf!' Cleo pouted. 'I do not like him. He has only one idea.'

'Disgusting!' Johan winked at Rohrbach who thought, damn his lights, he's tight.

Before they finished with her Mariotta had promised to ask Lindemann if she and Cleo could take them to a party in the *Hagenfels*. 'I am sure he will like you,' she was compellingly intense. 'He is very sympathetic.'

'I'm sure I shall like *him*,' said Rohrbach.

Johan kicked him under the table.

Mariotta said: 'It will have to be soon, or not at all.'

Then Rohrbach saw her embarrassment and signalled to Johan to shut up. *It will have to be soon or not at all.* So the rumour was true. The *Hagenfels* was standing by for a break out. German security wasn't so wonderful after all.

Rohrbach rescued her. 'Yes. Or we shall have gone. We have not much longer here.'

She was relieved, all right. No mistaking that.

A few nights later they met at the summer-house on the cliff drive below the Polana. The night was cool after a hot day, and an easterly wind came in from the sea. The Newt arrived first. Irritable because they were late and he'd left

Di Brett with a sugar planter from the Zambesia Province who was making a heavy pass at the young widow. The hell of it was, she seemed to enjoy it.

When he'd complained she said: 'Jealousy doesn't become you, James. I'm only being polite to him.'

'You're encouraging him.'

'*James!* That comes badly from you. You're a married man and look how *you've* encouraged *me*.'

'Well,' blast her, he thought, she's adding embarrassment to my frustration. 'I adore Betty, but she's six thousand miles away. Anyway—there's a war on.'

'One wouldn't think so, James, from your behaviour.' Illogically, that remark of her's hurt, and he left in a temper, and then this long wait in the dark for Johan and David. Blast their eyes, too.

But they had a good excuse; they'd been watching the drill at Ponta Vermelha.

'Saw the whole thing from A to Z,' said Rohrbach. 'It's a piece of cake. The ships are blacked out except for navigation lights. When they've rounded number nine buoy and headed up the dredged channel, they make their signal letters by lamp to Ponta Vermelha and the signal station acknowledges. No permission to proceed or any bull like that. We saw four of them go through the same drill.'

'Fair enough,' said Johan. 'They've got pilots on board at that stage, so there's no need for anything else.'

The Newt lit a cigarette, the flare of the match illuminating their faces for a moment.

'I was swotting up the Admiralty sailing directions and charts this afternoon. The South Channel's the normal one out of this harbour but it's fantastically complicated. Buoyed and lighted, but stinking with hazards. Navigator's nightmare—shoals to the left of you, shoals to the right of you . . .'

'God, what a cliché,' said Johan.

The Newt sighed. 'It's not funny. Out towards Cabo da Inhaca, there's a chain of shoals across the entrance to the bay. The channel runs through them—Canal do Sul—it's a ninety degree turn on to it. Then a run up to Inhaca on a transit of two lights. Gave me the twitch reading about it. That's where our troubles will start, unless Steve agrees to use the northern channel. Not buoyed and lighted and

54

only used by fishing craft and Portuguese coasters, but there's plenty of water.'

'My bet,' said Rohrbach quietly, 'is that our troubles will start in the anchorage.'

The Newt puffed at his cigarette. 'If you really want to be gloomy, remember that when we reach Inhaca there's a pilot cutter waiting for us—slap in the fairway.'

Johan made a rude noise. 'Let's go the whole hog. Beyond the pilot cutter there are U-boats and Jerry raiders. So what!'

The Newt cleared his throat and fingered his moustache. 'I checked up on the *Hagenfels*'s gangway routine. She doesn't keep a quartermaster on it all the time. Only when a boat comes off. When it's gone, they hoist the foot about six feet clear of the water.'

'Could be a nuisance.' Rohrbach didn't sound happy.

'Saw an interesting bod go off to the *Hagenfels* this afternoon, David.'

'Who was that, Newt?'

'The shipping agent—gent known as Herr Stauch. Got his name from Artur.'

'What did he look like?'

'Large, fat Hun, perspiring freely. Very busy, important character. He came ashore later with the Captain, this Lindemann chap. He looked a good type. Salt horse, I'd say.'

'Anything else?'

'Not really.'

They told him about their night out with Mariotta and Cleo, the possibility of a party in the *Hagenfels*, and Mariotta's remark: *It will have to be soon or not at all.*

The Newt said: 'Doesn't know how right she is. But is a party on board wise, David? Hell of a risk, isn't it?'

'Not at all. She knows I'm German. She reckons Johan's English-hater number one in these parts. It'll be marvellous to get on board and have a look-see. With the vino flowing and the girls giggling, somebody'll spill the beans.'

The Newt was sceptical. 'Probably, Johan. I wonder what Steve'll think?'

'He'll be all for it,' Johan was emphatic. 'Right up his alley. I know, we were shipmates.'

They decided they now had enough information for the

rest of the party to come down. It was the fifteenth of November and the period of no moon was drawing closer.

Next morning Rohrbach handed in a telegram at the post office on the Avenida da Republica and it read: *Many happy returns. Wish you were with us. Love from all. Peterkins.*

It was addressed to Stephen Widmark.

Chapter Six

The long car journey with McFadden took some sleeping off, and it was almost eight o'clock when Widmark woke to the screech of seagulls.

He went to the window and looked out across the bay. It had rained during the night and the sky was overcast, the sea beneath it a steely grey. In the distance Chefine Island and Cape Inhaca stood out on the skyline, etched in deepest blue, the tongue of land enclosing the bay clearly visible. To the east, the line of the horizon revealed the break where the bay opened to the sea.

In the fairway he could see the marker buoys, some fishing boats, and a dredger low in the water puffing out into the bay to dump its load. A breeze, cool and refreshing, came in over the water, and there was a steady drip from the trees and shrubs in the garden below him.

Dressed as a tourist, Widmark spent much of the morning in the docks checking various details, but speaking to no one; he wore dark glasses, something he now wished he'd done at the frontier posts. For some time he watched the four ships in the anchorage below the coaling berths, sorting them out and putting names to them on the basis of the information he had collected in Cape Town. As he looked he felt once again the exhilaration that precedes action: the stimulating synthesis of fear and excitement. For months he had been scheming and planning, and here at last was the object of it all: the big freighter with the raked bow, cruiser stern and squat funnel. He wondered about the men on board: what they looked like and what sort of account they'd give of themselves when the day came. Later he drove about the town, refamiliarising himself with its layout and the names of the wide tree-lined avenidas. Opposite the Old Fort near the harbour he found the Port Captain's office, the high gable decorated with a frieze above which hung the Portuguese flag. The whites and greys, the tessellated balconies, the deep shadows behind the tall doors and french windows, gave the building a cool tranquillity.

Widmark parked the car and walked down past the dry-dock to the boat harbour; beyond it he could see the upper works of two Portuguese gunboats at the Gorjao Quay. Wondering what rôle they might play in the events that lay ahead, he went into the boat harbour. The Catembe Ferry was taking on its load of Africans, the women wearing bright sarongs and coloured *doeks*, the men in khaki shorts and white singlets. The women carried a variety of things on their heads: sacks of beans, crates of fowls, jars of water and sometimes parcels. When he'd seen all he wanted to he drove back to the Polana where he found an envelope which had been pushed under the door of his room. The note read: *Number nine hooks are best. Peter.* It was from the Newt and confirmed the rendezvous for nine o'clock that night on the road to Peter's.

For the next hour or so he wrote up his diary. Something he'd not done for days.

Then, after a bath and change, he went down to the cocktail bar and brooded in the shadows over a dry Martini, thinking of what lay ahead.

Later, on his way through the dining-room, he saw Olympia Stavropoulous, voluptuous, magnificent, the glitter of her jewels heightened the illusion of majesty. His mild panic was followed by relief and embarrassment, for she was looking through him; there was not a flicker of recognition.

At his table on the veranda he breathed deeply, shrugging his shoulders. What shattering luck that he should have run across her here when she ought to have been safely bedded down in Alexandria. Of course there was nothing exceptional about her being in LM; a lot of wealthy women, and some of their men, had hurried down to Southern Africa when Rommel threatened Cairo and Alex. Olympia Stavropoulus would certainly be in the van of that sort of exodus: she had no loyalties, no cause, only beautiful clothes, priceless jewellery and a thirst for pleasure which little Dimitri Stavropoulus, engrossed in expanding his millions, seemed to encourage, perhaps to expand the area of his own freedom.

Widmark had met them in 1941 soon after his arrival in Alex., by way of a letter from his father, who handled Dimitri's business interests in the Union. The Stavropoul-uses lived and entertained on the grand scale and Widmark had dined twice in the big house above Sidi Bishr. These had been large cosmopolitan affairs, men from the fighting services sprinkled with sophisticated locals: Greeks, Frenchmen, Levantines, Egyptians; smooth, clever bankers and stockbrokers, professional men, business men and their cultured decorative wives. Olympia, superb, robust, full bosomed, presided over these gatherings with vice-regal hauteur, capturing the men and subduing the women with the sheer scale of her physical magnificence. But Widmark, still obsessed with the events in the Kasos Strait and his mother's death, paid little attention to Olympia or her friends. Then came the occasion of his third visit to the Stavropouluses' house; the note inviting him could not have been briefer: 'Stephen dear, come and dine with us on Saturday.' And since her food was excellent and he felt pleasantly anonymous among the glitter of her guests, since Dimitri had a good billiard table and Napoleon that really was Napoleon, and because Widmark liked at times to get away from the Union Bar and Pastroudis, so full of the Services, he accepted. But when Saturday came and he was shown by an Arab servant into the vaulted drawing-room he found himself alone—that is, until Olympia arrived. If possible a more sumptuous, more statuesque Olympia, the elegant revealing frock making of her fine breasts more than if she had bared them.

She was enormously surprised. What was he doing there? Dinner? Heavens, no! It was Saturday of *next* week. Had the note not made that clear? But how utterly stupid of her! And Dimitri away in Beirut, and the house practically servantless for she had been going to stay with her sister in Cairo and had given them all time off but for some reason she'd had to change her plans. She would not hear of his going. And, no, certainly not! She would not let him take her into Alex. to dine. What a thought! Mahmoud would prepare a meal for them. It would be simple, of course—she shrugged her shoulders and they reminded Widmark of alabaster.

The supper was exquisite; so were Dimitri's wines and Dimitri's Napoleon, and it was not until Mahmoud had gone—'. . . these dreadful Arab servants,' complained Olympia, 'You may be *sure*, Stephen, that we shall not see him again tonight.'—that Widmark through a haze of euphoria began to suspect that neither the occasion nor the supper were extemporary, for Olympia's importunings were remarkable. For the first time in his life he found the rôles reversed: the woman the seducer and he, the man, the defender, if not of his virtue at least of his person.

Why he had so stoutly defended this he had never been quite sure: some mixture of intoxication, obfuscation, ebullience, boredom and shock, he supposed. Perhaps because she had been so tediously obvious—in any event he had decided suddenly that not only would she not get what she wanted, but that he was bored and wanted to get back to his ship.

All that, he reflected, sitting on the veranda of the Polana, was perfectly understandable; but why had he been so rude, so brutally rude? He boggled at the recollection. Olympia like a felled giantess weeping noisily on the divan, her humiliation abject, and he lurching across the patio to the street, walking unsteadily through the blackout of the warm Mediterranean night. All terribly undignified. Then the 'clip-clop' of a passing gharry which he stopped and hired for the journey to the harbour where he took a felucca off to his ship.

He had not seen Olympia Stavropoulus again—not until this night in the Polana. And her chilling bright-eyed stare confirmed what he'd long suspected: that he'd made an implacable enemy.

The launch went alongside the *Hagenfels* and a tall man in a tropical suit got out of the sternsheets, carrying a roll of paper under his arm. He spoke to the African coxswain in Portuguese. 'Wait for me. I won't be long.' Then he went up the gangway to the upper deck where he was met by an officer who saluted. 'I am Günther Moewe, sir. Navigating Officer.' He was formal and precise.

The tall man smiled faintly. 'I am von Falkenhausen. You are expecting me?'

Moewe nodded. 'Of course, Herr Baron.' So this was the Freiherr! Somehow he had not expected such a big man, nor one with so much charm. He looked young for a *Kapitän zur See*.

'Come this way, sir,' said Moewe, 'the Captain is expecting you.' It was not yet noon and the second officer hoped that the Captain would not be drinking when this distinguished naval officer was shown into his cabin. They

60

went along the steel deck and up two companion ladders to the accommodation below the bridge. Moewe knocked on the door and they went in. Lindemann was sitting at a desk in the large day cabin, writing. He got up at once, bowed, and shook his visitor's hand. 'Welcome on board, Herr Baron.' This was done before Moewe could perform the formal introduction he'd been rehearsing. It was not often one had the opportunity of introducing such a distinguished man. Von Falkenhausen and Lindemann were soon relaxed and at ease and this irritated the second officer, who was a stickler for ceremonial. Nor did he approve of the tray of beer and the bottle of schnapps.

Lindemann showed his visitor to a chair and sat down opposite him; Moewe remained standing, cap under arm, until Lindemann looked up and said: 'Thank you, Moewe. I shall not be needing you.' The second officer said: 'Very good, Herr Kapitän,' and withdrew.

The two men made small talk while Lindemann poured the beer, and von Falkenhausen took the brown-paper wrapping from the roll he was carrying and unfolded the charts.

'These are the latest, amended and up-to-date.' He passed them to Lindemann. 'They are from the British Admiralty so they ought to be good.'

Lindemann looked at him curiously, taking in the frank brown eyes, the scarred left cheek. 'How did you get them, Herr Baron?'

'From a contact in South Africa. I picked them up at Ressano Garcia yesterday.'

Lindemann looked at the charts. 'This is excellent. You have everything here. Eight of them. North and South Atlantic, and Indian Ocean from the East African to the Australian coasts.'

'They are small scale, but they are all we need, Kapitän.'

Still looking at the charts, Lindemann said quietly: 'When do you think we go?'

'It is impossible to say. It is almost the period of no moon. I think the signal from the Wilhelmstrasse will come soon.'

'When will you join us?'

'On the night of sailing, Kapitän.'

'We shall be very glad to have you with us.' It was evident that Lindemann was sincere.

61

'I too. I shall be glad. It is a long time since I was at sea.'

It was a dark night, the thin moon had not yet risen, and to seaward sky and sea merged so that there was no horizon. In the headlights of the car there was little to be seen but the bush on either side of the road and occasionally the loom of a tree. The winding road was rough in places where the tar skim had broken and the car bounced and bumped. Through breaks in the dunes they saw the lights of the fairway buoys, and beyond them those of Chefine and Inhaca. A cool wind came in from the sea. A few miles down the road they turned left on to a dirt-track and soon after they saw, in the thin reflection of the tail lights of a car which had pulled off the road, two dark shapes.

Widmark slowed down. 'Probably them. We'll drive past slowly.'

They passed the stationary car and the Newt and McFadden confirmed that it was the rest of the party. Widmark stopped and reversed, parking the Buick in front of the Studebaker so that both cars were clear of the roadway. They got out of the car and David Rohrbach and Johan le Roux came up to them. Hans le Roux and Mike Kent got out of Rohrbach's car and there was some leg-pulling and laughter. They lifted the bonnet of the Studebaker and with a torch and some tools pretended to work on its engine. The others gathered round and for the next thirty minutes Rohrbach, Johan and the Newt gave the newcomers all the information they could. After questioning them Widmark seemed satisfied with what had been done.

'We'll have to work fast now,' he said. 'It's only three days to the no moon period. What's the latest gen on the sailing of *Clan McPhilly* and *Tactician*?'

Hans hissed, 'Car coming!' and they bent over the bonnet. The headlights of the passing car lit up the scene momentarily, then it was gone.

The Newt lit a cigarette and went back to Widmark's question. 'Artur—the tugboat chap—reckons they'll finish loading on the twenty-fourth.'

'What's the drill after that?'

'They leave the loading berth and anchor in the stream until two or three of them are ready. Then they sail during the hours of darkness, sometimes joining up with a convoy outside or if they're fast enough sailing independently.'

'Which of the two are we going to use?' David Rohrbach asked.

'Preferably the bigger ship, the *Clan McPhilly*. But I'm going to have a look at their captains before I decide.'

Widmark was keenly interested when he heard that Rohrbach and Johan might be invited to a party on the *Hagenfels*. 'Terrific!' he said, 'but you'll have to make it snappy. There isn't much time left, David.'

Rohrbach laughed dryly. 'That's what Mariotta said. They're seeing Lindemann tonight. She'll let us know at breakfast tomorrow, Steve.'

'Don't drop any bricks. Be careful if it's on. But you may get some marvellous gen. Try and get the skipper and his chums plastered. See if they let on in any way about being ready for sea.' He lit a cigarette, the flare of the match revealing his dark intense face. 'Mariotta's remark may not mean much. You tell me she's going back to her people in Northern Mozambique in a few days. That was probably what she meant by *soon or not at all.*'

'Maybe, Steve. But she looked as though she'd dropped a clanger.'

Widmark stroked his chin. 'The latest intelligence reports I saw in Cape Town were very vague. Rather played down what they'd said before. You know the sort of thing— *Hagenfels may* run for it or she *may not.* Take your choice.'

'That's precisely what we're going to do,' said the Newt.

'Yes, it is.' The way Widmark said it didn't sound as though failure was one of the things he was worrying about.

Ten minutes later the party broke up, the cars pulled away from the side of the road and turned and re-entered the main road, the Studebaker making for Peter's, and the Buick going back up the road towards the Polana. When the two cars dropped their passengers in darkened streets in the Polana and Ponta Vermelha areas, the breeze from the sea had become an easterly wind, and stars shone through gaps in fast-moving clouds.

Widmark parked his car and went into the hotel. It was late and the bar was empty but for two befuddled young men who drooled at each other in owl-like seriousness. He sat at the far end, refusing the bartender's attempts at conversation, and drank two Courvoisiers in fairly quick succession. Then, responding to their stimulation, he ordered a third and when it was finished gazed moodily at the empty glass, weighing the possibility of a fourth but deciding against it and for bed.

The lift stopped at an upper floor, he said good night to the African and made for his room. He saw that the door was on the latch and was mildly surprised because he thought he'd locked it. Opening it, he switched on the light and realised at once that he'd got out of the lift on the wrong floor for, upon the bed, her fine head precisely in the middle of the small embroidered pillow, lay Olympia Stavropoulus. The light could have been on for only a few seconds when he switched it off, but he left the room wondering furiously if she'd been awake and whether she'd seen him. If she had what on earth would she think? Worried and rattled, he cursed himself and the liftman for the stupid mistake and went up the stairs to the next floor. As he had suspected his bedroom door was locked. Again he cursed. Of all the wrong rooms he might have walked into, why had he chosen Olympia's?

The next day was Sunday.

Shortly before lunch Widmark came up from the harbour, swung his car into the courtyard, gay with portulaca, and parked in the shade of the magnolia trees. The heat rose from the paving stones in waves as he walked to the front door of the Polana past the palm trees with plantains growing at their feet, past the concrete tubs of red geraniums and the beds of tropical plants where the variegated leaves of the crotons and the deep carmines of the cannas predominated. The glare from the white walls of the hotel struck into his eyes like fine sand.

In the foyer he was asking the Goanese porter for a newspaper, when there was a touch on his arm and a woman said: 'Hallo, Stephen! What on earth are you doing here?'

He turned slowly, alarm signals jangling in his mind, wondering who it was and what he was going to say. Then with relief he saw that it was Di Brett, a woman he'd met at parties in the Cape in 1940 and once danced with at Kelvin Grove and then, somehow, she'd passed out of his ken, and when he got back from the Mediterranean he'd heard that she'd left the Cape.

As he said 'Hallo, Di!' he saw the Newt walking away, back towards them, and with cold unbelief heard her call after him. 'Do be a darling, James, and bring down my sunglasses.' The Newt's shoulders twitched and he mumbled 'Righto!' but he didn't turn round.

Widmark knew that Di Brett was a widow. 'Your new husband?' he smiled thinly, inclining his head towards the retreating figure.

'Heavens, no! A charming young Englishman from Portugal who is staying here. I've only known him for a week.'

'You haven't wasted much time.'

Her eyebrows arched. 'I call everybody "darling." You should know that, Stephen! Anyway what are you doing here? I thought you were at sea fighting the enemy.'

'Invalided out. Asthma. Just happened. I was bored stiff in the Cape, so I went up to Johannesburg and when that died on me I thought I'd come down here and loaf in the sun.'

'Married?' Her smile was half indolent, half curious.

'No. What are you doing here?'

'Oh! Waiting for the time to pass.' She looked away and her mouth drooped. 'I tried Durban after the Cape. Then Salisbury. Then Johannesburg. But everywhere I went it was people in uniform and the talk was war, war, *war*, and I couldn't bear it any longer so I came here. There's something to be said for a neutral country. You escape from the uniform and—and the things you're trying to forget.' She smiled gaily and said: 'And to be quite honest, the food and the atmosphere here are much less stodgy than the Union. This place is quaintly gay and cosmopolitan. There's even a casino.'

'I know. Costa's. I'm going to give it a thrash to-night.'

'Be careful, Steve! Lots of pretty girls there.'

He looked round the foyer, bored with the conversation, anxious to escape, worried about the Newt's friendship with this attractive woman. The Newt was highly susceptible and Widmark didn't want him involved in that sort of thing now. There was too much at stake. And why hadn't the Newt mentioned her?

At that moment Olympia Stavropoulus rounded a corner and sailed past them, looking to Widmark like a battle cruiser on the measured mile. Without appearing to notice him, she managed a general glare which was a mixture of hatred and triumph. Widmark shuddered and looked at his watch. God! he thought. She must have seen me in her room! To Di he said: 'I'll have to get under way. I'm astern of station.'

'That sounds terribly naval.' She thought of something and her eyes and voice were contrite. 'Oh, Steve! I haven't congratulated you. I heard you did terribly well in the Med. Two DSCs and buckets of glory.'

The lines round his mouth tightened and he gave her a wintry look. 'I'm not so sure about the glory.' Then he was gone.

Chapter Seven

To Otto Stauch it was intensely irritating that he had to go and see von Falkenhausen and not the reverse. Whereas Stauch had been in Mozambique for fifteen years, the Freiherr was a comparatively new arrival in the territory; indeed, it was only four months ago that he had come and then after six weeks he had disappeared again and of course they were not permitted to know where. Oh, no! He was too important for that. The first time he had stayed at the Polana, but now on this return visit he had a flat in the Ponta Vermelha area and what was more all the work of finding and renting it had fallen upon Stauch. *'Mein Gott!'* The fat man puffed and blew as he climbed the stairs to the flat. 'Anyone would think I am his servant.' Then he comforted himself with the thought that what he did was for the Fatherland and not for the Freiherr, and with that uppermost in his mind he reached the landing and pressed the bell. While he waited he saw that the name on the white card in the brass frame was still 'Jorge Andrada Cavalho.' That was sensible.

The door was opened by an African. Stauch followed him down a book-lined passage into a study which was clearly a bachelor's. There was a tray on a low table, with a whisky decanter, soda siphon, beer and glasses. The African disappeared and Stauch was alone. He walked round the room examining the pictures on the walls, some prints of early Lisbon, shelves of well-bound books with an unread look about them and various other odds and ends including a collection of ivory elephants. He stopped before a framed photograph taken on safari: Senhor Cavalho, evidently, standing with his foot on the trunk of a dead elephant, the tusks gleaming large and white behind him, a rifle in the crook of his arm.

Stauch's thoughts were interrupted by von Falkenhausen coming down the staircase into the study; tall, brown eyes unsmiling, he moved quietly for a big man. There was no friendship between these two. The Freiherr, warm and sympathetic by nature, had learnt on his last visit that Stauch was unapproachable, and he accepted this with the philosophy of a man who has other and more important things to worry about. He knew that Stauch was loyal; a painstaking man whose services in Mozambique were of great value to the Third Reich, but Stauch was, the Freiherr knew, inordinately jealous and given to ambitions which far outran his capabilities.

The men greeted each other formally and sat down. Von Falkenhausen offered his guest a cheroot.

'No thank you, Herr Baron.'

'A drink, then, Herr Stauch?'

The fat man would have liked to refuse, but his thirst and the appeal of the frosted bottles were too much. 'If you please,' he said curtly.

The Freiherr poured the beer into a porcelain stein with a pewter top, passed it to Stauch, and helped himself to a whisky and soda.

Without waiting for his host, Stauch raised his glass. '*Prosit!*'

The Freiherr said: '*Prosit!*' and smiled thinly at Stauch whose long look round the flat ended with a censorious, 'You live very comfortably.'

'In the moments when I'm here, Herr Stauch. At other times not quite so comfortably.'

The rebuke had its effect. Stauch sank back into his chair and applied himself to the stein of chilled Pilsener. It was excellent.

The Freiherr lit his cheroot, spinning the match into a wastepaper basket. 'Today I delivered the charts to Captain Lindemann.'

'Your first meeting with him? What do you think of him?'

'I liked him. He's uncomplicated. A real seaman. No beating about the bush.'

'And his navigating officer? Günther Moewe?' Stauch's small eyes watched the Freiherr curiously.

'How should I know? We met for only a moment. Possibly he is a good man.'

'He *is*. He is also a good member of the party.' This was said with some relish. Stauch, too, was a good member of the party; but with the German aristocracy, the old junker officer class, one could never be sure. The von Falkenhausens came from East Prussia and they were great landowners. Stauch felt sure their party loyalties would be lukewarm.

The Freiherr ignored the remark. 'Lindemann tells me that the *Hagenfels* is in all respects ready for sea. The period of no moon commences in three days. At any moment a signal will come from the Wilhelmstrasse. On the night of the sailing, during the hours of darkness, we will reinforce her crew from the other ships. The time of sailing must coincide with the outward movement of allied vessels. To give *Hagenfels* cover in the harbour as she leaves, and outside when she reaches the open sea.'

Stauch loosened his belt. It was hot and his stomach strained against the leather strap. 'Did you inform Kapitän Lindemann of what is intended?'

'Only in outline. That the ship will become a supply vessel for U-boats and raiders. No other details. He knows that I shall take command.'

They discussed the matter further, and then Stauch changed the subject. 'You have seen the signals we have been intercepting? The sinkings off here and to the south are excellent, are they not, Herr Baron?' His little eyes, conscious of the part he had played, shone with pride.

Von Falkenhausen nodded. 'Very good indeed! The U-cruisers are not wasting time. But the supply situation is serious and much depends on getting the *Hagenfels* out.'

Stauch looked at his watch and got up to go. The Freiherr waved him down. 'One moment, Herr Stauch! There is another matter I must discuss with you. It is important.'

The fat man sank back into his chair, his small eyes a mixture of suspicion and curiosity.

Von Falkenhausen filled the empty stein and poured himself another whisky and soda. 'At Ressano Garcia yesterday, when I collected the charts, two South African naval officers came through. They didn't recognise me, but I recognised them. I saw them in Alexandria last year on many occasions. They were serving in the same group.' He paused. 'An anti-submarine group.'

Stauch was not particularly interested. 'I imagine they are here on leave. It is not unusual.'

'No. But it is unusual to give incorrect information on immigration forms.'

Stauch sat up and began to take notice. 'How do you know this?'

'Andrada Gouviea was on duty in the customs house. He

69

let me look at the forms they'd just completed. Widmark—he was a lieutenant when I last saw him—described himself as a salesman. The other man, McFadden—he was engineer officer in Widmark's ship—described himself as an accountant.'

'That is normal, Herr Baron. These were probably their peacetime occupations and coming to a neutral country they can only come as civilians.'

'Their peacetime occupations happened to be "lawyer" and "marine engineer." But there is more. They gave addresses in Johannesburg at which they are not known.' The tall man's eyes glinted.

'Are you sure, Herr Baron?'

'I telephoned Johannesburg last night. Spoke to Leuthen. He checked and phoned me back this morning.'

'Another thing,' von Falkenhausen was holding his drink against the light, revolving the glass slowly, squinting at it with one eye shut. 'These two,' he paused, *friends*—down here on *holiday*—are staying at different hotels. That is not very friendly, Herr Stauch. Widmark at the Polana, McFadden at the Cardoso. This information, too, I got from the immigration forms.'

Stauch tapped on the arm of his chair, frowning at the problem. 'What is Widmark like?'

'That,' said the Freiherr quietly, 'is what worries me. He's a dangerous man. Known in Alex. as "The Butcher," and for good reason.'

He told Stauch what he knew of Widmark and how he had earned his nickname. After long discussion they decided on two things: first, that it would be unwise to inform the Portuguese authorities that these men had given false information at the border, because the Portuguese, though neutral, were unquestionably pro-Allies; secondly, the Freiherr would visit the Polana and reintroduce himself to Widmark: such a confrontation could do no harm. It might conceivably do some good. Give a clue, for example, as to why these two men were in Lourenço Marques.

Widmark was pretty certain that the oily, bald man with the sunglasses was watching him, putting aside his newspaper at times and inclining his head towards where Widmark sat alone in the corner of the lounge reading. Irritated by this attention, Widmark looked up and stared hard at the bald man who backed behind the paper again.

It was the first time he had seen the man, and his plump, swarthy oiliness did not commend him. He tried to classify him: Belgian? Portuguese? Greek? Roumanian? Hungarian? Merchant? Money-lender? Filthy postcard vendor? He gave up. The fellow looked like all or any of them—someone who belonged to the deeper shadows of the market place. Having put the man in his place, metaphorically at least, Widmark went back to his book with some satisfaction.

David Rohrbach and Johan spent that Sunday out in the bay fishing in one of Domingos Parao's boats. It was a sultry day and they ran out into the lee of Chefine Island, fishing along the reef Parao had recommended. They discussed various things including their disappointment that Mariotta had not appeared at breakfast that morning, so that they still didn't know whether the party was on.

In the late afternoon, when it clouded over and the wind came in from the east, they started up the motor and made for the harbour, passing an inward-bound tanker on the way. As they rounded the fairway buoy off Ponta Vermelha, they were overtaken by the sloop *Bartolomeu Dias* and on her upper deck they saw clusters of men in tattered clothing, many covered in fuel oil, some wearing bandages, most with haggard, strained faces. Johan realised they were survivors.

'Poor devils!' he said.

David Rohrbach nodded. 'I chatted to a German in the Central Bar last night. He told me there's a U-boat group outside raising hell. Apparently this place has become stiff with survivors in the last few days.'

'I've come across a few in the Rua Araújo.'

'Can't think why we still allow independent sailings.'

The entrance to the boat harbour loomed up, and they turned into it and secured alongside. After tidying up the boat and stowing away the gear, they paid Domingos Parao what they owed him, gave most of the fish they'd caught to Africans waiting at the Catembe Ferry, and drove back to the Cardoso.

That night there was a rendezvous down at the Aterro de Machaquene and to it went Rohrbach, Johan, Widmark and Mike Kent. They sat in Widmark's car, parked in the dark under the casuarina trees, well back from the road.

Widmark lit a cigarette. 'What's the buzz, David?'

'The party's on. We saw Mariotta and Cleo about an hour ago. Mariotta says Lindemann's all for it. When she suggested bringing me and Johan, he wasn't madly keen. Said there'd be too many men, but later he relented. Mariotta's pretty hard to resist. But he said not to let anyone know because his agent didn't like parties on board.'

'When's it for?'

'Any night this week. The girls are to let Lindemann know. We told them we couldn't make a date until tomorrow, because until then we wouldn't know which night Domingos had fixed for our fishing.'

Widmark was silent, thinking hard, then he said: 'Tomorrow's the twenty-second, isn't it? Beginning of the no moon period.'

Rohrbach confirmed that it was, and Widmark was silent again until he said: 'I was on the Gorjao Quay today. The *Clan McPhilly* and *Tactician* are still working cargo. They're working through tonight. The Newt's tugboat chap says they'll finish loading on Monday or Tuesday and go out into the stream. Sail on Wednesday or Thursday night.'

Widmark's laconic announcement jolted them. It meant they would be in action on Wednesday or Thursday night, and though they'd known the time was coming closer they tingled with apprehension at the approach of reality.

Rohrbach said: 'Sooner the better, I suppose. Shall we suggest tomorrow for the party?'

'What—Monday?' Widmark shook his head. 'I'd like to say "Yes," but it's too soon. We *must* sail on the same night as *Tactician* and *Clan McPhilly* and that means Wednesday or Thursday, and we're not ready in other ways.'

'But you'll want the party before that, won't you, Steve? That only leaves Tuesday.'

There was a moment of silence, then Widmark said: 'I'm afraid the party'll have to be on the night of sailing.'

Mike Kent's puzzled voice expressed their bewilderment. 'But what about the women, sir?'

'They'll have to come with us, Mike. A trip down the coast won't do them any harm.'

'Are you sure this is a good idea, Steve?' Rohrbach's

tone made it clear that he didn't think so. But Widmark was not compromising. 'I've given this a lot of thought. Ever since you mentioned the party. From every point of view it's the best thing. Means we'll have two of you on board at the beginning of the operation.' He chuckled dryly, 'You may even be able to do something with the Newt's love potion.' He paused, only to become serious again. 'If there's a party, Lindemann and his officers will be drinking. They'll be off their guard. We're counting on the element of surprise. It's going to be twice as easy if there's a party going on in the Captain's cabin with two of you there.'

'You mean you want us to go to the party armed?' Johan was mildly shocked—this was something quite beyond the social pale.

'Of course,' said Widmark, 'to the bloody teeth!'

'*Wragtig*—struth!' muttered Johan.

'I'm not happy about the women being there,' grumbled Rohrbach. 'They may get hurt.'

Widmark's nerves were on edge and he snapped: 'It's not a tea-party. We're hi-jacking an enemy ship.'

There was a long silence while they thought about the new plan and wondered how it would work. When Widmark spoke next his tone had changed and they knew he was making amends. 'The thing is, David, this party's a priceless opportunity. We *must* use it. We can't put the women ashore after it, because if we did the whole world'd know that the break out was a British operation. Another thing. If we staged it a day or so after the party, the girls might connect the disappearance on the same night of you two and the *Hagenfels*. They'd probably talk. I'm afraid there's nothing for it. They've got to come with us.'

They discussed the new plan and it was agreed that Widmark would visit the *Clan McPhilly* and the *Tactician* the next morning, so that he could by lunch time let Rohrbach know the night for the party. Rohrbach would then tell Mariotta. The others were to be informed of the new plan and there was to be a full attendance at a rendezvous the night before D-night for a final rehearsal. On Monday night, Rohrbach and Johan were to go fishing but this time they were to pick up Hans le Roux and Mike Kent at the native fish dock, take them into the bay, and land them at the fish dock again on the way in. It was essential that they should learn how to handle the boat and know their way about that part of the Espirito Santo at night.

Rohrbach turned the car and drove back into the suburbs, dropping his passengers in dark streets not far from their hotels.

It was a thoughtful Mike Kent who made his way on foot up Avenida Aquiar, past the Vasco Da Gama Park to his hotel.

Inside he was frightened. This he acknowledged with a curious clinical interest and with no sense of shame. Frightened and vaguely sick and wishing that he'd not volunteered for this hare-brained operation. He'd longed for action and now that he was about to get it he wasn't at all happy with the prospect.

Now that it was so close, the fun and excitement of the early days of planning seemed to have gone. He'd tried to recapture the zest but couldn't. Instead he thought of his mother and wished that he were with her. It was a childish and most inappropriate thought, he knew, but intellectually he was too honest to deny it, so he set about analysing its cause and this took his mind off the unpleasantness.

After they'd dropped him in a side street near the Avenida da Republica, Widmark walked over to his car and drove down Alexandre Herculano, turned left at the bottom and made through the Aterro do Machaquene to the sea front where he parked facing the sea, absorbed in his thoughts.

Not for the first time he was thinking of the consequences of what he had done. He was certain that the decision he had made was right, and he excluded the likelihood of failure though it remained a remote possibility, an unpleasant shapeless thing in the background which he refused to contemplate. But he was troubled tonight by a picture which formed obstinately in his mind of a court-martial, with himself on trial, the red-bearded Commodore testifying: 'Yes. I showed him the Commander-in-Chief's signal which flatly rejected the operation and forbade any . . .'

Widmark shook off these thoughts and fell to worrying about the Newt and Di Brett—this had been gnawing at his mind ever since her 'Oh, James, be a darling and fetch my glasses'; then he checked mentally every detail of the plan, examining it meticulously, making sure he'd forgotten nothing. Finally his thoughts turned to the next day. He knew that everything now depended on what he found when he visited the British ships at the Gorjao Quay.

Without the full co-operation of one of them it would not be possible to go ahead with the operation. If both captains refused to co-operate he would be confronted with defeat. For a long time he brooded over this and then, as if that were not enough, he was troubled by a lively picture of Olympia Stavropoulus sweeping past in the foyer as he spoke to Di Brett, her eyes flashing their twin messages of hatred and triumph. The hatred he understood, but triumph for what? Because she'd found him speaking to a pretty woman?

Dismissing these cheerless thoughts, he drove into the town and parked below the Port Captain's office. It was close on midnight. He walked over to the Rua Araújo and then along it to Rua Salazar. In the Central Bar he ordered a double whisky and felt all the better for it. Then he worked his way back through Rua Araújo, past The Emperor with its brassy blast of music to the Carlton. It was as he passed it that he had this very strong feeling that he was being followed: whether he had heard footsteps, which he doubted because the night was full of sound, or whether it was instinct he did not know, but the feeling grew until the desire to look round was overwhelming. He turned and there was the balding man with the sunglasses. Farther down the road Widmark twice stopped and on each occasion his shadower did so too.

Widmark reversed his course, walked straight back past the man who was examining a shop window, apparently oblivious of Widmark who continued on his way until he was abreast of the Carlton where he slipped abruptly into the dark lane adjoining it. He went through a courtyard and up an iron staircase to the first-floor landing of an old and rambling building. In the main hall the band was playing and the dance floor and the tables round it were packed. He stood against the wall in the shadows, watching, getting his bearings. Johan le Roux and David Rohrbach were with a dark beauty at a far table and he wondered briefly if she were Mariotta. Then he began worrying about the oily man. There was no doubt that he'd been following him, and this on top of the incident in the Polana. But why, puzzled Widmark, is he interested in me? Why is he following me? Unable to answer these questions but conscious that he'd succeeded in shaking off his shadower, Widmark went over to the bar, collected another whisky, plopped in ice from a bucket on the counter, and made for the roulette room. He edged in between some women at the crowded table and watched the play with the absorbed attention of the gambler. But he held back, waiting until he'd got the feel of the table, watching the stakes go on, the wheel spinning, the croupiers calling and raking the table. When he'd bought twenty-five pounds worth of escudos counters from the cashier he went back to the table. As always he started with the equivalent of two pounds each on *odd* and *red*. The wheel spun, the small white ball ran round the rim, came lower as the wheel slowed and dropped into one of the thirty-seven cups. The croupier called *twenty-two*, even and black, and Widmark's bets were raked away. That decided him. He'd work up to an odd red, since he always followed a losing bet. He raised his stakes, putting five pounds on the table, again on *odd* and *red* and this time the croupier called *twelve,* so it was even and red and Widmark was still four pounds down. He shifted his counters to *manque,* the wheel spun, and when it stopped the croupier called *thirty-one*. A woman cried out in dismay, and Widmark saw the rake take his money, and he made a mental note of his losses—fourteen pounds. He moped round the table to get away from the bad luck and put his remaining eleven pounds *carré* on seventeen, eighteen, twenty and twenty-one, and it was then that he looked up and saw the girl watching him. The croupier was intoning, and with his mind now more on the girl than the table Widmark was slow to register that *twenty-one* was a win for him; he saw the rake push a heap of counters against his stake, and woke up. The odds on the *carré* were eight to one, so this was ninety-nine pounds—the eleven pounds he'd staked plus the win of eighty-eight. Pocketing half the counters, he put those still on the table on twenty-seven, chasing his luck with odd and red, pre-occupied now with the girl rather than the game.

The wheel spun, the white ball scampered and he waited impatiently for the croupier's call; it came at last—*ten,* and Widmark saw his fifty pounds disappear.

Hunching his shoulders, he stood up, nodded to the croupier, exchanged his remaining counters for a pile of escudos which he reckoned at fifty pounds, and then looked for the girl. She was still standing against the wall at the far end of the bar, and beyond all doubt she was watching him.

The light from a wall lamp reflected on her face and their eyes met and held in one of those extraordinary moments of recognition; not of two people who'd known each other, but of a man and woman seeing each other for the first time both conscious of an irresistible attraction and acknowledging it without inhibition. She was tall and slim, and from an oval high-cheek-boned face, slanted hazel eyes watched him with a curious mixture of sympathy and inquiry.

Without consciously making the decision, he went over to her and said: 'Hallo!'

She smiled and said 'Hallo!' and he knew then that she wasn't English; but her smile did something to him which he knew he'd never be able to describe.

For what seemed a long time they looked at each other, conscious of the strange thing that had happened. Then he said: 'Come and dance,' and they went through the crowded tables to the small floor where he took her in his arms as if he'd known her all his life.

'I should not be doing this,' she said, mildly shocked. 'I am with other people.' One eyebrow lifted as if she wanted some reassurance from him.

'You could have refused.'

'I could not!' Her eyes were serious but there was the hint of a smile. 'You shouldn't have asked me.'

'I *had* to. The moment I saw you.'

'I know. I felt like that. I couldn't stop looking at you. Is it not strange?' Again the eyebrows registered interrogation.

'Very strange.' His hand tightened on hers. 'I think I've been waiting for you for a long time.'

'I too.' She said it serenely, looking away from him, as if the remark were commonplace.

'Who are you?'

'Cleo Melanides. I live in Lourenço Marques. We are Greek.' This was added with a proud little tilt of the head.

He looked at her hand. 'You're not married?'

'No.'

'Thank God!'

'And you?' She laughed gaily.

'No.'

'Thank God!' she mimicked. More seriously, she said: 'What is your name. Tell me about yourself.'

She noticed his hesitation before he said: 'Stephen

Widmark, from Johannesburg.'

The band stopped and they stood waiting, clapping, hoping that it would begin again, but the lights went up and the floor emptied. She touched his arm. 'I shall have to go back to the others.' As she said it she saw his disappointment and her eyes softened. 'Shall I see you again?'

Holding her hand, oblivious of their surroundings, of the people round the empty floor, he said: 'Of course. What's your telephone number?'

As they walked off the floor she gave him the number and then, before he knew what was happening, she had stopped at a table and was saying: 'These are my friends—Mariotta Pereira, David Rohrbach and Johan le Roux.' The three men looked at each other blankly, and Johan bowed. 'It was nice of you to bring back *our* guest.'

'Not at all,' Widmark smiled remotely and was conscious of the other girl, Mariotta, looking at him.

Rohrbach pointed to a chair. 'Won't you sit down?' It wasn't a warm invitation and, embarrassed at the turn of events, and torn between leaving Cleo and staying for what might be an unwise exercise in wits, Widmark shook his head. 'I'd love to, but I must be going. It's late.'

Johan looked at his watch and said: 'Yes, it is,' with heavy emphasis.

The band started and Johan and Rohrbach took Mariotta and Cleo on to the floor. Widmark watched them go and from what seemed an eternity away Cleo gave him a sad little smile before she was engulfed by Johan.

Still tingling from the excitement of meeting the girl, Widmark made his way back to the bar. Everything was a pleasant blur until he found himself looking at short range into the face of an oily balding man who sat on a bar stool with his back to the room, smoking a cheroot. Because of the sunglasses Widmark couldn't be sure that the man was looking at him, but as his face was less than four feet away it seemed highly probable that he was. Widmark gave him the sort of look reserved for bad smells, decided not to have a drink, and went down to the street. There he thought anxiously about this latest encounter, eventually deciding that he was getting jumpy and that it could all be coincidence; even the apparent shadowing in Rua Araújo. After all, why shouldn't they both have walked in the same direction at the same time? And while it was

78

true that when he'd stopped the bald man had stopped too, it was probably because he'd been embarrassed by Widmark's stare in the Polana lounge. And surely there was nothing odd about his presence in the Casino? After all, he was essentially the Casino type. Where better to flog his wares, filthy postcards or otherwise? Widmark dismissed him from his thoughts.

Had he been asked to, he couldn't have described his walk to the car and drive back to the Polana; his thoughts soared and he felt tremendously excited; he had never before experienced such a state of euphoria and, thinking about it, he realised that he was in love—in love with a girl he'd just met in Costa's: a girl about whom he knew nothing but that she was Greek, lived in Lourenço Marques, and evidently felt about him as he did about her.

The nearest thing to this experience, but a long way from it, had been in 1937, in San Francisco, a few days after they'd arrived in the *Albatross*.

At a party in the Mark he'd met a girl, fallen, he thought, deeply in love with her, and on the strength of a wild five days and a good deal of encouragement followed her across the North American continent to New York where he'd found she had a husband and two small children. Vowing never again to let a woman make a fool of him, he'd flown back to San Francisco, sad and chastened, to attend to the sale of the *Albatross*.

Then the war had come and what with the Kasos Strait affair, the loss of his mother, and the private disgrace of his return to South Africa, he'd become gloomy and preoccupied, and one way and another he'd not had much time or inclination for the company of women.

And now, sitting in his room at the Polana, thinking of Cleo, of that incredible meeting, of how she had looked and what she had said, he accepted with sombre resignation that in the few days left to him in Lourenço Marques he'd have to keep away from her. He couldn't afford to get involved in anything which might interfere with or endanger the task ahead. Afterwards, when it was all over, he'd come back. It wouldn't be long and she'd wait. Then, with a distinct sense of disquiet, he remembered something: Cleo would be at the party in the *Hagenfels*—she, too, would be coming with them to Durban.

For a moment he panicked: thought of warning her that

she mustn't come, that she might be in danger; but even as he had them he discarded these thoughts. How could he tell her that? She knew Kurt Lindemann! There could be no change in the plans. For better or worse she'd have to come. His feeling of unease gave way to the agreeable prospect of seeing her again so soon. Of one thing he had no doubt: she was the future Mrs Stephen Widmark.

At 2 a.m. Widmark made his way downstairs and along the passage to number 214. He tried the door, found it locked, frowned with irritation, and knocked on it quietly. But there was no response although he did this several times; then, just as he was about to go, thoroughly angry, the Newt came up the passage, winked heavily, unlocked the door and let him in.

'Where've you been?' said Widmark coldly.

'Having a pee, old boy! Any objections?'

Widmark gave him another frosty look. 'Let's see those charts and sailing directions.'

For some time they worked on them, and they decided eventually to abandon the idea of taking the normal course on leaving, Canal do Sul and Cabo da Inhaca, because of possible trouble with the pilot vessel.

Instead they would use the northern channel, Canal do Norte, which had ample water although it was not buoyed or lighted and was never used by large vessels.

When all this had been agreed, Widmark said what had been on his mind for some time: 'Look, Newt! Your private life's none of my business, but for God's sake don't get involved with Di Brett. She's easy on the eye, I know, but we've got a hell of a lot at stake, and this isn't the time for necking.'

The Newt became distinctly offhand. 'My dear Steve, *please*! I didn't come down in the last shower of rain. I enjoy her company, it's no more than that. And since I'm supposed to be here on holiday I might as well behave as if I were. After all, it wouldn't be very convincing if I spent all day on my own. On the contrary, I'd say it'd look damned suspicious.'

'Well, maybe you've got something there. But for God's sake be careful.'

'Of course I will,' said the Newt huffily. 'I'm not a bloody fool.'

80

Chapter Eight

It was Monday, and Widmark was down at the docks early. He'd discarded the casual dress of a tourist for a tropical suit, a Hawks tie, a silk shirt and sunglasses.

His first call along the Gorjao Quay was at the *Clan McPhilly* where he showed his boarding permit to the gangway guard. On the upper deck he found all the bustle and activity of a merchant ship loading: shouting African stevedores, whirring electric cranes, and the thud of loaded cargo nets landing in the holds. There was the customary litter of dunnage, of wooden hatch covers, steel hatch beams, folded tarpaulins and cordage.

At number three hold he found the third officer, a red-haired young man with a freckled face, uniform cap pushed well back on his head. Widmark showed him the letter and asked to be taken to the Captain. They went forward along the starboard side and by way of various ladders and alleyways to the Captain's cabin.

He turned out to be a thick-set Scot from Glasgow with a weather-beaten face, beaky nose, and challenging grey eyes.

After the introductions, the third officer left and Widmark handed the Captain a letter from the chief agents in Cape Town.

It was brief and to the point.

Dear Captain McRobert,
*   This will introduce to you Lieutenant-Commander Stephen Widmark of the SA Naval Forces. I shall be grateful if you will give him every assistance.*
                                    Yours sincerely,
                                    R. L. Hendry

From his wallet Widmark produced his Naval Identity Card which the Captain examined carefully, his eyes moving from the photograph to Widmark and back. Then he said: 'Take a seat, Commander.'

They sat down and McRobert began to fill his pipe. 'What

can I do for you?'

Widmark produced an Admiralty envelope marked 'Most Secret.'

In the few minutes he'd been in McRobert's cabin he'd decided that this was his man, and that it wouldn't be necessary to visit the *Tactician*. Had it been otherwise, had the Captain not so favourably impressed him, he wouldn't have produced the second letter. Instead he would have asked whether he could ship his car to Cape Town in the *Clan McPhilly*; the answer he knew would be 'no,' because her next port of call was Durban, whence she would sail direct to Liverpool.

'Before I hand you this letter from the Naval Chief of Staff, Captain, I must emphasise that you are under no compulsion to help us. Your part, *if* you decide to help, will be voluntary. But you are bound to secrecy whether or not you agree to co-operate. Do you accept those conditions?'

McRobert grunted his assent.

Widmark handed him the envelope. The Captain looked at the 'Most Secret,' then at Widmark, put it down on the table and lit his pipe. 'It's early yet. No cause to hurry.' He puffed away at the pipe and put his lighter and tobacco pouch away with slow deliberation; then he picked up the envelope and took out the letter. It was typed on Admiralty paper and addressed to the Master of the *Clan McPhilly*. It read:

1. You are asked to give every assistance to the bearer, Lieutenant-Commander Stephen Widmark, DSC, South African Naval Forces, once he has identified himself to your satisfaction.

2. It is necessary to enjoin you to the strictest secrecy and to emphasise that this matter may not be mentioned to anyone outside those of your ship's officers whose help is essential. Under no circumstances may it be mentioned to shipping agency, consular, port or other authorities or persons with whom you are or may in future be in touch.

3. Upon conclusion of the matter concerned you are to continue to maintain this secrecy. For reasons which Lieutenant-Commander Widmark will explain, the Naval Staff will be obliged to deny the existence of this com-

munication and any knowledge of the subject with which it deals.

4. The successful conclusion of this officer's most important task will depend in large measure upon your co-operation, which the Royal Navy feels sure will be forthcoming.

Lieutenant-Commander Widmark will in your presence destroy this letter by burning once you have read it.

(Signed) A. J. F. Cardington
Commodore
Chief of the Naval Staff

The letter was stamped, Cape Town, 5th November, 1942, with an official Admiralty stamp.

While the Captain was reading, Widmark's thoughts went back to his visits to the Clan and Harrison Line agents in Cape Town to get the boarding permits and letters of introduction. There had been no mention of Lourenço Marques; the agents had understood that he intended visiting the ships in Cape Town on their way up the coast, to discuss operational matters with their captains. He remembered, too, his anxiety while typing the Admiralty letters—one for the master of each ship—that they might not look sufficiently authentic and the many attempts he'd made before he was satisfied. Finally, he recalled the time he'd spent copying Cardington's signature before signing the letter.

Now through clouds of tobacco smoke McRobert's rough homespun voice and piercing eyes challenged him. 'What's all this aboot, laddie?'

Widmark met the disconcerting stare. 'You'll be sailing on Wednesday or Thursday, Captain—lying in the stream a day or so before that, I understand?'

'Correct. It's Wednesday we're sailing. Finish loading tomorrow. Anchoring in the stream as soon as the last sling of cargo's aboard.'

Widmark watched him intently. 'When you go out into the stream, Captain, we want you to anchor close to one of the German ships—the *Hagenfels*.'

McRobert gave him a sharp look. 'That's a bit far upstream. Port Captain might not like it. But go on. I'll be telling you what can be done when I've heard more about it.'

'There's one other thing we want you to do, Captain. Delay your sailing on Wednesday night from 22.00 to 23.15.' He paused. 'On account of windlass trouble. That's why you had to anchor upstream. You discovered the trouble as you cleared your starboard cable for lowering. You decided then to anchor at once.'

'Windlass trouble,' echoed McRobert. 'That's something the *Clan McPhilly's* never had.' But he was uneasily aware of the compulsion in the younger man's stare and of his air of authority when he said: 'Yes, windlass trouble, Captain. Rivets have worked loose in the base plates. You daren't put the strain of weighing on to the gypsies. You'll have to drive rivets on that fo'c'sle of yours from 22.00 to 23.00 on Thursday night, Captain. The more noise you make the merrier.'

'For what reason?'

Widmark looked away. 'It's better for both of us if I don't go into too much detail. Afterwards, if you're asked questions, you'll be able to answer them more truthfully.'

'What sort of questions?'

'Like what was happening on the *Hagenfels* between ten and eleven on Wednesday night.'

From under shaggy brows the Captain's eyes questioned him. 'And what will be happening?'

Widmark hesitated, sizing up McRobert. Then he decided it was better to tell him. 'I'm going to board her with a British naval party.'

'My God! So that's it.'

Widmark nodded, his mouth shut in a firm line.

McRobert sucked at his pipe, looking at the bulkhead clock behind Widmark's head, thinking about what he'd been told, trying to grasp all its implications. 'And the Portuguese? What about them?'

'They'll know nothing until the *Hagenfels* has gone. And when she has, they'll think it was a break out by the Germans. The Portuguese haven't a clue that we're here or what's on the go.'

'And this riveting. This noise you want, laddie. What's the idea?'

Widmark looked at him quizzically, shrugging his shoulders. 'We shall have to use force. Our coshes may not be enough.'

84

'Aye.' McRobert's eyes glinted. 'Use them if you can, laddie. Better not to spill blood.' Intensely practical, he added: 'At least not in a neutral port.'

'So you're prepared to help?' For the first time Widmark's calm deserted him.

'I'd be a damned poor Scot if I wasn't. Of course I'll help. Man alive! How often d'ye think we can hit back at Jerry with his bluidy U-boats and the like.' He put down his pipe. 'But there's a man I'll have to take into ma confidence. The chief engineer. We can't get to riveting without Fergus Duncan gie'ing a hand. And the mate. We'll no weigh anchor without him.'

'Of course, Captain.'

For some time they discussed the plan as it affected the *Clan McPhilly*, settling how the port authorities would be told of the sailing delay, how the pilot would be dealt with, and the eventual sailing of the Clan ship herself.

Before they'd finished, Widmark had destroyed the 'Admiralty' letter by burning and explained to the Captain why the Royal Navy would have to deny any knowledge of the operation if things went wrong—and, for that matter, if they didn't.

He went down the gangway of the *Clan McPhilly* feeling that he could not have found a better man for the part than Captain McRobert, but as he stepped on to the quay this acceptable thought received an ugly jolt, for standing on the quay opposite the foot of the gangway, perhaps twenty yards from it, reading a newspaper and smoking the inevitable cheroot, was the oily man.

Widmark went quickly down the quay, turning once to see if he was being followed. He was not, but now he really was worried. *This* was more than a coincidence. The oily man was shadowing him. Widmark decided to find out who he was. That might provide some sort of clue. But he was frantically worried. The man was almost certainly a German agent. If he was, the one place Widmark would prefer him not to have been was at the foot of the Clan ship's gangway. He decided to alert the rest of the party as soon as possible. If necessary they'd have to bump the fellow off, but that was actually the last thing Widmark wanted. It would, he decided, have been a pleasure in almost any other circumstance, but not now when there was so much at stake and the one thing absolutely essential to their operation was the element of surprise.

It was a hot day, the sun a fireball in a patchwork sky, the sea reflecting blues and browns and mauves, the horizon quivering with heat, and Chefine Island dancing in the haze.

Widmark walked down Bartolomeu Dias past the red-fezzed sentries of the Quartel-General, behind them white walls splashed with bougainvillaea; down a side street past a vacant site filled with sunflowers, the pavements lined with flamboyants. He came next to an overgrown garden where an old wood and iron house stood back in the shadows, the top of the stone wall surrounding it feathery with antigna, and beneath it a hedge of plumbago.

At Bellegarde da Silva he turned north, went up the road between the houses, their pastel shades holding off the heat of high noon, turned into Rua Dos Aviadores, from there crossed over Avenida do Duque de Connaught into Rua San Rafael where he saw them waiting: Rohrbach and Johan, sitting on a bench under a wild-fig tree. He sat down at the far end of the bench, opened his newspaper and told them in undertones of the visit to the *Clan McPhilly*. The operation, he confirmed, was for Wednesday night.

Much had to be done in the time remaining; there would be a final rendezvous the next night, Tuesday, on the road to Marracuene, soon after midnight, when there would be few cars about. Arms and equipment would be issued. Wednesday to be spent resting in their hotels. Mariotta must be told that Wednesday was the night for the party as they'd be leaving for the Transvaal on Friday, and had another engagement for Thursday. Rohrbach must arrange with Domingos Parao for the hire of the fishing boat for Wednesday night.

Widmark turned the sheets of his newspaper. 'That's all, I think. Any queries?'

Rohrbach said: 'You say the *Clan McPhilly*'s due to sail at 22.00 on Wednesday. What time does the *Tactician* sail?'

'23.10.'

'So we take the *Hagenfels* out just ahead of her.'

'That's right.'

'What time do you come alongside the *Hagenfels*?'

'22.00. Should have the situation under control within fifteen minutes. There'll be seven of us, and with their libertymen ashore we'll easily cope with ten or eleven Jerries. They won't be expecting us. Won't have time to arm, though we must reckon on the night watchman carrying a revolver.'

Three Africans came down the road, and conversation on the bench stopped until they'd passed. Widmark turned the sheets of his newspaper, frowning at the picture of a torpedoed merchant ship sinking in heavy weather.

'We'll tackle the upper deck and fo'c'sle as soon as we get on board,' he said. 'The crew live for'ard. The officers will probably be in Lindemann's cabin—the steward nearby. There'll be a night watchman on the upper deck, and a greaser or two in the engine-room. That leaves two or three men in the fo'c'sle. Should be a piece of cake. Don't start anything in the Captain's cabin unless the Jerries raise the alarm. Wait for us to join you. But if we haven't arrived by 22.30 you'll know we've come to a sticky end.'

'The chap I'm going to mark,' said Johan, 'is that big bastard who looks like a prize-fighter.'

'Heinrich Schäffer,' said Rohrbach.

'That's it, Heinrich. He's my baby.'

Widmark looked at Johan's fifteen stone. 'Don't be brutal,' he said dryly.

'That's nice, coming from you,' Johan said and immediately regretted it.

Rohrbach came to his rescue. 'Well, that's about all for now, isn't it, Steve? Hadn't we better get back and brief our oppos. Johan and I've got a date with the girls. They're lunching with us.'

Widmark looked at him curiously. 'You'll be seeing Cleo?'

There was something in Widmark's voice, a wistfulness perhaps, Rohrbach had not heard before. 'Yes. Nice girl, isn't she?'

Widmark got up and folded the newspaper deliberately. Down the Rua San Rafael bright patches of sunlight were scattering the shade from the flamboyants which spread their branches like scarlet umbrellas. At the end of the street the sea shimmered with heat and the horizon melted into the sky. 'Yes,' he said quietly, 'she is.' Then he walked away, down the road towards the sea.

At lunch Widmark sent for the head waiter, a Goan with whom he had already established a sound customer-client relationship. He began circumspectly: would there be any difficulty about getting a picnic lunch from the hotel if he decided to drive down to the Maputo elephant reserve for the day. The head waiter assured him there wouldn't be. After that there were various questions about Maputo until finally, as the Goan was about to leave, Widmark said with studied casualness: 'Who's the man sitting inside the window behind me? Bald with sunglasses. Looks like somebody I know, but I can't place him.'

The head waiter walked down the veranda, came back and held the menu in front of Widmark. He was a discreet and understanding man, the Goan. 'It's a Mr Jules Kemathi, sir.'

'Kemathi—Kemathi——' Widmark repeated the name softly. 'No. That doesn't ring a bell. And yet——'

He looked at the menu, then at the table-cloth, then at the head waiter. 'Where's he from?'

'I don't know, sir. I'll find out.'

Widmark shrugged his shoulders. 'It's not important. I just wondered. Feel I know him. I'll have the iced consommé.'

The head waiter saw the possibility of a tip. 'It's no trouble, sir.' He raised his voice. 'The iced consommé, sir.'

Towards the end of the meal he was back at Widmark's side, bending over him, holding the menu with studied solicitude. 'He came a week ago, sir. From Egypt.'

'From Egypt,' echoed Widmark quietly. 'Happen to know what part?'

'Alexandria, sir.' Then louder: 'Try the scampis, sir. Bought on the market this morning. Excellent. I can recommend them.'

When the head waiter had gone, Widmark thought about Kemathi. From Alexandria. How many more from Alex.? And yet, of course, that was exactly what Kemathi looked like. Straight out of the Levant. Hence the oily look. But what was he doing here and why was he following Widmark? That was a question which had to be answered.

Kemathi was from Alexandria. Widmark had been well known in Alex. Could there be any connection? *Was* Kemathi an enemy agent? Lourenço Marques was said to teem with them. And if he were, could the Germans draw any worthwhile conclusions from his visit to the *Clan McPhilly*? He doubted it. What more natural than that a British naval officer, even if recently invalided, should go on board a British merchant ship in a foreign port. Widmark thought, I'm getting nervy. Must keep a grip on myself, and not see something sinister in every goddam thing that happens.

As he went through the lounge Olympia Stavropoulus bore in sight on a converging course, aglitter with jewels; tall, erect, her bosom, mien and bearing more imperial than ever. She swept past him with a swish of silk, a trail of Chanel behind her; but he might have been a chair for all the attention she paid him. Never again, he decided, did he want to see Alex., or anyone from that ancient city.

Later that afternoon Widmark drove into town and parked in the Praça McMahon. From there he walked to the Gorjao Quay passing down long lines of railway trucks. Between the rails lay pools of water from the afternoon's thunderstorm, and steam was still rising from the tarmac. At the far end of the quay he stopped and looked across the Espirito Santo to the Catembe side where he could see the beach at Ponta Chaluquene with its array of small craft. Off shore were the wrecks of old lighters, and behind the beach a cluster of bungalows with iron roofs. He was as near now as he could get to the German ships. Absorbed in his thoughts he watched them: the *Dortmund*, the *Aller* and then to the right the *Hagenfels* and behind her the tall masts of the sailing ship.

The *Hagenfels* still rode to two anchors, the gangway hoisted clear of the water. Men moved about her upper deck.

The tide was ebbing and the ships lay with their bows upstream towards Matola; in the distance he saw a tanker at the oil berths, to its left the mangrove swamps and beyond them the low line of the Lebombos. The sky was streaked with grey cloud, and smoke curled up from an unseen fire. In the foreground the river was all greys and silvers, the smooth surface mirroring the hot sky.

Widmark noted the position of the German ships, of the Italian *Gerusalemme*, and of the berth where the *Clan McPhilly* would anchor near the *Hagenfels*. In the anchorage down river towards the harbour mouth many ships were waiting to go alongside the Gorjao Quay. It was on the far side of the Espirito Santo, off the Catembe shore and past Ponta Chaluquene, that his party would make their approach in the fishing boat and he took good note of what he saw. The night would be dark and they could not afford mistakes.

Walking back along the Gorjao Quay he saw that the Portuguese gunboats were still there. Satisfied, he went out through the dock gates to the Praça McMahon.

Widmark got back to the Polana at seven that evening and stopped in the lounge for a drink before going up to his room. The waiter had brought the whisky and soda and he was signing the chit when he heard Di Brett's 'Do you mind if we join you?' Tense and on guard he stood up. The Newt was with her. With studied indifference Widmark said: 'If you want to.' She introduced the Newt, the men looked at each other with blank faces, Widmark mumbled 'How d'you do?', more drinks were ordered and they sat down. Di Brett took a mirror from her handbag and fiddled with her lips. 'Well—what have you done with yourself today, Stephen?'

He held his glass up to the light, looked at it, then at her, and finally at the Newt. 'Nothing,' he said. It was as near being rude as made no difference and the Newt blushed for him. He looked at Widmark coldly. 'You here on holiday?'

Widmark nodded, his eyes on a tall figure coming from the foyer into the lounge. The light was behind the man so that his face was in shadow. As he approached, two small scars on his left cheek stood out clearly. Widmark stiffened, his mind preoccupied once again with the problem of where he'd seen the face. The tall man stopped in front of them, the trace of a smile on his lips, his eyes on Widmark. He clicked his heels, and bowed. 'Lieutenant-Commander Widmark?' The German accent was unmistakable. The men stood up. Di Brett watched them, frowning.

Widmark's face was blank. 'What do you want?'

The tall man relaxed. 'Merely to renew an old acquaintanceship. I saw you at Ressano Garcia the other day and thought it was you, and now——', he looked round the crowded lounge, 'I came here to see friends and again I see you, so I thought I'd come and say "hallo." May I sit down?'

Widmark thought quickly. It wouldn't be difficult to be rude to this fellow and get rid of him, but if he did he'd lose the chance of finding out who he was, so he said: 'Yes, of course. But let me introduce you. Your name?'

The tall man bowed. 'Von Falkenhausen. Baron von Falkenhausen.' The name meant nothing to Widmark. He introduced the Baron to Di Brett, and then looking at the Newt and raising his eyebrows, he said: 'Didn't get your name, I'm afraid.'

'James Newton,' said the Englishman unhappily.

They sat down. The Freiherr got to work quickly. 'You don't remember me?' He leaned forward, brown eyes smiling.

Widmark was cold, guarded, full of suspicion and curiosity.

'Frankly, I don't.'

'Alexandria, 1941—in the Montelémar!'

That made Widmark look at him really hard. The Montelémar was a night club, a favourite stamping ground for naval officers, and he'd spent a good deal of time there one way and another. 'There's something familiar about you. Those scars,' he admitted. 'But I still can't place you.'

'Don't you remember Swiss Fritz, the barman?'

Widmark started. That was it. By God! That was him. Of course. 'But you had black hair and a waxed moustache!'

Von Falkenhausen laughed. 'What a lot of time I spent waxing that moustache and how I *loathed* it, especially in the hot weather.'

'Why the disguise?' Widmark said it in his chilliest manner.

The Freiherr shrugged his shoulders. 'In war these things are necessary.'

'So you were a spy?'

'Call it that if you like. I was serving my country.'

There was an awkward moment, until the German said: 'And you, Commander, what are you doing here?'

Widmark felt inclined to be rude but he realised that it wouldn't help. 'Holidaying. I'm out of the Navy. Invalided. Asthma. Live in Johannesburg these days.'

'Invalided out?' The German's eyebrows lifted in polite concern. 'Not, er, *removed* from the Active List?' The brown eyes smiled but it was a quizzical, insolent smile.

'May I ask what you mean?' If the Freiherr had known Widmark well he'd have realised that trouble was coming.

'Well, Commander, you were not called "The Butcher" for nothing, and you *did* return to South Africa rather suddenly.'

The colour went from Widmark's face. He stood up, hands clenched, eyes bright with anger. 'Like most members of your race, Baron, or whatever you call yourself, you lack manners. Will you now please *go!*'

Von Falkenhausen saw the thinly controlled rage and hesitated, caught off guard by this sudden onslaught. Then he stood up, bowed to Di Brett and the Newt and said: 'My apologies' and, without looking at Widmark again, crossed the room to a table on the far side where he joined a group of local Germans. Di Brett was pale. 'That was horrible, Stephen. I loathe scenes. Did you have to?'

Without answering, Widmark left the room.

In the far corner of the lounge a plump, balding man in sunglasses put down his paper, stubbed out a cheroot and moved silently towards the door through which Widmark had gone.

Much later that night, it was in fact ten minutes before midnight, von Falkenhausen heard the bell of his flat ringing downstairs; three shorts in quick succession. Looking at his watch, he smiled. His visitor was punctual. There was the sound of a key turning in the latch, of footsteps on the stairs, the door opened and Di Brett came into the study, her blue raincoat and scarf accentuating the cornflower blue of her eyes.

Von Falkenhausen jumped to his feet and took her in his arms. '*Liebling!*' he said, 'You are not only the most beautiful woman in the world but the most punctual.'

The Freiherr was a man of great charm and he understood perfectly the psychology of women.

Chapter Nine

Di Brett took off the blue raincoat and scarf and for some moments they sat on the settee busy with the small play of a man and woman in love; then von Falkenhausen laughed, said: 'Duty before pleasure, Helga,' and jumped up and poured her a mixed vermouth, packing the glass with ice.

He stood waiting, drink in hand, while she finished fussing with her hair and lips; then she took the glass and said: 'Thank you, Ernst. It looks lovely.' He poured himself a whisky and soda and sat down next to her. 'Now, *liebling*, what have you to tell me?'

Sipping her drink, she looked at him over the rim of the glass. 'It was an awful moment this evening when that Widmark insulted you. I could have killed him.'

Von Falkenhausen shrugged his shoulders. 'It was my fault. I was in too much of a hurry. But I wanted to see how he reacted to the shock of recognition.'

'Well, you certainly saw!'

'Yes. It was interesting. His anger was not only because I called him "The Butcher." It was also shock because I had turned up here out of the blue and recognised him.'

'Do you believe the asthma story?'

'Of course not! Why the false addresses for him and his friend McFadden, and their choice of different hotels?'

She stroked the scars on his cheek with the back of her fingers. 'Ernst, it is even more than that.'

'What d'you mean?' He watched her with a half smile, indulgently, as if she were a child.

'James Newton and Stephen Widmark pretended not to know each other this evening and I had to introduce them. It was just before you came. But last night, very late, I saw them go into Newton's room together.' She watched his face, seeing what effect this would have and she was not disappointed. He blinked with astonishment. 'Good God! Another one.'

She nodded. 'There's more to come, Ernst. I was in Newton's room myself tonight——'

'Was that not risky?' he interrupted. 'He might have

come in and caught you.'

She fluttered her eyes at him. 'Grow up, Ernst! I was *with* him.'

Von Falkenhausen frowned. 'Did you——?'

'No, of course not. But *he* would like to. That is how I got there. You men are all the same. You have only one idea.'

'It's a very good one, Helga,' said the Freiherr complacently.

'Anyway, the visit was worthwhile. I saw some things I wasn't meant to see.'

'Such as?'

'Charts. Two of them. On the table. I looked at them and said "What are these, James?" and he was embarrassed and said: "Oh, some local charts. I'm a yachtsman. Borrowed them from a chap in the harbour. Wanted to see what sailing conditions were like here." There was also a book on the table. It was called *Africa Pilot, Vol. III*.'

The Freiherr's eyes gleamed. 'Ah! The sailing directions. This is tremendously important, Helga! Widmark, McFadden, and now Newton. All pretending to be strangers to each other. I wonder if Newton's a naval officer?'

'I'm sure he is, Ernst, in spite of the moustache. They all speak the same language, the same clichés. He always says "Let's get under way" if we are to go anywhere. Or if I'm late he says "You're astern of station." In the morning when it's time for a drink before lunch he says "Well, the sun's over the yardarm now." That is what they all say. I didn't spend two years in Cape Town and Durban for nothing.' She paused. 'What are they here for, Ernst?'

For some time he sat silent, frowning at the problem. 'I don't know,' he said at last. 'Those charts and sailing directions puzzle me. You know that heavy sinkings are taking place between here and Durban. The U-cruisers are not wasting time, and the raiders *Köln* and *Speewald* are also about. The British must suspect that we give raiders and U-boats information about sailings from Lourenço Marques. Somehow Widmark and his men are here in that connection. It *must* be that. But the charts and the sailing directions, I wonder?' he said softly, 'I wonder?'

She looked at him archly, her eyes just clear of the edge of the glass. 'Are you pleased with me, Ernst?'

'But of course, *liebling*.' He took her in his arms and gave

94

her a long kiss. 'You have been *brilliant*! Now let us go to my room and see if you can be equally brilliant in bed.'

She tweeked his nose affectionately. 'Don't be vulgar, Ernst.' He picked her up and carried her into his room.

Next morning von Falkenhausen was in Herr Stauch's office when the doors opened at eight o'clock, and to him he confided Helga Bauer's news. They discussed the problem at length, but Stauch's nimble brain could not add much to the Freiherr's conclusion that Widmark and his men were in Lourenço Marques on counter-espionage. Urgent inquiries were set in train and by noon useful information had been elicited. None of the three men had visited the British or South African Consulates or were known there; Stauch had trustworthy contacts at both places and the information could be relied upon. This caused the mystery to deepen. Telephone inquiries to Ressano Garcia, and thereafter to Johannesburg, revealed that Newton, like Widmark and McFadden, had given the frontier post an address in Johannesburg at which he was not known. But the Germans were still not any the wiser.

The Freiherr switched the subject. 'Anything from the Wilhelmstrasse?'

Stauch shook his head. 'Nothing. She remains at twenty-four hours' notice.'

Von Falkenhausen got up and paced the room, hands clasped behind his back. 'It will come soon,' he said confidently. 'There will be four days of no moon from tomorrow. The signal will come soon.'

'Unless they postpone it again.' Stauch scratched at his stomach.

'I think it's unlikely. This is the first time she's on twenty-four hours' notice.'

'Well, I hope it's soon, this business——'

Von Falkenhausen interrupted him with a low whistle. '*Mein Gott!* Is Widmark here in connection with that?'

'With what?' Stauch mopped the perspiration from his face with a large handkerchief.

'The sailing of the *Hagenfels*.' Von Falkenhausen's eyes narrowed. 'Maybe the British have picked up a hint from somewhere. Perhaps the people in the harbour. They may have seen the provisions going on board over the last few weeks. Then the information goes to the British consulate.

Thereafter to Simonstown. Then Widmark and his men are sent here to keep a watch on things. To check the rumour about sailing. To keep the ship under observation. To report the moment that she has gone, so that interception can quickly take place outside.'

'It's possible.' Herr Stauch was grudging, irritated that this quite feasible explanation should have occurred to the Freiherr and not to him. 'But why the charts and sailing directions?' He said it triumphantly, his small eyes bright with pleasure at this spanner in the works.

'That is a mystery,' conceded the Freiherr. 'But there's one possible explanation. Widmark may be checking whether there is an alternative route the *Hagenfels* can take out of Lourenço Marques other than the Canal do Sul and Inhaca. Maybe to look, also, for places along the coast where she might hide.'

Stauch shook his head gloomily. 'There's a daily air reconnaissance by the South African Air Force from Durban. No eight thousand ton ship can hide from that.'

'Nevertheless, Herr Stauch, I have suggested a possible reason for the charts and sailing directions. Unless you can think of a better one, I suggest we pay some attention to it.'

Stauch winced at the reproof, and disliked the Freiherr more than ever because he suspected he was right.

'Now we shall go on board the *Hagenfels* and discuss this matter with Kapitän Lindemann. We can also question Moewe about the charts. He may have some ideas.'

'Very well, Herr Baron.' Stauch was submissive again, hating the other man. 'As you wish.'

They went on board the *Hagenfels* just before lunch and explained to Lindemann the purpose of their visit; he sent for Günther Moewe, who produced charts of the approaches to Lourenço Marques and of the coast north and south of the port.

It was Admiralty Chart no. 644, the Bay of Lourenço Marques, that decided them in the end that the Freiherr was probably right and that Widmark and Newton had been checking alternative routes. At this stage, Lindemann suggested that the *Hagenfels* should not take the normal passage by way of Canal do Sul and the pilot vessel at Cabo da Inhaca, but should alter course to the north after passing the Ribeiro Shoal and take the rarely used Canal do Norte, keeping as close inshore as possible.

'In this way we avoid the pilot vessel, we keep to territorial waters, and by daylight we should be a hundred miles to the north. We can turn to the east, get out into the shipping lanes and steer a southerly course before the morning air patrol gets here. Then we will seem to be a vessel inward-bound for Lourenço Marques.'

All agreed with the soundness of this plan and von Falkenhausen voiced their thoughts: 'Even if Widmark and company spot our sailing—and it won't be easy on a dark night—they won't know which passage we've taken. We'll be seventeen miles out, and not a light showing, before we alter course at the Ribeiro Shoal.'

The steward, Müller, brought a tray and over large steins of chilled beer they again discussed the problem of what Widmark, Newton and McFadden were doing in Lourenço Marques and agreed that it must be counter-espionage of some sort; either in connection with breaking the German system for passing information about the movements of Allied ships, or to intensify the watch on the *Hagenfels* in case she made for the sea—or both.

At this stage Moewe said to Lindemann: 'Since the signal may come from the Wilhelmstrasse at any moment, Herr Kapitän, do you think it wise to have a party on board tomorrow night?'

Lindemann knew his second officer well enough to know that this was said for the benefit of the Freiherr and Herr Stauch, and it confirmed his belief that Moewe was untrustworthy.

Herr Stauch's small eyes narrowed and his voice was censorious. '*Another* party, Kapitän?'

'Yes,' said Lindemann. 'We have a few guests coming on board after dinner tomorrow. If you wish, it can be cancelled.'

Von Falkenhausen held up his hand imperiously, and Günther Moewe wetted his lips in anticipation of the slating the Captain was about to receive.

'Certainly not!' said the Freiherr. 'Of course the party must go on. Otherwise the people concerned may conclude that the *Hagenfels* is sailing. How do we know to whom they will not talk? No! The party is essential, and what is more I have two other guests for you, Kapitän.'

Lindemann was puzzled, and Stauch and Moewe, with the sad faces of bloodhounds called to heel, showed interest again.

'They are Di Brett, better known to you as Fräulein Helga Bauer, and her friend, Mr James Newton, a very un-naval looking gentleman who I'm convinced is a British naval officer.'

Lindemann remained calm, but not Herr Stauch. 'Is this wise, Herr Baron?' he protested excitedly. 'To bring such a man on board?'

'What can he learn by coming on board? You are fore-warned. You must feed him with so much incorrect information that he will leave the *Hagenfels* convinced that we cannot take her to sea. That is why I want him on board. If his job is espionage this is the best thing that can happen. Do you understand?'

Grudgingly they admitted that they did, while Linde-mann made no secret of his admiration for the Freiherr's idea.

'There is one other reason why I want him on board,' continued von Falkenhausen. 'I shall be coming to the party myself—somewhat later than your other guests—and I may confront Mr James Newton with what I know about him. He doesn't look a very tough customer, and I think he may talk if he's frightened. By the way, who are the other guests, Kapitän?'

Lindemann smiled, faintly embarrassed. 'Two local ladies, Herr Baron. Senhoras Mariotta Pereira and Cleo Melanides and their two men friends. One is a German from South Africa, his name is Rohrbach, and the other an Afrikaans farmer from the Western Transvaal, le Roux. Moewe is also bringing off a lady—Fräulein Hester Smit. That is the entire party.'

The Freiherr was thoughtful, his searching brown eyes on Lindemann. 'What do you know about these men, Kapitän?'

'I understand that le Roux is anti-British and that Rohr-bach, under the pretence of being a German Jew, is passing information to our side.'

'You *understand*! Do you not know them?'

'No. But they are friends of the young ladies.'

Von Falkenhausen drummed on the desk, his forehead puckered. 'Rohrbach—Rohrbach—I do not know the name.

But then of course it might be anything. The Abwehr do not tell us of these men unless we have to contact them. And the ladies?' For a moment his face relaxed and he smiled. 'They are—*ladies*—I take it?'

Lindemann nodded stiffly. 'Most certainly they are, Herr Baron. I would not permit the other sort in my ship. One is Portuguese and the other Greek. Fräulein Hester Smit is Afrikaans and, like so many of her people, pro-German. I can vouch for them. But they will talk, of course, if there is trouble on board.'

'There will not be trouble, I hope, Kapitän. Possibly, if *Mister* Newton becomes difficult, we may have to ask him and Mrs Brett to leave, but there will be no rough stuff—of that I can assure you. We may stage a bluff, to frighten him into talking, but no more. Of course,' he shrugged his shoulders, 'we cannot guarantee Mr Newton's safety *after* he leaves the *Hagenfels*. Unfortunate accidents do occur—especially in harbours when a man is drunk.'

'What sort of accidents, Herr Baron?' Lindemann's blue eyes searched the Freiherr's.

'Oh! Stabbed by natives in the dock area. Run over by a hit-and-run motorist. You know how easily these things happen when a man is not sober.'

Lindemann shook his head. 'I don't like that sort of thing, Herr Baron.'

'Nor I,' sighed the Freiherr, 'but war is a nasty untidy business and *quite* dangerous. We are at war, unfortunately. There are U-boats and raiders outside and they are counting on us. I am afraid we cannot allow people like "Butcher" Widmark and Newton to stand in our way.'

Stauch scratched the back of his neck with a thick finger. 'Do you think this Newton will accept the invitation to the party?'

'I think so. If he is looking for information about the *Hagenfels* he will jump at it. If not, Fräulein Bauer has powerful weapons of persuasion.'

'She is a remarkable woman,' agreed Stauch, wishing that Paula had half the other woman's charm. Only half. He was not greedy.

Chapter Ten

Early that Tuesday morning, on Widmark's instructions, the Newt met Johan and McFadden near the bathing kiosk to warn them that von Falkenhausen was Swiss Fritz of the Montelémar—now blond and clean shaven, and to be recognised only by the twin scars on his left cheek—that he had recognised Widmark, and that McFadden and Johan, who had often visited the Montelémar, should be on their guard. Then he told them about Kemathi. Described him and said that he, too, was from Alexandria, that he was evidently shadowing Widmark and had seen him coming down the *Clan McPhilly*'s gangway. It was clear that he was von Falkenhausen's man. They were also reminded that the final rendezvous would take place that night, five miles out of Lourenço Marques on the road to Marracuene, down a dirt-track leading off to the right several hundred yards beyond the eighth kilometre post; the usual 'break-down' drill would be followed and they were to bring empty bathing bags.

Rohrbach and Widmark would make arrangements during the day for storing their cars in garages for several weeks, as taxis would be used on the night of the party.

'Got all that?' asked the Newt.

Johan gave him a thumbs up sign. '*Ja, meneer*—yes, sir.'

'How are you chaps feeling about tomorrow, Chiefy?'

'Och! A wee bit queezy, laddie. Usual feeling before the show starts. And you?'

The Newt patted the underside of his moustache with his forefinger. 'Pretty fit. Actually a bit windy, I dare say.'

'How's Steve?'

'Rather tense and ratty. Burning with determination as usual.'

Johan chipped in. 'Mariotta says Cleo's been in a trance since she met him at Costa's on Sunday. He promised to phone her but hasn't.'

'He's not likely to, either, Johan. Until this job's over. She doesn't know Steve. He's a man that keeps his eye on the ball.'

There was no more to be said so they went their separate ways.

That Tuesday was a busy one for a number of people: for Rohrbach and Johan, who arranged for storing the Studebaker at a garage at Pinheiro Chagas and then saw Domingos Parao about the fishing boat.

They explained that they would collect it at six the next evening, and return it at midnight. They were anxious, they said, to try their luck on the reef off Chefine.

'You won't be back at midnight if the feeshings ees good.' Domingos hitched his trousers over his large stomach.

Rohrbach frowned: 'That's a point, Johan. I mean, we never know what the night may produce.'

'Yes! He's dead right. We might get stuck into something really big.'

'Tell you what, Senhor.' Rohrbach pulled at his beard. 'Let's say we should let you have the boat back by morning.' The 'should' salved Rohrbach's conscience.

'Of course,' Domingos beamed. 'You no worry, I trust you. You take plenty time. You still young. Take pretty girl in boat. If feesh no bite, you still got plenty fun. Ha! Ha! Very good, isn't eet?' Beneath the black curling moustache, his teeth gleamed like pearls.

'Ha! Ha!' Johan held his sides. 'Very good!'

So with that arranged they left Domingos and called next at a hardware store where they bought a steel hack-saw and some spare blades. After that they went to the upstream end of the Gorjao Quay, checked on the *Hagenfels*'s anchors, saw that she was still lying to both, that the gangway was down and that a launch was alongside. 'The eleven-thirty trip,' said Rohrbach. 'Taken the mail off.'

'Hope they enjoy it,' said Johan. 'They won't be getting much more.'

While they watched, they saw a familiar churn of white under the stern. 'The chief's turning the engines, Johan.'

'Yes. He's a stickler for routine.'

'Hallo! Look what's happening!' Rohrbach pointed down river to where tugs were pulling a merchant ship clear of the quay. 'That does my heart good.'

'If it isn't our old friend, the *Clan McPhilly*. The Butcher should be here to see this.'

While they watched, the Clan ship came clear of the

quay, cast off the tug and drifted up river on the tide past where they were standing. Presently she started her engines and altered course to port, towards the anchorage where the German ships were lying. She was about a quarter of a mile from the *Aller*, when they heard the roar of cable and saw the splash as her starboard anchor was dropped and she swung slowly, paying out more cable as the tide caught her. Then she let go her port anchor and they heard again the noise of running cable. Eventually the cables were checked and she rode to her anchors, her stern a few hundred yards from the *Hagenfels*'s bow.

'Nice piece of seamanship, David.'

'Wizard! She's just where Steve wanted her.'

As was their custom, they counted the ships lying at anchor in the stream. The day's total was sixteen; well up to average. Already a cargo ship was warping slowly into the vacant berth left by the *Clan McPhilly*, and as they walked back along the quay they saw that the *Tactician* had singled up fore-and-aft and was standing by, waiting for the tug to assist her out into the anchorage.

'You know, David,' said Johan. 'These are the chaps who are winning the war. These merchantmen. Look at them. As defenceless as lame ducks. They're being sunk day and night all over the show, and yet nothing stops them. It's bloody marvellous and every time I hear some blithering idiot in the Union moaning about the difficulty of getting golf balls, or the hardships of petrol rationing, I feel sick.'

'I couldn't agree more. In the club in Cape Town the other day there was a commercial type in the bar boasting that so far this war he'd not missed motoring to the Game Reserve and back with wifey each year. A little over two thousand five hundred miles! "I get the coupons from the company's ration," he said. "Just *have* to get away. With so many chaps on active service, we're under terrific pressure." '

'Poor chap!' breathed Johan. 'What did you say?'

'Nothing. But there was a pongo there called du Toit who was a major in something or other—he'd lost an eye at Sidi Rezegh—and he said: "Can't you recommend yourself for a decoration," and walked away.'

Another busy trio that day were von Falkenhausen, Stauch

and Captain Lindemann; they had met by arrangement in Stauch's office off the Rua Araújo, where they were sitting round his desk talking. It was a hot morning and the large fans were doing little more than exchange one lot of stale air for another. Normally the door of Herr Stauch's office was open and this would have helped, but today the subject under discussion was too confidential and the door was shut.

Herr Stauch, his face glistening with sweat, had loosened his tie, opened his collar, taken off his linen jacket and eased his belt several notches—but he was still far from comfortable. Lindemann wore a white drill suit and perspired freely. The Freiherr in tussore silk somehow contrived to look cool and elegant.

He leant towards Lindemann. 'You say that two officers and seven men will be coming ashore tomorrow night, Kapitän?'

'That is correct. Moewe and I will be on board with eight others including Müller, the steward. We have one man in hospital.'

'Which officers are going ashore?'

'Kuhn, the chief engineer, and Schäffer, the second engineer.'

'He's that big man?'

'Yes, Herr Baron. That is him.'

'Good! That should convince our curious friends that we're not staging a break out tomorrow. At what time did you say you expect your guests?'

'The launch will pick them up in the boat harbour at eight-thirty. They should be on board fifteen minutes later.'

The Freiherr smiled. 'Splendid! I shall be coming off later. About ten o'clock. I want Kuhn to stay on board with you. Not to go ashore. And I want Schäffer to come off with me at nine-forty with one of his men. A good man. You may explain to them what is happening. Ask Schäffer to meet me in the boat harbour at twenty-five minutes to ten.'

'Do you really think that precaution is necessary, Herr Baron?' Stauch, looking worried, mopped his face.

Von Falkenhausen nodded. 'Probably not, but I don't want to take any chances. Better to play safe. This way—

from ten o'clock—there will be five of us in your cabin and only three of them.'

'*Three* of them,' echoed Lindemann with surprise. 'What do you mean?'

Von Falkenhausen's eyes were calculating. 'Kapitän, I have checked on Rohrbach and le Roux. I have no idea who they are, but I can tell you they gave false addresses at the frontier. Like Widmark, McFadden and Newton, they are not known at the addresses they used. Quite a coincidence, is it not? Like the coincidence that they should be asked to a party on board the *Hagenfels*. I've no doubt they made a point of cultivating Senhora Pereira at the Cardoso, once they knew that she was a friend of yours. Some time we must find out how they knew *that*. But it's all beginning to take shape now. The British are very thorough. Five officers sent to Lourenço Marques to check on the *Hagenfels*. That looks as though they've got a pretty good idea that we're standing by for a break out, and they attach a great deal of importance to it. That is a very serious matter, gentlemen. The information should not have got out. When the signal comes from the Wilhelmstrasse we cannot fail. That is why I am taking no chances tomorrow night.'

Lindemann was confused. 'Herr Baron, I regret that I have invited these men on board. Mariotta Pereira made the suggestion but I have been careless, and——'

Von Falkenhausen interrupted him. 'Don't worry, Kapitän. No harm has been done. Indeed, it is fortunate that matters have turned out as they have. Now we have three of the five on board. But I have no desire for violence. It would be a great mistake in a neutral port. It might well ensure that the *Hagenfels* does not get out. What we must do is convince them that the ship cannot sail. That will be a task for you, Kapitän, and your chief engineer. When I arrive on board with Schäffer you should have completed it. I hope we shall find you having a gay party—especially your guests. By then I trust they will have had much to drink.' Von Falkenhausen smiled. 'They must have no cause for complaint about German hospitality. And it will make my task easier, for I intend to make them talk.'

After a number of other matters had been discussed, the Freiherr got up to go. 'A final detail.' He looked at Lindemann. 'Schäffer and I will be armed. You and Moewe should have revolvers within easy reach. I don't think they will be necessary, but it is as well to be prepared.'

At midnight the Buick turned to the right down the dirt-track beyond the eight kilometre post on the Marracuene road. After a mile they saw on the left the rear lights of a car pulled off the road, and soon established that it was Rohrbach and his men. The usual 'break-down' drill was followed once they were together.

The back seats of the cars were taken out and the covers removed from the concealed compartments. An automatic pistol, a shoulder-holster and twenty-five rounds of ammunition were issued to each man. The fishing boat party—Widmark, McFadden, the Newt, Mike Kent and Hans le Roux—were given a light hook rope and a scaling ladder made from signal halyard, the paddles, hammer, punch and steel hack-saw. Belts, sheath-knives and torches were handed out. The blue light of the small torches ensured that in the darkness anybody using white torchlight would be known to be the enemy. Two large signal torches, and tins of stove-black, went to the boat party, who also took the charts and sailing directions. Coshes were given to everyone, except Rohrbach and Johan, who could not take them to the party.

Each man stowed his equipment in a canvas bathing bag, the last item in being a bathing towel.

After the compartment covers had been screwed back into the car, they gathered round Widmark for the final briefing.

The night was dark but the sky shimmered in its brilliance of stars, and a warm breeze drifted through the bush. Occasionally a nightbird cried, frogs croaked in a pond, and the smell of wood smoke, of African blankets and cattle dung, came from a nearby kraal.

Widmark took them once again through the detail of the plan, making certain that each man knew exactly what was to happen and what was expected of him.

The challenge and reply—'Tally-Ho' and 'Break out'—were confirmed, and it was agreed to settle hotel accounts and book out at five o'clock the next evening. The small amount of luggage they had, apart from the bathing bags and the clothes they were to wear, would be locked in the boots of the stored cars.

'Stay in your hotel rooms most of the day,' said Widmark.

'Don't let the equipment out of sight unless it's locked away. Rest as much as you can. You won't get any sleep from the time the operation starts until we get to Durban—that'll be not less than thirty-six hours. I've got Benzedrine tablets but I don't propose to issue them until you're really exhausted. Have plenty to eat, but go easy on the drink. You two party-goers,' he looked toward Rohrbach and Johan, 'have a problem about that one. You'll have to use your wits. Drink slowly, spill your drinks, take them to the lavatory, swop full glasses for empty ones, anything you bloody well like. But don't get tight. That's strictly for your hosts.'

Mike Kent said: 'When do I go to the wireless cabin, sir?'

'As soon as we've got control of the ship. Get familiar with the R/T and W/T gear but don't make any transmissions until I tell you, or——' he paused, 'the Newt if anything's happened to me—and David if anything's happened to the Newt. If David's laid out, Johan takes over. By then we'll have lost the battle, so forget it.' He chuckled dryly.

'What about our prisoners, laddie?'

'Put the lot—officers and men—in the chain locker. It'll be hot and stuffy down there but they'll have to lump it. We can't spare guards, and we can't put them in compartments with portholes or other openings. There's only one door to a cable-locker and we'll secure that on the outside.'

McFadden was silent for a moment. 'And the women?'

'Until we're clear of the harbour, we'll lock them in the Captain's sleeping cabin. After that they can come out, but they mustn't leave midships. They're welcome to the run of that.'

There was a long thoughtful silence, broken by Widmark. 'Quite happy about starting those engines, Chiefy?'

'Don't worry about that, laddie. A marine diesel's a marine diesel whatever its nationality. Hans and I'll have things moving in no time. We know they turn the main engines twice a week. The air bottles must be topped up for that. Don't be fashin' yourself about the *engines*.'

It was the typical you-keep-off-my-pitch-and-I'll-keep-off-yours that had always existed between the engine-room and the upper deck, and in the dark Widmark smiled.

Hans had a question: 'What about the fishing boat, sir?

Once we've got on board the *Hagenfels*?'

'Last man out pulls the seaplug. She'll sink alongside. Poor old Domingos'll assume she sank in the bay and that David and Johan have drowned. Very sad!'

There were one or two more questions, then Widmark said: 'Well. That's the lot. Good luck to you all. I've never felt more confident.' He hesitated. 'And I've never had a better bunch of chaps with me.'

Johan had the last word: 'Don't forget that big bastard Schäffer's mine,' and they went back to their cars and drove off into the darkness.

Sleep was not easy for Widmark that night. Perhaps it was because he knew how important it was that he *should* sleep that he failed and lay there struggling with his thoughts, trying hopelessly to shake them off. An endless succession of faces paraded across his mind: von Falkenhausen, the scars on his cheek sinister, the brown eyes menacing; the Commodore, red-bearded, tall and angular, saying: 'My dear chap, we can't stage a naval operation in a neutral port!' Kemathi, oily, bland and anonymous behind his sunglasses; Andrew McFadden, hair tousled, loyal and dependable; Rohrbach, dark, clever, alert, and compassionate; Mike Kent, ardent and serious, and then—as if to disturb these pleasant thoughts—Olympia Stavropoulus, thrusting and purposeful, her eyes flashing contempt, scornful and unforgiving. . . .

It was no use. He couldn't sleep. Getting out of bed, he switched on the light and looked at his watch. It was just after eleven. He pulled on flannels and a shirt, slipped his feet into canvas beach shoes, locked the door, pocketed the key and went downstairs, leaving the hotel by a side door near the billiard room. There were still people about; he could hear the rise and fall of voices and occasional laughter.

Outside the hotel gates he set off down the pavement, keeping to the dark shadows of the trees, enjoying the breeze from the sea and the solitude of the night. An occasional car passed and sometimes a lone African, but for the most part there was nothing but the slanting street lights and the long shadows of the flamboyants.

More than an hour later, refreshed, his mind at rest, he got back to the Polana, went in through the same door and up the stairs.

He let himself into his room, switched on the light, drank a glass of water, and was about to undress when he heard what sounded like a muffled sneeze on the balcony outside the french windows to his room. There was no access to it except from the room, and yet beyond all doubt somebody was there. He sensed danger and his mind, cold and alert, quickly took over from his tensed body. He had no weapons, the automatic pistol and sheath-knife were in the bathing bag locked in the wardrobe—it would be foolhardy to attempt to get at them; the intruder might well be armed, indeed, probably was. In the brief moment between hearing the sound and registering these thoughts, he decided to behave as if he had heard nothing. His best defence would be to secure the advantage of surprise. Keyed up, he went on undressing. For the second time that night he cleaned his teeth with quiet deliberation, put on his pyjamas, brushed his hair—and while doing that picked up the pocket knife lying with some coins on the dressing-table. The moment was approaching now. He went to the door and turned off the ceiling light, then to the wall near the french windows where he switched off the wall lights. After that he crossed over to his bed, pulled back the sheets, got in and put off the bedside light—in the same movement he slipped out of bed on the far side, reached the wall in two cat-like strides and with his back to it edged along as far as the open french windows. He was now within a few feet of the intruder on the balcony. He thought he could hear breathing.

In one hand he held the open pocket knife, the other was on the switch of the wall lights, and his head was turned towards the french windows. Tensed, he waited. Five, ten minutes went by and nothing happened. Then there came from the balcony what sounded like a stifled sigh. Soon after that there was the faintest sound of movement and to his left a dark form, just discernible, came through the french window. Widmark held his breath, his eyes straining to make something of the slowly moving shape. It passed and was fractionally ahead of him as he snapped on the wall lights to see, not three feet away, the back of Kemathi's bald head. From it there came a muffled cry as Widmark's arm closed round the thick neck and bent Kemathi over backwards with a choking headlock. Widmark frisked the hot limp body with the back of his left hand in which he still held the pocket knife. But there was no gun and then, with the headlock still tightly applied, he hissed: 'I'm going to let you go, Kemathi, but if you make a sound I'll kick your teeth into the back of your head.'

This threat was unnecessary for Kemathi was shaking with fright, the perspiration gathering and running down his face. When Widmark let him go, Kemathi staggered to the small settee and slumped down, gasping, his dark eyes —it was the first time Widmark had seen them—wide with fright, his hands feeling his throat.

Widmark stood over him, suspicious and angry. 'Well,' he said icily. 'What are you doing in my room?'

Kemathi looked up in misery. He lifted his shoulders and dropped them, his middle eastern voice husky: 'Sorry, sir. It's a bad mistake.'

'So you unlocked the door by mistake, did you?' Widmark's sarcasm made Kemathi's shoulders lift again and he held out his hands in a gesture of hopelessness.

Widmark brought the pocket knife closer to Kemathi's throat. 'You'd better speak up, my friend, and make it snappy. This little knife is sufficient for my purpose. Now out with it. You've been following me. I'm not a complete bloody fool. What's your game? And incidentally, how did you get a key to this room?'

Kemathi, who had been looking at the floor, breathing heavily, now looked at Widmark and then away as if the whole thing pained him beyond words.

'From wax.' It was almost a whisper.

'What d'you mean?'

'A wax impression. I got the key from the board when the porter was out of the office for a couple of minutes. Then I made a wax impression. For the locksmith.' He looked up to see how Widmark was taking this, but was evidently not encouraged for he soon turned away again.

'Bloody cheek, I must say,' breathed Widmark. 'But what's the idea? Come on. What's it all about?'

Kemathi's arms went out again in a tired gesture. 'It's her fault.'

'Whose fault?'

'Mrs Stavropoulus.'

'Wha-a-at, Mrs Stavropoulus? What d'you mean?'

'I'm her bodyguard. Her husband employs me to look

after her and her jewels. Very rich man, Mr Stavropoulus.'

Widmark relaxed. All the tenseness went. He wanted to laugh but couldn't. He felt better disposed towards Kemathi now. A great weight had been lifted from his mind. 'But what the devil's that got to do with me?'

'You went into her room the other night.' Kemathi looked at him reproachfully. 'She saw you.'

'So what?' exploded Widmark. 'I made a mistake. It's in the same position as this room, but on the floor below. Liftman's fault. That's no reason for you to trail me round the town and break into my room.'

There was a long pause, Kemathi breathing heavily and fingering his neck. 'You got her worried. She reckons you're after her jewels.'

'Her jewels,' said Widmark incredulously. 'What on earth for?'

'More than a hundred thousand pounds' worth.' Kemathi shook his head sadly. 'Dat's big money.' He cleared his throat. 'Another thing. She doesn't like you. She says to me: "Jules, I hate that man. He's a crook. Never let him out of your sight. Follow him everywhere. Make his life a damn' misery for him. Look in his room one night. Perhaps you'll find clues there. Perhaps——" ' he stopped and looked at Widmark apologetically. ' "Perhaps, Jules," she says, "perhaps you'll find him in bed with a woman. And that's good, too. You tell me whatever you see, Jules. But worry him plenty, he's crook." That's what she says to me.'

Whether it was relief, or the bizarre nature of Olympia's revenge, Widmark did not know but he began to laugh, a low rumble which worked itself up into a high cackle, and he was still at it when Kemathi slid out of the room.

110

Chapter Eleven

Wednesday the twenty-fourth of November broke fine and clear, and Widmark, who'd had a bad night, was up early to inspect the sea and sky and to check once again the times of moonrise and moonset and of high and low water. After a bath and shave, he slipped on shorts and a beach shirt, locked the canvas bathing bag with its equipment in his B-4 bag, locked that in the cupboard and pocketed the key.

It was seven o'clock. Early yet for breakfast and he was too restless to stay in the room. Downstairs he got into the Buick and drove out through the hotel gates along the road to Peter's. But for a few Africans cleaning the verandas the roadhouse was deserted. Parking the car, he went through a strip of bush to the beach and then north along it towards Costa do Sol.

The tide was low and small wavelets slopped over his bare feet as he walked along the wet sand. It was a narrow beach with clean white sand, and shells and driftwood and leaves and pieces of cork and seed-pods from the islands offshore marked the line of high tide. In front of him scurried seven little ring-plovers, heads down, stopping every now and then to look back and then, when he got too close, flying low over the sea and alighting on the beach ahead of him. There were seven in his party and he wondered if the ring-plovers were a good omen.

Throughout a restless night he had worried about the way things were going. There had always been a high probability that he would meet people he knew in LM but he had certainly not expected them to include 'Swiss Fritz' of the Montelémar—now von Falkenhausen, a self-confessed German spy. That confrontation in The Polana? What was behind it? Curiosity about Widmark's presence in LM. Or was it more sinister. Lesser worries were the presence of Olympia Stavropoulus and Di Brett, but even they had assumed formidable proportions in the middle of that hot and sleepless night.

Later, accepting that he could do nothing about these

things but be on his guard, he had transferred his thoughts to the operation itself—not only had he worried about the detail and how the operation would go once they'd embarked upon it, but he'd had a last minute attack of conscience about all that he'd done: the faked letters, the involvement of the men of his own party and, to a lesser extent, of Captain McRobert. And what would the Chief of Staff's attitude be once they'd got the *Hagenfels* safely to Durban? Would the success of the operation itself condone disobedience of the Commander-in-Chief's unequivocal instructions? Widmark sighed. It was too late to raise these issues now. He worried, too, about the women who would be on board, and the possibility that they might come to some harm. This had caused him little concern at first, but now it was different because of Cleo. When he thought of her, and it was often, he became confused. It had all happened so suddenly. In one moment of his life there had been no one and in the next there was Cleo. Twice he'd been on the point of telephoning her but, realising that it could do no good, he'd checked himself. That night they would see each other; travel together in the same ship; he, prepared for the journey; she, taken unawares. What would her family think when she didn't return? What would Cleo herself think? He gave it up. There was a war on. They were going to cut out an enemy ship. One couldn't tie up all the ends—think out everything to its logical conclusion. Strange, unexpected, unpleasant things were happening to men and women all over the world. There was no reason why people in Lourenço Marques should be exceptions. It was just one of those things. He drove back to the Polana, breakfasted well, picked up the Johannesburg *Star* of the day before, and made his way to his room which an African servant had just finished cleaning.

It was after 10 a.m. when the telephone next to his bed rang. It was the Newt with an urgent request to see him. Since Di Brett had introduced them officially, it was no longer necessary to behave as strangers, so Widmark told him to come down.

A few minutes later he came in, smoking a cigarette, as unruffled as ever.

Widmark sat on the bed, the Newt straddling the chair next to the writing-table.

'What's the trouble, Newt?'

The Englishman blew a smoke-ring. 'Di Brett's asked me to a party tonight.'

'So what! You know you can't go.'

'I'm not so sure. The party's on board the *Hagenfels*.' He watched curiously to see the effect this had on Widmark.

'Good God! Another ruddy woman on board. How can *she* ask *you* to a party there?'

'She knows Lindemann. Says he used to come here often in the evenings for a drink. It's quite a gathering place for Germans, you know. Apparently he had some sort of row with the management and has stopped coming. She says he's a charming man. Definitely not a Nazi, though he's pro-German, of course.'

'They all say they're not Nazis if the occasion warrants. Doesn't mean a thing, Newt. They're all tarred with the same brush. But why did she ask you?'

'Lindemann bumped into her in town last night, said he was having a party on board and asked her to come and bring a boy friend. Told her there'd be a couple of Portuguese girls. She knows I speak the lingo so she asked me.'

Chin in hand, Widmark eyed the Newt, thinking about this new development. After a bit he said: 'What did you say?'

'I told her I'd love to come, but that I had a date. Said that if I could duck it, I might make it. What d'you think I should do? If I go, it gets three of us on board before you chaps arrive which is quite a point.'

'It is, Newt. Only snag is we counted on having you in the fishing boat to reply in Portuguese if we're challenged at any stage of our journey up-river.'

For some time they discussed the pros and cons of this, and finally agreed that on balance the Newt should accept the invitation. It was too good a chance to miss.

The change in plans would not involve anything much; the fishing boat party would be reduced from five to four, but that was about all there was to it.

Widmark stubbed out his cigarette. 'We'll tell the others when we meet at the fish dock this evening. You know, a point I forgot to mention at the briefing last night was this: if you people in the Captain's cabin hear firing on deck, you'll have to get cracking. Nobody must get out of that cabin. Pity you won't have your coshes with you, but it

113

can't be helped. You'll have your automatics.'

The Newt went off to tell Di Brett that he'd be delighted to join her for the party on board the *Hagenfels*.

Much as he disapproved of mixed parties on board while the Third Reich was locked in mortal combat, while German blood flowed in Russia, in North Africa and on the high seas, Günther Moewe had nevertheless succumbed to Lindemann's suggestion that he should invite his girl friend to the party on Wednesday night. On only one other occasion had she been on board—to a lunch party—but thereafter Moewe had resolved that he would entertain her ashore. This had not been so much a matter of principle as of expedience. Heinrich Schäffer had been so importunate on that occasion, and Hester with her sparkling humour and roguish eyes so amenable to his advances, that Moewe had fancied he saw his treasure slipping through his fingers; and since Hester provided him with many comforts and was excellent company, dispelling the gloom which so often lay heavily upon him, he was not anxious to tempt fate. On this occasion, however, it would be different: for one thing it was to be the last party on board; the no-moon period had begun; the ship was at twenty-four hours' notice; at any moment the signal from the Wilhelmstrasse would come, so that this was really a farewell party to Hester. It was for these reasons he had asked her and she had readily accepted.

But on this Wednesday morning there had been a development which worried Moewe: Lindemann had called him into his cabin to give him the extraordinary news that the three men coming on board as guests that night were in fact British naval officers, and that they were almost certainly looking for confirmation of the *Hagenfels*'s impending flight; that it was the duty of the ship's officers to give no inkling that they knew their guests' identity, but to entertain them right royally and to leave them under no doubt that even if the ship wished to sail, for one reason and another she could not.

When Lindemann added that though it was unlikely, there *might* be trouble, and that revolvers . . . out of sight but handy . . . would be in the cabin, Günther Moewe had felt a thrill of excitement, mixed with some apprehension, at the prospect of what the night might hold. Later his thoughts, becoming more sober, had turned to Hester of whom he was genuinely fond.

That morning he had to go ashore with documents for Herr Stauch and he took the opportunity when he had delivered them to the office—much to his regret, because Stauch was a good Party man and Moewe had looked forward to a confidential chat, Stauch was not there—to call at the department store in the Avenida da Republica where Hester worked on the glove and handbag counter. When he got there she was busy with a customer, so he sought out Cleo Melanides who worked as a learner buyer in the store which was owned by her father. She was a good friend of Hester's, and Moewe had met her on a number of occasions when she had been on board the *Hagenfels* with Mariotta. He found her in low spirits, which was strange for she was normally a cheerful girl. Soon, however, Hester was free and she was, he found, in excellent form and obviously pleased to see him.

Günther Moewe believed that he was Hester's *steady*, and she had cultivated this impression; but she was a gay girl who found men irresistible, and she had other suitors on some of the five nights a week when Günther did not come ashore. Her good humour was infectious and though she could not speak German—they had to use English in which he was proficient—he knew that she was Afrikaans and from her manner and conversation he had concluded that she was pro-German. The truth of the matter was that Hester, still only twenty-two, young and attractive, had not really sorted herself out about the war. She was too busy enjoying life to worry overmuch about the rights and wrongs of what seemed a remote struggle, notwithstanding the survivors she met from time to time; she was equally kind to those of either side although her loyalties—had she been obliged to acknowledge them—probably lay with the Allies, for she had a brother in the Western Desert who was an anti-tank gunner with the South African Sixth Division—something she had never mentioned to Günther.

She greeted him with bright eyes. 'Hallo, sweetie! What are you doing here?'

Frowning, he took her aside where they could not be overheard. 'It's about tonight's party,' he said.

'What's wrong? Is it off?'

He shook his head, his dark eyes grim. 'No. But it might be a funny sort of party.'

'Not indecent, I hope, Günther?' She said it so cheerfully, he wondered if she wished it might be.

'No! No! But first I must swear you to secrecy. You must not tell Mariotta or Cleo.' He hesitated and then dropped his voice. 'It might damage the Third Reich.'

She noted the air of portentous gloom and realised that he had something important to tell her, so she said: 'Of course I'll treat it as secret. But why are you telling *me*?'

'Because I don't want you to get hurt.' Moewe felt a tickle of gallantry as he said that and saw her eyes soften.

'Tell me all about it.' She patted her hair and fiddled with her frock in the irrelevant way women do in moments of crisis. She was an attractive girl: tall with regular features and smiling eyes.

Guardedly, Moewe told her all he knew and when he finished she clapped her hands, looking quite entranced. 'But how thrilling. British naval officers in disguise. Spies. Guns!' She became serious. 'But Cleo and Mariotta will be terribly upset. I've not met these boys, David and Johan, but they are always talking about them. They say they are *marvellous*. The one is a German, the other an Afrikaner. Are you sure you're right?'

'Absolutely,' said Moewe, adding darkly, 'We have our sources of information.'

'So what do you want me to do?'

'Nothing, Hester. Keep your eyes and ears open and if trouble starts in the cabin—the Captain says it's most unlikely—fall down flat on the floor. That's the safest place in a fight.'

'Ooh! Sounds terrible.' Hester's eyes shone.

'Anyway, *liebling*, I'll be there to protect you.'

Rather tactlessly, she said: 'Will Heinrich Schäffer be there. He's so strong.'

'And stupid,' said Moewe ungraciously. 'Beware of him, Hester. He's a womaniser. Even native women, they say.'

'But of course, darling. I wasn't thinking of *that*! It's just that he's so big and strong.'

Irritated that Schäffer had been brought into the conversation, Günther Moewe got ready to go. 'The launch will be waiting for you in the fishing harbour at eight-thirty.

Cleo and Mariotta will be there with their *friends*, and Di Brett and her *friend*.'

'Who is Di, Günther?'

Only that morning Kapitän Lindemann had told him who she was, but this was not information he could pass on to Hester. 'She is an Englishwoman who lives at the Polana,' he said briefly.

Had some omniscient being that Wednesday been able to see into the minds of those connected in one way or another with 'Operation Break Out,' what a strange miscellany of thought he would have observed: for example, Otto Stauch working in his office off the Rua Araújo, hot and perspiring as usual, wondering what the night would yield, inevitably his thoughts wandering into his particular dream world: the *Berghof* at Berchtesgaden, the great room he had never seen, its wall of windows overlooking the valley, rich with the art treasures the Führer had pilfered as his legions drove across Europe. The Führer himself standing in God-like solitude looking out over the Bavarian mountains to the Tyrol, then turning, his mesmeric eyes burning into Stauch, the outstretched hand, the rare but engaging smile, and the magic voice: 'Ah, Herr Stauch. I congratulate you in the name of the Third Reich for your services to Germany . . .'

On board the *Hagenfels* Lindemann was sitting at the desk in his day-cabin, writing a letter to his wife. At times he would stop, his thoughts far away with her and the children, then he would write again.

When he'd finished the letter he began to worry about the night ahead. He was a man of peace and he felt uneasy. The sea, not war, was his love. His thoughts went back to the early days when he had trained in sail: once again he was out on the foretop yard, his bare feet gripping the foot rope, one frozen hand clawing at the flapping fore-topsail, the other holding on for dear life. The wind screaming and tearing at his body so that he was involved in a personal struggle with the gale—beyond these things he was conscious of nothing but the dark pit of the night. Each time he grasped the wet canvas it was whipped from his hand and he knew that soon he would lack the strength to go back along the yard and down the rigging . . .

A deck above Kapitän Lindemann, second officer Gün-

117

ther Moewe was in the chartroom looking at the chart of Lourenço Marques. The signal from the Wilhelmstrasse would come at any moment now and he wished to be in all respects ready: to know by heart the configuration of the bay with its many shoals, the courses they would have to steer, the depths of water they would encounter, the lights they would see, the tides and currents. Nothing must be left to chance. As he rolled the parallel rulers from the compass rose to the chosen points, drawing the pencilled course lines with neat, firm strokes, his thoughts turned to the coming night. He burned with inward fire at the impertinence of these British swine, coming on board a German ship under the pretext of friendship. Disguised. Ready to spy. *To cheat!* Enemies of the Third Reich! The British were being taught a sharp lesson by Hitler. They had discovered what the armed might of the new Germany meant. They were under no illusion now as to the courage and tenacity of German troops. The British were an effete anachronism; a once great people who had grown soft and lost their way. The mantle of imperial glory had fallen upon the Aryan master race. Moewe dropped the pencil on to the chart and rested his head in his hands, his thoughts soaring until he saw once again the camp-fires of the *Hitler Jugend* in the Black Forest, the marching songs, the fair-haired Brunhildes waiting for their Siegfrieds—a little irreverently he remembered the night he'd seduced his Brunhilde in a haystack. It was the first time for her—she was fifteen—and afterwards she had cried and he'd felt embarrassed at first and then annoyed that the prospect of bearing a warrior in arms for the Third Reich could evoke any emotion other than pride. He tried to remember her name . . .

Siegfried Kuhn, the chief engineer, was in his cabin one deck below, entering the fuel and water registers. His thoughts were uncomplicated, for as always they were about his engines. To be precise, the need to renew the glands of the main fresh-water feed pump. It would be a two-day job; with the ship at twenty-four hours' notice it could not be tackled. In any case it was not urgent. A matter of routine maintenance. The pump would lose a little of its efficiency but that was not serious.

Heinrich Schäffer, the second engineer, was down in the engine-room writing up the log-book, but his thoughts were not on what he was doing; they were as usual confused. One part of his mind considered the strange situation which required him to come back on board at ten o'clock that night with the Freiherr, armed and ready for trouble, but under strict orders not to start anything.

Schäffer liked a fight. He'd been in many. For three Britishers he didn't need a gun. His fists would be enough. The other part of his mind toyed with its perennial thought —it concerned women, and there is little point in pursuing it. . . .

Ashore, Freiherr Ernst Joachim Sigismund von Falken- hausen was in his study resting, his mind much on coming events and what they might bring. Somehow or other he must neutralise Widmark and his men. How, he was not clear. Violence on board with the women present was out of the question. Ashore, discreetly handled, it was always a possibility. But not for all of them. They couldn't all be dealt with that way. Widmark, yes, and perhaps McFadden, or the man Newton. But Widmark and McFadden were not coming to the party. Still, there might be other opportun- ities, though not much time was left. The cool rational part of the Freiherr's mind told him, however, that violence was not really the solution. The answer was to so mislead these people that they would be put off the scent, so that when they woke up to what was happening the *Hagenfels* would already have gone. The Freiherr sighed; he longed to get to sea again, to have done with espionage. While he had been risking his freedom and his life to gather information, brother naval officers had been gathering Iron Crosses, oak leaves and swords; not only that, they had had all the thrills and solid achievements—the hard- ships, too, he had to admit—of the war at sea. Spying was an anxious uncertain business. There was no recogni- tion, no protection. The grandfather clock struck and he was reminded of the family *schloss* outside Schneidemühl. He thought of his mother and father and of his sisters; of his favourite rides; of his falcons and the hundreds of hours he had spent training them, and the thrill of hunting them. Of them all, Atilla was his favourite. Wicked, fiendish Atilla, straining at his jesses, talons clawing at the gloved fist, upside down, bating, aquiver with rage. Then he saw Gina, his Italian wife, and thinking of her pale beauty he felt alone and sad. Gina was dead. What was the use of thinking about her. It could only hurt. After Gina, life had been empty and aimless and women no more than passing fountains at which he had refreshed himself. Helga was one of these. Attractive? Yes. But how could she really mean anything to him after Gina?

Ridding himself of these desolate thoughts, he went to the small table and poured himself a schnapps. . . .

And what were the others thinking about? Widmark's men? Mostly of what the night might bring, but interwoven with these were other thoughts: Mike Kent, for example, in between checking the W/T call signs he would have to use—the challenges and replies, the drill when they passed Ponta Vermelha signal station—and wondering what sort of wireless set-up he'd find in the *Hagenfels*, and whether he'd know his way about it—in between these, Mike Kent was thinking about his climbs on Table Mountain and the Drakensberg; he was thinking, too, of the days spent birdwatching and some of the exciting finds—the Nerina Trogon he'd seen early one morning while walking down a fire-break in the Knysa forests and once, standing on a high slope of the Drakensberg near Himeville, he'd seen a peregrine falcon go into a stoop which ended far below him when it struck a rock pigeon in flight. Once again he saw the moment of the strike, the puff of feathers and what seemed a long time afterwards the sound of it— like a muffled handclap. In the Drakensberg, near Garden Castle, he had heard a shrill sad cry and looking for its source had seen a Lammergeier sitting on a rock. He was ten then and it had been one of the most exciting moments of his life, for this great eagle was rarely seen . . .

Johan and Hans le Roux, confident in their strength and in Widmark's leadership, were probably the least worried but they, too, suffered from that queeziness and loss of appetite which precedes action. These two were not only remarkably alike physically, but their outlook on life, their beliefs, were much the same. Both had been brought up in the Calvinist mould, so that God was often in their thoughts and like their frontiersmen forefathers they put their faith in equal measure in the Almighty and their strong right arms; the one, they were convinced, could not do without the other. As to their other thoughts that day they were largely of the farm at Zwartruggens where they had been born and reared, of their family who lived there and of the girls on adjoining farms whom they planned to marry.

Thinking of the farm they saw not only the old stone farmhouse, *Veelsgeluk*, but the whole six thousand morgen, the ploughed lands, the mealie and teff lands, the kopjes and dry watercourses, the dusty tracks winding through the thorn bush; the stone kraals and wattle and daub huts of the Africans; the herds of beef cattle, sturdy brown Afrikaners with humped shoulders, and the rough coated black Aberdeen Angus; the tractor sheds and the corn grinders; the muddy water-pans and the windmills, and the endless veld grass—and these pictures evoked the smell of wood fires, of dung-filled cattle kraals, and of the veld after rain had fallen on parched land . . .

Andrew McFadden thought mostly of the diesels he would have to start that night and keep running until the *Hagenfels* had reached the safety of Durban; and of the auxiliary machinery, the generators and circulating pumps and ventilation motors that would have to be kept going. But he never doubted his ability to do these things with the assistance of Hans.

Outside these compulsive thoughts' were private ones of the small house in Rondesbosch where his wife and three small children lived, Jeannie no doubt worrying about where he was and what he was doing, for he had told her nothing more than that he would be gone for a few weeks. Discreet and understanding, accepting this as yet another of the unpleasant things the war required of her husband, she had kissed him good-bye and kept back her tears. Other thoughts, irrelevant but vivid, tumbled in and out of his mind: the launching of a ship on the Clyde when he was an apprentice in a shipyard; a cycling trip with Jeannie from Gourock to Largs on a glorious summer's day in 1932 when they were engaged. Half-way there he had tussled with a faulty bicycle pedal and she had chided him: 'You're no' an engineer's foot, Andy, if ye let a wee thing like that get the better o' you . . .'

David Rohrbach, serious, intensely committed to the task ahead, thought much of his family in Germany, of his time at Munich University and, characteristically, of some of the great music he had heard. For some reason his thoughts dwelt on a trip up the Rhine with his mother, father and two sisters. They had boarded the steamer at

Frankfurt and left it in Cologne to return by train. It had rained most of the day and now looking back, sadly, he recalled with what pride his father had recounted the history and legends of the great river, of Pfalz and the Lorelei and other famous landmarks they had seen, and how he had spoken of the glory of Germany. The Germany which was now doing God knows what to that father and those sisters—the Germany which had embarked on the most obscene orgy of murder that the world had ever known. These things hardened his heart and made him look forward to the night in a way which none of the others could, except perhaps Widmark. Revenge was something he had to reject intellectually, yet emotionally he was dominated by the Old Testament's eye for an eye and tooth for a tooth . . .

James Fellowes Newton was perhaps the member of the party whose sensibilities were least involved. He disliked the Germans because they had disturbed the peace he'd so much enjoyed, and he resented with an inward and controlled anger the bombing of London and other British cities.

To him as an Englishman it was incomprehensible that the nation which had produced Goethe, Wagner, Bach, Mann and Einstein should have fallen for a rabble-rouser like Hitler—that it could have gone to so much trouble to be beastly to so many different people. His general view of the enemy now was that they were a bunch of misguided bounders who would have to be put in their place whatever the price.

He looked forward to the night's work in a casual, partly eager, partly fearful fashion. It would be the first action to come his way for a long time and he was grateful for the relief from boredom. He had enjoyed the time in Lourenço Marques: the sleuthing round the docks and the more sophisticated pleasures of Di Brett's company. While he resolved that he would do all he could to keep her out of harm's way on board the *Hagenfels*, he felt at the same time that the journey to Durban would be all the better for her company.

Inevitably he thought a good deal about his wife Betty and his family's home in Oporto, and for an hour he engaged in his favourite piece of escapism: planning with pencil and paper the house he hoped to build for her there after the war. That led his thoughts to the cruising ketch he'd designed while in the *Dorsetshire* and which, come the peace, he intended to have built in Lisbon.

Finally there was Stephen Widmark, alone in his room at the Polana writing up his diary and, when he had finished, adddressing it to himself, care of his father in Cape Town, going downstairs and asking the hall porter to dispatch it by registered post. This he did not because he envisaged failure, but because he could not exclude the possibility that something might happen to him and he knew that the diary was the sole evidence of his personal responsibility for 'Operation Break Out,' and of the innocence of his companions. He wished, too, to ensure that those concerned would know—should he not be there— by what process of reasoning he had arrived at the decision to take matters into his own hands.

Later, back in his room, he spent some time reading Francis Thompson, ending with *The Hound of Heaven* which left him, as always, strangely agitated and restless. Cleo came into his thoughts then and he made vague but satisfying plans for their future. Then he embarked upon an imaginary dialogue with her but gave it up because— knowing nothing of her other than those ten minutes in Costa's—he had no idea what she might say or think in other circumstances. Later he became depressed and his thoughts went back to the Kasos Strait, and to the gale in which his mother had drowned. Once again his mind re-enacted in all their vivid horror these events from which it was never really free, and he ended up on the bed, straining, his body taut, and his nerves jangling.

Chapter Twelve

'Operation Break Out' went into action at five o'clock that afternoon when Widmark and Rohrbach took their cars to garages in different parts of the town, handed them over for storing, luggage locked in the boot, charges paid in advance.

At six o'clock the Newt, telephoning Widmark from a public booth at the docks, said he had counted nine men getting into the 5.30 p.m. launch when it went alongside the *Hagenfels* to take liberty men ashore.

At about the same time Rohrbach and Johan le Roux took a taxi from the Cardoso to the boat harbour; with them went their bathing bags and fishing gear. Domingos Parao handed over the boat and bait, expressed regret that they had disregarded his advice to take ladies with them, and wished them good fishing. As usual, and notwithstanding his protestations, they paid him in advance. They left the harbour and set course down river; to port the Aterro do Machaquene, the native fish dock, and Ponta Vermelha passed in quick succession. The evening wind had begun to come in from the east, there was a light lop on the water, the sky was overcast, and there was the feel of rain in the air.

When Ponta Vermelha was abeam they turned to the south-east and by six-thirty they were off the reef at Ponta Maone. Johan stopped the engine and they anchored, put the baited lines over the side, and although they had no great desire to catch fish that evening it so happened they caught many. It began to rain and at seven o'clock when it was dark they weighed anchor, started the engine and steered in on the light at Esparcelado; at seven-fifteen it was abeam and they made a wide alteration of course which put number nine buoy ahead. When they reached it they switched on navigation lights and ran in for the fish dock. It was raining, visibility was poor, and they had some difficulty in finding the entrance. Once inside, Rohrbach ran the boat gently up into the shallow waters of the beach until the bows grounded. There were a few fishing boats in the harbour, but no signs of life in the darkness other than the flicker of two oil lanterns and the murmur of African voices around a fire under the trees. At 7.30 p.m. three flashes of blue light showed up in the darkness to their left. Johan raised his torch and gave three flashes in reply. There was the scuffle of feet ahead of them: Johan called 'Tally-Ho' and they heard Widmark's reply 'Break out.' Soon afterwards, he, McFadden, Hans le Roux and Mike Kent came out of the darkness, dropped their bathing bags into the boat and climbed aboard.

There were last minute handshakes, whispered 'Good lucks!' Johan said: 'Sorry you types weren't invited to the party,' and he and Rohrbach went off to where the taxi was waiting. Complaining that the fishing was poor, they asked the driver to take them to the Cardoso. There they paid him off, made their way through a side entrance to their rooms where they washed and changed, strapped on their shoulder-holsters, put their coats on over them, and slipped the spare ammunition into their pockets.

'How do I look?' said Rohrbach, turning round self-consciously. 'See anything?'

Johan looked at him with a critical eye: much depended on what he saw. '*Eerste klas*—first-class, can't see a sausage.'

'I feel such a bloody fool, toting this,' complained Rohrbach. 'Too dramatic!'

'I don't,' Johan patted his holster. 'Makes me feel good. Only wish I had my cosh.'

Rohrbach looked at Johan's big hands. 'Why the hell you want a cosh when nature gave you clubs like that, beats me.'

For a few minutes they practised drawing the automatics—sitting down, standing up, and on the move. In the end they finished up on the floor helpless with laughter. 'Talk about cowboys and crooks!' croaked Johan. 'What a couple of clots we must look.'

They learnt a valuable lesson: to bring the right hand down from the chin so that it fell easily on to the butt of the pistol; they learnt, too, not to draw too fast or hitches occurred.

Taking their raincoats, they went down to the lounge and joined Mariotta and Cleo, took a taxi and arrived at the boat harbour just after 8.30 p.m. The launch was waiting. The lights on the quay shone through a curtain of rain into the cabin where the Newt was sitting with two women. Since Rohrbach and Johan weren't supposed to know him, and as none of them knew Di Brett, there was a moment of embarrassment when they got into the launch.

Then Mariotta and Cleo recognised Hester Smit, greeted her warmly and introduced her to David and Johan: that done Hester introduced them all to 'Mr James Newton and Mrs Brett.' 'We introduced ourselves while we were waiting,' she explained.

'Sorry we're late,' said Rohrbach.

'It's nothing. We were early.'

'Pity it's raining.' The Newt looked at the cabin windows streaming with rain. 'But it won't worry us once we're on board.'

The African coxswain told the bowman to shove off, the engine started and the launch went up river past the ships at the Gorjao Quay, the light clusters on the cranes looking like blurred moons in the rain. As they made for the anchorage below Ponta Chaluquene, they saw the lights of ships lying in the stream but could not see their hulls.

The women chatted inconsequentially, while the men were silent as men are when they've just met. All very convincing, thought Di Brett. But she did not know that the real reason for their silence was their awareness that the operation had started, that they were committed from now on to action.

Presently the engine slowed and the African coxswain answered a hail from the night, disembodied and peremptory. The launch shuddered as the engine went astern, there was a bump and the next moment a sailor in oilskins was helping them on to the foot of the gangway and they were climbing the wet steps which reflected the light from above.

Rohrbach reached the top and stepped out of the rain into the shelter of a covered deck. An officer with two stripes saluted him. 'Good evening, sir.' The accent was unmistakably German.

'*Guten abend!*' replied Rohrbach.

They were on board the *Hagenfels.*

As the launch left the boat harbour, two dark shapes stepped from behind a pile of sleepers.

126

'Well,' said von Falkenhausen, 'that's that. Three flies in the parlour.'

'I envy you,' said Herr Stauch. 'Can't I go off to the ship with you, Herr Baron?'

In the light of a dock lamp the Freiherr looked at the fat man's stomach, somehow more prominent under the wet raincoat. 'No,' he said evenly. 'You are too valuable ashore, Stauch.'

As Rohrbach and Johan disappeared into the night, Widmark put the engine astern and backed the boat out from the fish dock until they were clear of the breakwater; then with navigation lights burning they turned and headed across the river to where the Esparcelado Light glowed every second through the rain. The wind was blustering and when they cleared Ponta Vermelha the boat began to feel the sea and speed was eased. Widmark looked at the luminous hands of his watch—it was 19.40—7.40 p.m.; they had to be in position off the *Hagenfels* at 21.30, so they had nearly two hours in hand. To port he saw the flashing green light of number nine buoy and, altering course to the north-east, he headed the boat up the dredged channel, the buoy ahead a winking pinpoint of red light.

Under their coats they wore their shoulder-holsters and automatics; the spare ammunition clips, torches and other small items were in their pockets.

The fishing boat was decked-in forward where there was a small store for stowing the anchor, ropes, fenders and other gear. Crouching, a man could just get into it. The sternsheets were open to the weather, but the engine round which they sat was protected by a wooden and canvas cover.

The wind and sea were on the starboard bow and at times spray sluiced back over them, but the night and the water were warm and the discomfort slight.

Fortunately all of them except Mike Kent had served in small ships, or seasickness might have been embarrassing. As it was, he was the only sufferer. He sat weak and retching, miserably ashamed, as the boat butted into short seas, passing first number eight buoy and then number seven. A few minutes later, at 20.00, Widmark ordered the dousing of the navigation lights. After consulting the chart in the fo'c'sle, he brought the boat's head round to the south for the run in to Ponta Maone. This put the wind and sea on the port-quarter and the motion became easier; Hans gave the engine full throttle and the boat worked up to its maximum speed of eight knots. The darkness was black and complete, but in the west a few stars blinked through the overcast and there seemed less rain. When the Esparcelado Light bore due west they altered course, heading back into the Espirito Santo on the Catembe side. At 20.27 they were abeam of the light on the new course and they slowed down. The engine note dropped and sounds from the shore came down to them in the wind; the distant clamour of traffic and the ringing of church bells.

They made their way slowly down harbour, the lights of the ships at anchor misty balls of yellow, the black bulk of hulls shutting out the city's lights. Near the pier at Catembe, they stopped the engine.

Widmark stood up in the sternsheets. 'Righto, chaps. Get busy. Blacken your hands and faces, and lay out the gear.' He turned to Mike Kent. 'You okay now, Mike.'

'Much better, sir,' he whispered. The retching had stopped, but he still felt weak and was unhappy about the prospect of climbing a rope ladder up a steel side in the dark.

They took it in turns to go into the fo'c'sle where, with the aid of torches and a small mirror, they dried their hands and faces and blackened them with stove-polish, put on the rope-soled shoes and the belts with the sheath-knives. While this was going on the others laid out the hook rope and scaling ladder, checked that the hammer, punch and hack-saw were in one bathing bag, and that the charts and sailing directions were in another.

Widmark said: 'I've stuck a small White Ensign into the bag with the charts.'

They found this strangely reassuring, for they were pleased about the White Ensign. That was a nice touch he'd kept to himself.

Within twenty minutes everything was ready.

'We must be looking a fine lot of thugs,' said Andrew McFadden.

Hans laughed. 'Glad my girl friend's not around or I'd have had it.'

'That'll do,' said Widmark. 'Pipe down! Our job's to listen. All set?'

There were answering 'okays.' The engine started and the boat moved slowly upstream, the throttle well back.

It was 21.10.

They had about a mile to go and twenty minutes in hand.

It began to rain again as Ponta Chaluquene came abeam to port. Ahead of them lay the *Gerusalemme*, the German ships and the sailing ship. The tide was ebbing and the ships faced up river, their port sides towards the fishing boat as it made its way slowly against the tide. The relative positions of the ships as he'd last seen them were fixed in Widmark's mind. Rohrbach had told him where the *Clan McPhilly* had anchored the evening before, and it was for her he was now looking. Presently he saw a light-cluster on the fo'c'sle of a ship ahead and to starboard of them. McRobert had been as good as his word.

They came level with the *Clan McPhilly*'s fo'c'sle, and men could be seen at the windlass where there was the sound of hammering. The fishing boat drew slowly ahead. Widmark knew that the next ship in the line was the *Hagenfels*, and the blur of her lights was already visible through the rain; beyond her those of the *Dortmund* and *Aller* shone weakly. Widmark altered course to port to open the distance from the German ship, and the fishing boat went closer inshore. With the tide against them, they barely made headway and he ordered more throttle. They were about four hundred yards from the *Hagenfels* and downwind from her, so there was no danger of being heard. When they'd drawn well ahead they reduced speed and made a wide turn to starboard until the bows of the fishing boat faced down river and the *Hagenfels* lay ahead. They could now see both sides of the German ship. To starboard the foot of the gangway was hoisted clear of the water.

Widmark watched her lights, judging the distance as best he could. Then in a low voice he called: 'Stand by to anchor!'

The engine stopped and they drifted down with the tide towards the *Hagenfels* until, when the distance had closed to about a hundred and fifty yards, he ordered: 'Let go!'

The small anchor was lowered into the water so that

there should be no splash, and the anchor rope was paid out until it held and the boat swung to the tide.

It was 21.33.

Seventeen minutes to go.

On board the *Hagenfels* the party in the Captain's cabin had got off to a difficult start. It would have been bad enough under normal circumstances with so many strangers, but circumstances weren't normal and everybody in the cabin knew it except Mariotta Pereira and Cleo Melanides.

The Captain's day-cabin was a large one, well furnished, and off it to port were his sleeping-cabin, bathroom and pantry. There were two separate entrances to the day-cabin, but they both led on to the same alleyway; one directly into the cabin and the other via the pantry. Müller, the steward, was on duty and he came out of the pantry from time to time with plates of snacks, sausages, cakes and fruit, which he put on a table already well equipped with drinks. Immediately inside the main door on the starboard side there was a leather settee and on this Hester Smit sat between Günther Moewe and Johan. On the settee opposite were Mariotta, the Newt and Rohrbach. Against the foremost bulkhead there was a mahogany desk with book-cases on either side, and in the corner a fire-place with an electric fire, a carved mantelpiece above it. Di Brett was in the desk chair, turned to face the centre of the cabin, to her right Kuhn, to her left Lindemann.

Cleo Melanides was alone in an arm-chair opposite Lindemann.

The introductions had been performed with much bowing and heel clicking. Now they were talking, but the conversation was stilted and the party seemed bogged down, uncertain, the guests ill at ease.

Moewe and Kuhn got up from time to time to pour drinks and go round with the snacks.

The room was clouded with cigarette smoke, and though the large insect-screened portholes were open and there were two fans and a punkah-louvre at work, it was hot. The main door to the cabin was open, but inside it a light screen-door kept out mosquitoes.

Günther Moewe had gone the rounds with a plate of sandwiches, finishing up next to Rohrbach. 'So, Herr Rohr-bach,' he said in German. 'You are a Bavarian?'

130

'Yes. From Munich, Herr Moewe.'

'When did you last see Bavaria?' Moewe watched him intently, the morose eyes expressionless.

David Rohrbach half smiled, shaking his head. 'Some things one cannot mention before strangers, Herr Moewe.' He nodded in the direction of the Newt, who was listening to their conversation.

'Quite, Herr Rohrbach. One cannot be too careful, though I doubt if he speaks German.' As he said it, Moewe's mouth curled with contempt; there was no doubt in his mind, now that he had seen him, that this fellow Rohrbach was a Semite. No wonder he was a traitor to the Fatherland.

'As you say, Herr Moewe, one cannot be too careful. Maybe he does speak German. Who is he?'

Günther Moewe resented having to continue this game but he had no option. 'An Englishman who lives in Portugal, I understand.'

Rohrbach's eyebrows went up and he turned to look at the Newt. 'An *Englishman*! I am surprised you have him on board a German ship!'

'In time of war one does strange things, Herr Rohrbach. We would even invite *pigs* to our ship, if necessary.'

Rohrbach drew deeply on his cheroot before blowing a cloud of smoke into the second officer's face. 'Quite, Herr Moewe.' He'd blown the smoke into the man's face to get rid of him; he didn't like him standing at his side, looking down on him—the automatic and shoulder-holster felt unpleasantly conspicuous. The smoke trick worked and, disgusted, Moewe went over and sat next to Hester Smit who was carrying on a lively conversation in Afrikaans with Johan, her eyes shining—details which the German noted with irritation.

There was a lull in the conversation. Lindemann chose it to lean across Di Brett and say to Kuhn, quietly but in a voice all could hear: 'I saw you had the shore engineers on board this afternoon, Kuhn. Any progress?'

Kuhn shook his head. He looked careworn. 'None, Herr Kapitän. They examined it in their workshops yesterday and today. They cannot repair it here and they have not the resources for local manufacture.'

Lindemann frowned. 'That is serious, Kuhn.'

'Are you having engine trouble, Kapitän Lindemann?'

Rohrbach sensed a calamity.

Lindemann looked round the room, lowered his voice. 'Unfortunately, yes. The main crankshaft has a fracture. Due to metal fatigue, Herr Kuhn tells me.'

Rohrbach's stomach knotted with anxiety. This was shattering news. 'Operation Break Out' could only end in disaster. There was about to be a fight for the *Hagenfels*— no way of stopping it now—but when they'd got control they wouldn't be able to move her. It meant, at the least, internment in a Portuguese gaol for the rest of the war. With difficulty he fought down his rising panic. There was no way of getting word to Widmark. It was too late! Then the words used by Kuhn, still ringing in Rohrbach's ears, soaked through to the inner recesses of his mind: *They examined it in their workshops yesterday and today*. A main crankshaft would take the best part of three days to dismantle and lift out of the engine-room and yet from the Gorjao Quay yesterday, he and Johan had seen the froth of disturbed water under *Hagenfels*'s stern as the engines were turned. She was a single-screw ship so somebody was lying, or he had not heard aright.

'Fortunate that you have plenty of time for repairs, Kapitän Lindemann,' he heard himself saying, and he tried to smile. 'But how did you discover the trouble here? I mean, with the ship in harbour like this?'

Kuhn chipped in then. 'Sometimes in harbour we turn the main engines to keep them in condition. When we last did this'—he looked thoughtful—'about a week ago, we found excessive vibration. We knew at once that something was wrong.'

'Is it a big job taking out the main crankshaft, Herr Kuhn?'

'A very big job. With the few men I have here and some help from the shore it took us four days.'

Rohrbach hoped that his face didn't show his relief. He felt like jumping up and hugging the little chief engineer. But why had they troubled to tell such an elaborate lie? With this thought uppermost he followed Kuhn's remark with: 'How many men *have* you got on board, Kapitän?'

Lindemann made a small gesture of despair. 'Not enough to take the ship to sea. Less than half our complement.'

Rohrbach wondered what it was, but didn't like to ask.

The Newt's tugboat friend had said about twenty; he was probably not far off the mark.

With the aid of alcohol the conversation brightened and within half an hour the ice had broken, both sides privately pleased with the night's work so far. The Germans were pressing hosts—not holding themselves back—and this complicated the slow drinking act, for there were limits to how slow it could be without arousing suspicion. Fortunately Johan acted as barman for the third round and managed to pour ginger ale only for his companions' 'Horses' Necks,' the drink they'd agreed on with an eye to leaving out the brandy whenever possible. Hester Smit and Johan's interest in each other grew with the night, to Moewe's intense annoyance; the Newt and Di Brett concentrated on each other, and Mariotta and Lindemann flirted so openly that Rohrbach suspected they were more than old friends. Perhaps she'd had a romance with him when she'd travelled out in the passenger ship of which he was chief officer before the war. It was none of his business, but it seemed to explain Mariotta's influence with the Captain.

Only Cleo, sitting by herself in the big arm-chair, pale and withdrawn, seemed out of the party. Occasionally the Newt would speak to her, and once or twice Johan tried to cheer her up, but she smiled sadly and when he chided her she said she didn't feel well. At that, Hester Smit whispered in his ear: 'She's in love. Madly! With a South African she met the other night at Costa's. He promised to phone her and never did. *Men!*' She shook her head.

'You'd be miserable without them.'

'Drop dead!' She squeezed his hand on the side away from Moewe who was sitting on her right.

The Newt had a hand in his coat pocket and was fingering the sodium seconal capsules, wondering how and when, if ever, he could use them, when Lindemann invited Mariotta to accompany him to the bridge to settle an argument they were having about the stars. Rohrbach heard them and looked at his watch. It was 21.40. There were unlikely to be any stars on view, but in ten minutes' time the fishing boat would begin moving down on the *Hagenfels*, and the fewer people on the upper deck of the German ship the better. There was nothing he could do, however, but pray. Pray that they might go no farther than the chart-house—that love and not the stars was the object of the exercise. He suspected it was.

It was now time to put into operation a small detail of the plan. He stood up and said to Kuhn in German: 'Excuse me, Herr Kuhn, but—the toilet?' He spoke with the slight embarrassment which overcomes young men in mixed company on these occasions.

Kuhn smiled understandingly, nodding towards the door leading into the Captain's sleeping cabin. 'Through that door and to the left.'

Rohrbach looked over towards Johan and the Newt and said: 'Hookey's this way, chaps.' In the sleeping cabin he found the door which led into a small WC with wash-basin. Soon he was joined there by the Newt and Johan, who had left the Germans in the cabin suspicious but powerless to do anything about this altogether plausible move. In a whisper Rohrbach told them of Kuhn's and Lindemann's pretence that the main engines were out of order, and how he knew they were lying.

'Thank God for that!' breathed Johan. 'Nearly went round the bend when Moewe told the same sad tale to Hester and me. I'd forgotten about the engines turning yesterday.'

The Newt nodded. 'I heard Moewe telling you. Must say I felt a bit put out, too. It looked as if we were bitched at the start.'

Rohrbach looked at his watch. 'Another fifteen minutes and the balloon goes up.'

Through his coat the Newt patted his shoulder-holster. 'Comforting, aren't they?'

Johan, towering above him, said: 'Telling me!'

'I'm going to beat it,' whispered Rohrbach. 'Don't be too long.'

Mariotta and Lindemann were still missing when he got back to the day-cabin. Moewe was in a corner laying down the law about something to Hester Smit, who was saying: 'Don't be so childish, honey! He's a nice guy, that's all. I'm helping your party along.'

Di Brett had been talking to Kuhn, but as Rohrbach came in she stopped and went over to Cleo. Then Johan and the Newt came back and Moewe insisted on pouring them all drinks. Johan made a bee-line for Hester.

Kuhn disappeared into the pantry and the Newt found

himself standing near the desk alone. The Captain and Mariotta had not returned; Günther Moewe was pouring drinks, his back towards the room and everyone else was busy talking. The moment couldn't have been more propitious. Casually, using his left hand in which there was a cigarette, the Newt dropped the capsules into the partly filled steins left by Lindemann and Kuhn. Then he stopped in front of the bookcase, looked at his watch, and examined the titles of the books. Three minutes, he was thinking, can be an awful long time. The capsules didn't fizz. He'd tried them out at the Polana. No fizz, but three minutes to dissolve. Twelve minutes to act. That'd be 21.55!

On the far side of the cabin Rohrbach, talking to Cleo and Di Brett, was obsessed with the compulsive thought—when will Mariotta and Lindemann get back to the cabin? For Christ's sake when will they get back? Kuhn came in from the pantry with a plate of cakes and took them round. The Newt joined up with Hester and Johan, and Günther Moewe handed out the drinks he'd just mixed. There was no escaping the alcohol this time and, indeed, the male visitors were glad of it. Waiting for the show to start was a nerve-racking business.

Moewe put the tray down and questioned the Newt about his life in Oporto and South Africa—getting monosyllabic and unhelpful replies, he switched to Johan, whom he now doubly disliked because Hester had so clearly fallen for him. What was more they spoke to each other in Afrikaans, which he couldn't understand, and this infuriated him.

'You are a farmer, I believe, Herr le Roux?' From under thick eyebrows he peered morosely at the big Afrikaner.

Johan looked down on the German cheerfully. 'That's right.' Adroitly he changed the subject. 'You must be fed up with this place, Herr Moewe. Think you'll ever make a run for it?'

The question was so direct and unexpected that Moewe was off his guard. 'Well—er—no! I mean, we can't,' he stammered.

Johan nodded sympathetically. 'The *verdoemde* Royal Navy, I suppose. I mean, you couldn't get past them, could you?'

Moewe bristled with outraged national dignity: to think
135

that this ape should assume that they couldn't run the blockade! 'We are not interested in the Royal Navy. We have raiders, supply vessels and U-boats operating very successfully outside.' He pointed with his stein of beer in the general direction of the Indian Ocean. 'Perhaps you have seen some of the survivors coming in, Herr le Roux? The Royal Navy don't seem to have been much help to them.'

'Of course, Herr Moewe. You Germans are so efficient. And so *brave*,' he added enthusiastically. 'I mean, how could the decadent British worry you. But why is it, then, that you have not sailed?'

'I have already told you, Herr le Roux. There is a serious defect in the main engines.'

'Yes. That's *now*, Herr Moewe. But *before*. You've been here since the war started. Why haven't you sailed before?'

This was too much for Moewe. 'Because, Herr le Roux, we Germans obey orders. When we are told to go, we go.' He stood erect, resentful of Johan's height, the words more or less hissed from a half-shut mouth. Günther Moewe was on his fourth stein of Münchener. Valour had taken over from discretion.

Amusement flickered in Johan's eyes. 'I see, Herr Moewe. So you are waiting for orders to go?'

Moewe stiffened at once. 'I did *not* say that.'

'Of course. Forgive me. My mistake.' Johan patted his cauliflower ears. 'These don't work so well nowadays. They're always getting bent in the scrum.'

Hester Smit tittered.

'I do not know what you're talking about,' Moewe muttered; then, conscious of his blunder, he walked away.

In the alley-way outside, they heard Mariotta laughing and a moment later she and Lindemann came back. To the Newt's dismay, she sat down in what had been the Captain's chair and picked up his stein of beer. 'My goodness, I'm hot and thirsty!' She looked at Lindemann. 'Mind if I drink this, Kurt?'

'Of course not. Go ahead.'

She did. The Newt sighed. There was nothing he could do about it. To his relief, however, Kuhn had gone back to his old seat and was swallowing the Münchener.

Fifty per cent return, anyway, muttered the Newt, but poor old Mariotta . . .

The fly-screen door to the cabin swung open and the conversation stopped suddenly. Von Falkenhausen and Heinrich Schäffer stood in the doorway.

'Ah!' smiled the Freiherr, 'A party. Charming. May we join you?'

Rohrbach looked at his watch. It was 21.55.

'Dear God!' he breathed.

Chapter Thirteen

Time was dragging for the men huddled in the sternsheets of the fishing boat, silent but for an occasional mono-syllable, straining in the darkness for anything that might come to them from the *Hagenfels*. The dark bulk of the ship lay astern of them, the anchor and deck lights and those from the portholes under the bridge illuminating parts of her dimly, so that she was a disembodied complex of lights and shadows.

Occasionally they heard hammering from the direction of the *Clan McPhilly*, and sometimes the wind brought to them faintly the sound of voices and the laughter of men and women in the German ship.

'Seem to be enjoying themselves,' said Widmark caustically.

McFadden cleared his throat. 'They're no' round to fightin' yet, that's for sure.'

Widmark looked at the luminous hands of his watch— 21.43—seven minutes to go. In a low voice he ran once more through the probable disposition of the German crew at ten o'clock—22.00. 'Crew totals, say, twenty,' he began. 'Nine are ashore—that leaves ten or eleven. Let's say eleven. We don't know how many officers there are on board. Probably the lot, since Lindemann's giving a party. That puts four of them in the Captain's cabin. It's pretty certain the steward'll be there, too. That's five of the eleven. There'll be a night watchman somewhere on the upper deck. If he's like a British sailor he'll be between the gangway and the galley most of the time fixing himself cups of cha. That's six. Five still to be accounted for. There'll be one or two bodies in the engine-room watching the generators and auxiliaries—that leaves three or four. Crew accommodation is for'ard, so they may be there or, on a hot night like this, they could be hanging about on deck. Maybe somewhere near the Captain's cabin where they can listen to what goes on. You know what sailors are.

'Once on board we remain concentrated. We'll make first for the fo'c'sle and deal with whoever's there. Then we'll make for the Captain's cabin and join up with David and company. If trouble starts there before we arrive it's up to them to deal with it. After that we'll fan out and round off any odds and sods left over, like the bods in the engine-room. Got that?'

This was the plan they'd been through several times since they'd known that some of their number would start the operation in the Captain's cabin. But Widmark knew that this last-minute summary was a good thing—it helped the time to pass, it steadied nerves and freshened memories. His watch showed 22.47. Almost time to begin. 'Check your gear,' he said quietly. 'Off raincoats. Fix your cosh-thongs on your wrists.'

There was a bustle of activity in the boat.

'All set?'

There were answering 'okays.'

'Right!' he said tensely. 'Stand by to weigh. Out fenders.'

Four pudding fenders were hung over the starboard side to take the rub once the boat was alongside the German ship.

At that moment, faintly but distinctly, Widmark heard the sound of a motor boat. 'Shissh!' he warned. 'Belay everything! There's a boat approaching.'

They could all hear it now, the note of the engine growing stronger, coming from somewhere between the *Hagenfels* and the shore. Then it was shut out by the noise of hammering from the *Clan McPhilly*, and Widmark wished that Captain McRobert might not for the moment be so diligent. The hammering stopped. McFadden said: 'Look! The gangway.'

On the starboard side of the *Hagenfels* they saw the gangway being lowered, and a launch came out of the darkness into the circle of light and went alongside. Three men got out of the sternsheets and went up the gangway, the launch waited for a moment then the engine roared into life and it made for the shore.

'Name of a name!' said Widmark. 'What the bloody hell's going on?'

'Liberty men returning?' suggested McFadden.

'Not likely at this time,' said Widmark.

It was 21.55. Whatever this development might mean they were committed; there was no going back.

'Out paddles,' he ordered and then, after a pause, 'Weigh anchor!' Mike Kent and Hans le Roux pulled on the anchor rope and the fishing boat moved slowly ahead; they lifted the anchor a few feet clear of the bottom when the rope was up and down and secured the line round a bollard. Caught by the tide the boat drifted, slowly, stern first, towards the *Hagenfels*. They manned the paddles and from time to time Widmark would order: 'Paddle starboard!' 'Paddle port!' or 'Paddle together!' and in this way they steered the boat. It was not long before the *Hagenfels*'s bows loomed above them, black and forbidding shafts of light from the portholes penetrating the outer darkness, clouds of insects round the wire screens. They manhandled the boat round the stem to the port side and Hans released the anchor rope, paying it out until the anchor held again; then, hitching it round a bollard, he held the boat under the flare of the *Hagenfels*'s bow, where they were hidden from anyone on deck. There they waited, their minds full of the new complication, nerves and bodies taut.

It was 22.03.

Still no riveting.

Widmark ground his teeth in frustration. For Christ's sake, he thought, what has happened in the *Clan McPhilly*? He daren't start warping the boat down the side until the riveting started. They waited for another four minutes— 22.07—then he decided there was nothing for it but to go ahead, whatever the risk. Paying out the anchor rope, they drifted aft with the tide, down along the port side of the *Hagenfels*, McFadden and Hans holding the boat off the steel plating. It was no easy task but somehow they succeeded and a few minutes later, when Widmark judged they were opposite the after well-deck, the rope was secured and the boat rode to her anchor again, the pudding fenders taking the rub against the *Hagenfels*'s side.

Widmark prayed for the sound of riveting but nothing came. Even the hammering had stopped.

Hans le Roux climbed on to the bow of the boat and with a powerful throw sent the hook rope sailing up into the darkness on to the deck of the *Hagenfels*. In spite of the grapnel's foam rubber sheathing there was a metallic clang as it struck the steel deck. In the boat they shuddered. Hans pulled on the hook rope until it held and then went up it hand over hand, his feet braced against the side of the ship, the scaling ladder over his shoulder. From the boat they could see nothing of him for although the rain had stopped the sky was still overcast and the boat was shrouded in darkness. Night and time seemed to pause in fearful expectation while they stood in the sternsheets waiting, their nerves jarring, faces turned upwards, trying in their minds to picture what was happening in the blackness above. There was the sound of footsteps along the steel deck and a deep voice called: 'Wer ist da?' There was no answer and the call was repeated. With chilly apprehension, they waited.

There were the fragmented, unreal sounds of a scuffle, two solid thumps, what sounded like a groan—then silence —followed seconds later by the scrabbling noise of the scaling ladder coming down the side. From the rail above came Hans's rough whisper: 'Okay—come up.'

Widmark went first, followed by McFadden. Mike Kent, the last man to leave the boat, pulled the sea-plug and, once he could hear the water gushing into the bottom of the boat, he, too, went up the ladder.

In the dim glow of the lights on the winch island they saw Hans standing over a body which lay humped on the steel deck.

'Must have been the night watchman,' he whispered. 'The grapnel made a helluva noise. Soon as I got on deck I hid behind that ventilator cowl. Then I heard this bloke coming. Walked past me calling, "Wer ist da?" so I coshed him.'

'Think he's out for long?' Widmark spoke quickly but dispassionately, his eyes on the midship island of the *Hagenfels*, the direction from which more trouble was likely.

'For keeps, I reckon.' Hans shrugged. 'First time I've used a cosh. I don't know the dose. This bloke mumbled after the first one, so I gave him another for luck. His head made a nasty noise. Don't think it did him any good.'

Hans sounded hit up and slightly hysterical.

Widmark said: 'Okay, Hans. Take it easy.' He looked at his watch. 'We're way behind schedule.' It was 22.11.

At that moment, like a sudden but infinitely prolonged burst of machine-gun fire, the sound of riveting came down on the wind.

141

Widmark grinned sardonically; from the shoulder-holster beneath his coat, tucked away under his left armpit, he drew the automatic, transferring it to his left hand, gripping the cosh in his right. The others did the same.

It was no longer necessary to whisper.

'Come on,' he said. 'Let's go!'

At 21.50 the Port Authority launch delivered the pilot, Carlos Alberto d'Almeida, on board the *Clan McPhilly* where she lay at anchor in the Espirito Santo and having done so left immediately for the shore. As he went up the gangway, d'Almeida cursed the wet darkness of the night and the thoughtlessness of the Clan ship's Captain in anchoring so far upstream; with the ebb tide it meant that the ship would have to be turned as soon as the anchor was aweigh, and the river was narrow here and the anchorage crowded.

At the head of the gangway, d'Almeida was met by the second officer who took him to the Captain's cabin. The two men knew each other, McRobert having called at Lourenço Marques for many years. After formal greetings, inquiries about each other's health and families, and mutual expressions of regret at the heavy losses of Allied shipping taking place on the coast, McRobert invited the pilot to sit down. A steward brought coffee and toast, putting the tray on a small table between them. D'Almeida saw from the cabin clock that it was almost ten o'clock.

'Unfortunately there is not time, Captain. We must start weighing in three minutes.'

McRobert frowned. 'Did the Port Captain's office no' tell ye, then?'

The pilot threw out his hands in a gesture of interrogation. 'Tell me what, please?'

'We're delayed a wee bit, Pilot. We reported by voice radio to the Port Captain's office a short time back. Windlass trouble, would ye believe it? That's why we've had to let go down here. Rivets in the base plate sheered and we've got to put in new ones.' He cocked his head on one side, and pointed to the forward portholes. 'Hear that, now?'

From the fo'c'sle came the sound of hammering.

The pilot nodded, resigned, his mouth drooping. 'How long shall we be?'

McRobert poured the coffee. 'Shouldn't be too long. About an hour, I'd say. We'll be having a report from the Chief.'

D'Almeida looked at the bulkhead clock again. If he radioed the Port Captain's office now for a launch it would take at least fifteen minutes to reach the *Clan McPhilly*— then he'd have to come back after thirty minutes ashore. It wasn't worth it. With a small sigh, a click of the teeth, he accepted the inevitability of another late night.

McRobert remembered something about d'Almeida. 'What would ye be saying to a wee game of chess?' He got up and took a chess board and wooden box from the bookcase.

D'Almeida's eyes brightened and his teeth gleamed; this was something he understood. 'Excellent, Captain. What's the English saying?'

McRobert looked at him thoughtfully. Then he smiled. ' "It's an ill wind that blows nobody any good." The English say it's from Shakespeare. Wouldn't surprise me if it wasn't Burns.' He began to whistle under his breath, up-ending the box for the pieces to fall on the chessboard. But he was thinking of other things.

While they set out the chessmen he was listening to what was going on outside; but what he was waiting for did not come. When the cabin clock showed 22.03 he mumbled an apology to d'Almeida, left the cabin and hurried through the darkness to the fo'c'sle. At the top of the ladder he was met with the noise of hammering. Kneeling next to Angus Duncan he implored him: 'For the Lord's sake, Mr Duncan, start the riveting!' Under the light cluster the Captain's face showed agitation such as the chief engineer had never seen. The thin Scot shook his head and went on wrestling with the valve of the oxy-acetylene cylinder which lay next to the windlass. 'This bluidy valve's nae bluidy guid! We've been working on it for ten minutes.' With an impatient gesture he took the hammer from the chief officer. 'John,' he said through clenched teeth, 'git them bring anither cylinder from aft as quick as ye can, man!'

The chief officer slipped away and Duncan said: 'We'll have the riveting going in ten minutes, Captain.'

'Could be too late, Mr Duncan.'

Duncan kicked the cylinder. 'The damned thing. It's Satan's work. One in a thousand valves, maybe, will do that.

Should ha' tested it earlier.' He hammered frenziedly at the base plate making all the noise he could—but it was no substitute for riveting.

When the launch went alongside the *Hagenfels* and Widmark saw three men go up the gangway, he had thought of abandoning the plan to concentrate on the crew's accommodation first, and to make instead for the Captain's cabin. But he had no means of knowing who the new arrivals were, or to what part of the ship they had gone.

Crew returning from the shore early?

Unlikely because the launch's trip was an unscheduled one.

More guests for the party?

Scarcely at that hour.

Agents or other port authorities?

Possibly, but why?

Since Johan, Rohrbach and the Newt were already in the Captain's cabin, it was important to deal with other parts of the ship first.

So they kept to the original plan.

Widmark led as they moved up the port side, Johan behind him, then McFadden and Mike Kent, his seasickness forgotten in the excitement of action.

Passing along the midship deck-house they hugged the bulkhead, ducking under lighted portholes, moving silently on rope-soled shoes, revolvers and coshes at the ready.

At the forward end of the deck-house, Widmark signalled the others to stop; he edged up to the corner and looked across the well-deck.

There were a few blank spots: the winch island at the foot of the foremast, between numbers one and two holds, shut out a part of the starboard side, and there were ventilators which did the same thing. He said to the others. 'It's all clear along the port side as far as I can see. When we get to the winch island, Hans and Mike must deal with the starboard side. We'll move on up the port side. Meet you at the fo'c'sle doors.'

Hans and Mike Kent went over to the winch island, and Widmark and McFadden worked their way forward on the port side. The riveting from the *Clan McPhilly* shut out any sounds from the Captain's cabin the lights of which were now visible from the foredeck. But the breeze carried the smell of food and tobacco smoke and the tangy odour of beer. Widmark sniffed it and decided that the party was doing itself proud.

Hans moved silently along the after side of the winch island, with Mike Kent close behind him. At the end of the island he stopped and looked round the corner. Twenty feet from him two men leant over the side, elbows on the bulwark rail. They were talking in low voices, looking out over the river towards the lights of the town. Hans held up a hand.

'There's a couple of guys there!' he said. 'Watch me but don't come unless I'm in trouble.' With remarkable agility for such a big man, he slipped round the corner of the island, cosh in one hand, automatic in the other. It took him less than five seconds to come up behind the Germans who never knew what hit them.

Hans looked at the bodies sprawled grotesquely at his feet. 'Hell! That's two more,' he mumbled to himself. 'It's becoming a habit.' He felt the men's hearts. One was all right, but the other's was beating irregularly and a trickle of blood came from his mouth. Enemy or no enemy, Hans was unhappy about that. He'd seen it before, in rugby when a forward had been kicked on the head. The man had died. Hans was at heart a gentle man and all this ferocity appalled him. He sighed.

A moment later Mike Kent came up and they dragged the bodies behind the winch island. 'Out for a long count,' muttered Hans as he and Kent went over to where Widmark and McFadden were waiting. Hans told them what had happened. Widmark said: 'Well done!' in a quiet, quarter-deck voice and looked at his watch.

It was 22.14.

He touched Mike Kent on the shoulder. 'Wait outside the port door of the fo'c'sle and bash anyone who uses it. Watch those two at the winch house. They may come round. Put them to sleep again if they do. We'll go into the fo'c'sle and see what's cooking. Can't be more than two or three of them there.'

Followed by Hans and McFadden, he went into the fo'c'sle, quietly shut the starboard door, locked it and pocketed the key. Systematically they searched the seamen's and stokers' messes, the wash places and toilets, but they drew blanks. Then they started on the six cabins. Standing outside the second one, they heard voices. The door was ajar. Widmark kicked it open and there was a big man sitting in a chair, gnarled and sunburnt, with close-cropped hair, he was sweating profusely in a white singlet and khaki slacks. With him was a small man with the face of a ferret. Widmark pointed his automatic at the big German whose mouth opened in astonishment. He tried to get up but Hans pushed him down, frisked him and found a sheath-knife on his belt.

'Put your hands up!' Widmark's hard voice conveyed more meaning to the Germans than the words.

Their hands went up. Johan frisked the small man, but he had no weapons.

The large German began to lower his arms. Hans tapped him with his cosh. 'Keep 'em up, chum, if you want to live.'

Widmark kept the automatic on him. 'How many crew on board? Quick or I shoot!'

Watching all this from behind, McFadden felt an almost overwhelming compulsion to laugh. There was something incredibly music-hall about it all—the Germans' huge surprise at the sudden confrontation; the armed men, their blackened faces streaked with rain and sweat, behaving in the best traditions of villainy.

Widmark raised his cosh. 'Come on! How many men on board? Make it snappy!'

The German shook his head. '*Ich spreche klein Englisch.*'

McFadden picked up an English magazine from the table next to the bunk. 'What's this doing here, then?'

Solemnly the German protested: '*Ich spreche klein Englisch.*'

Widmark said: 'I'm going to shoot this bastard. He's wasting our time.' The effect on the German was immediate. Not only did he understand English, but he didn't like the way Widmark spoke it.

'Okay. Okay,' he muttered. 'What you want to know?'

'How many crew on board *now*?' The delay was making Widmark angry.

'Twenty.' The German watched stolidly for the effect of this information.

'Don't lie to me.' Widmark's eyes narrowed. 'Your total crew's only that and there are men ashore. Come on. Quick!' He poked the barrel of the automatic into the man's neck. 'Hear that riveting outside? Nobody'll hear me shoot. Out with it.'

Widmark meant what he said, and his determination was felt by the German with whom fear now got the upper hand. His hands went higher and his voice became hoarser.

'Okay. Okay. I tell truth. Three officers on board. One steward. Two greasers. Two seamen. Carpenter,' he nodded at the small German next to him, 'and myself. I am bosun.'

Widmark looked at him with cold, calculating eyes. 'If you've lied I'll kill you. A few dead Germans one way or another make no difference to me.' McFadden and Hans wondered if the German knew how accurate that remark was.

The bosun nodded emphatically. 'What I say is true.'

'Now,' said Widmark. 'Take us to the chain-locker. Both of you. Quick, and no tricks or you're dead ducks. We're short of time. Hans, fetch those Jerries you laid out by the winch island and get Mike to help you. Put them in the chain-locker with these customers. I'm not taking any chances.'

Hans doubled off and Widmark and McFadden followed the Germans down a companion ladder to a lower deck, then forward along a narrow alleyway which ended against a steel door. The bosun unbolted it and switched on a light. Widmark looked in. It was the chain-locker all right. Full of cable and mud and smelling like a sewer.

'In you go!' He pushed the two Germans through the steel door. 'We'll send you some chums in a moment. There'll be an armed guard outside.' Tapping his automatic, he pointed at the door.

The bosun's protest was half fear and half indignation. 'This is not a place for men. There is no air.'

Widmark snapped at him. 'Too bad. That's where you're going, my friend. Plenty of fresh air comes down the spurling-pipes.'

There was a noise behind them. It was Hans staggering down the alleyway with a body over his shoulder. 'This bastard weighs a ton,' he complained. They helped him lay the man down inside the chain-locker. Hans was soon back with the second unconscious German. They shut the door on the prisoners, bolted it on the outside and made their way back up the ladder. After a quick look through the remaining cabins they returned to the foredeck. Mike

Kent was there waiting for them.

'Okay?' he asked anxiously.

'Sure. Everything's fine.'

'Haven't seen a thing here, sir. Much quieter in the Captain's cabin now.'

'Right,' said Widmark. 'Leave the bag with the cable gear here. McFadden, take Hans and Mike down the port side into the midship deck-house. You'll have to go up two decks. You'll find the foremost alleyway running athwartships. The door to the Captain's cabin will be for'ard on the starboard side. Remember the plan? Stand by outside the door, or near it if it's open, and if you see any Jerries fix them. As long as this riveting lasts you can use your automatics, but try and make do with coshes. If you hear trouble in the cabin, go in at once and give a hand. Otherwise don't start anything until I arrive. Okay? I'm going to do a quick recce.'

Widmark went up two companion ladders to the boat-deck below the bridge and along the port side of the deck-house until he'd reached its forward end, rounded the corner and crossed slowly to starboard, keeping below the level of the portholes. From them came a voice he recognised—a man's voice. Taking a deep breath, he moved up until his eyes were level with the rim of the porthole. For a second he looked through the gauze fly-screen into the Captain's cabin, then ducked again. What he saw had shaken him badly.

The Newt, Johan and Rohrbach were sitting on a settee in an unmistakable attitude of surrender, their hands well above their heads. Opposite them, just inside the door, von Falkenhausen's and Schäffer's revolvers explained why. In the fraction of time he'd had to take this in, Widmark realised that these must be two of the men the launch had brought off.

But how had they learnt what was on the go?

Where had the plan miscarried?

The answers were beyond him. Then he thought of the Commodore in Cape Town: '. . . *in war there are too many imponderables, Widmark. It's a blinding certainty that something will go wrong. It always does.*'

Well, it certainly had and with a vengeance. He slithered round to the foreside of the deck-house and gingerly went up for another look. This time he could see Di Brett and Hester Smit, white-faced and huddled on the settee on the starboard side of the cabin. Mariotta was in an arm-chair in the middle of the cabin, and her eyes were closed. Why? Widmark had no idea. Günther Moewe, revolver in hand, stood behind the settee on which the Newt and his friends were sitting. To their right a small middle-aged man with close-cropped hair and steel-rimmed glasses sat in an arm-chair, but Widmark couldn't see his face clearly.

On the far left, a man's legs jutted forward; he was evidently sitting with his knees crossed. Widmark presumed it was Lindemann. Beyond him the neat shoes and ankles of female feet just showed and Widmark realised with a pleasant shock that they must be Cleo's. In the excitement of the last half-hour he'd forgotten her. Lowering his head after this briefest of looks, he heard von Falkenhausen say: 'You gentlemen are playing a dangerous game. This ship is German territory. There are penalties for spies in wartime and they are not pleasant . . .'

Widmark thought fast, his mind cool and clear, but his body tense, every sense alert to what was happening. He had to create a diversion. Moving back to the starboard side of the deck-house he lifted himself cautiously for the third time and took a snap view through the porthole. The Newt, Rohrbach and Johan were again opposite him, Moewe behind them, revolver in hand. Lindemann in the corner on his right was now visible and next to him a pale Cleo, head back and eyes half-closed, her hands on the arms of the chair. Lindemann was still in the arm-chair but there was a revolver in his right hand, the barrel pointing at the deck. The little man with close-cropped hair appeared to be asleep. Drunk, thought Widmark caustically.

From upwind the high-speed rat-a-tatter-rat-a-tatter of the *Clan McPhilly*'s riveting filled the night sky with over-whelming noise.

Widmark held his breath.

Chapter Fourteen

The screen door slammed behind von Falkenhausen and Heinrich Schäffer. 'Ah!' said the Freiherr. 'A party. Charming. May we join you?'

Lindemann went across to meet them. He clicked his heels and bowed. 'An unexpected pleasure, Herr Baron?' There was a note of interrogation.

The Freiherr bowed. 'I am sorry to disturb you, Kapitän, but Schäffer and I have been discussing the repair problem with the engineering people ashore. The position is highly unsatisfactory. I thought I should come at once and discuss it with you. I had no idea you were entertaining.' He looked round the room. 'We also brought off Francke, your chief mechanician. He was at the discussions with us.'

'We can discuss the matter in a moment, Freiherr,' said Lindemann. 'In the meantime let me introduce you.'

The Captain performed the introductions and the Freiherr bowed and smiled, his charm communicating itself to them all. When Lindemann introduced him to Di Brett and the Newt, the Freiherr nodded. 'I have already met Mrs Brett *and* Mr Newton. At the Polana the other evening.'

'The others,' Lindemann looked round the cabin, 'you already know. My officers: Herr Kuhn and Herr Moewe.' The Germans bowed stiffly, clicking their heels.

'Now,' said the Captain, 'Please sit down. Schäffer will get you a drink.'

Schäffer poured the drinks for the Freiherr and himself, *prosits* were exchanged and the new arrivals sat down.

An awkward silence was broken by the Freiherr, whose smile embraced all in the room. 'Forgive me, ladies and gentlemen, but I must talk shop for a moment.'

Turning to Lindemann, he lowered his voice as they discussed the defective crankshaft and the problem of its repair locally. Rohrbach listened to the conversation with amused cynicism; these two were undoubtedly working hard at their act. The Germans' conversation came to an end and another silence ensued.

'Lovely weather we're having.' The Newt beamed good-naturedly at the Freiherr.

'You like the rain, Herr Newton?'

'Cools things down rather, don't you think?'

In between wondering how the new arrivals were going to complicate what was about to happen, the Newt speculated on the precise geometry of the Freiherr's scars.

'Where do you normally live, Herr Newton?'

The Newt lit a cigarette and put the spent match in the ash-tray with exaggerated care. Blowing a cloud of smoke at the deckhead, he looked at the Freiherr. 'Oporto, actually.'

'Unusual,' said the Freiherr, frowning. 'An Englishman from Oporto? In Lourenço Marques? While his country is at war?'

The expression in the brown eyes didn't match the half-apologetic smile which accompanied the next statement. 'What brings you here at *this* time, Herr Newton?'

The atmosphere in the cabin was electric and the women began to feel the tension between the Germans and their guests.

The Newt's grey eyes stared unconcernedly at the Freiherr, while he strained for a sound from outside—for the sound of riveting. Johan and David Rohrbach were taut, wary of the conversation, Johan knowing that this was 'Swiss Fritz' of the Montelémar, trying to reconcile the face he now saw with the one he had known then; wondering exactly what the significance of this unexpected arrival was; sizing up Heinrich Schäffer at close range and deciding that he and the German were about the same height and weight but noting with an athlete's eye that the German was not fit, that he carried too much weight, that his neck and face muscles were flabby, his stomach too prominent.

Rohrbach, wondering much the same things, was tenser and more highly strung than Johan, but his keen brain was evaluating the new situation, recording the relative positions of those in the cabin, trying to anticipate their reactions when events outside aroused their suspicions.

The Newt's calm voice interrupted his thoughts: 'I'm here on business, actually.'

'What sort of business, Herr Newton?' The brown eyes, unblinking, had a curious intentness.

'My family has a wine export business in Oporto. We trade with Mozambique.'

The Freiherr stroked his chin, nodding as he weighed this

information. 'I see. And you, Herr le Roux?' He switched suddenly to Johan. 'What brings you here?'

'Holidaying. I like the place. The change from the Union.'

'Ah! You like the place.' He nodded again, slowly, then his eyes shifted to David Rohrbach. 'And you, Herr Rohrbach—what is it that brings you here?'

An element of theatre had entered into the proceedings: the Freiherr's slow, deliberate questioning which had silenced all other conversation in the cabin; the puzzled faces of the women who sensed that something was wrong; the quietness of the other Germans, each observing their male guests covertly—each of them, that is to say, except Kuhn, who appeared to be as drowsy as Mariotta whose eyelids kept drooping, only to be lifted with an embarrassed start each time she found herself dropping off to sleep.

Rohrbach said: 'I came down with le Roux—on holiday,' but his heart thumped so hard he wondered if it could be heard. 'I've always liked the place.'

'Yes. Delightful, isn't it?' Von Falkenhausen turned away from the men and spoke to Di Brett. 'Do you know Lourenço Marques well, Mrs Brett?'

The cornflower blue eyes dropped and she smiled nervously. 'Pretty well. I've been staying at the Polana for some months. There's something awfully attractive about LM, don't you think?'

'Indeed, Mrs Brett, I do.' He looked at the Captain. 'Forgive me, Kapitän. I seem to monopolise the conversation but—meeting so many charming strangers at once—one is naturally curious.' Turning to them again, he laughed. 'I can never go into a room and see strangers without wondering who they are and what they do. Appearances are so often deceptive.'

'Aren't they?' Johan grinned amiably. 'Now suppose you tell us what you do. And how you got those scars. Must be a good story, that.' This produced a ripple of laughter in which the Germans didn't join.

The Freiherr shook his head. 'The truth is very dull. I'm a shipping man. And the scars—well—I'm a German. We have duelling—the British have foxhunting—the French——' he shrugged his shoulders. 'I suppose they have something——'

Günther Moewe sniggered.

'The *Tour de France,* if you're thinking of sport,' said Rohrbach quietly. 'Apart from that a great deal of culture —a quality in short supply in Europe these days, wouldn't you say?'

Hester Smit made a moue. 'What about talking to us for a change? This party's getting very dull.'

'Hear! Hear!' Cleo smiled sadly. 'You'd think we weren't here.'

'I quite agree.' Di Brett, who was doing her lips, a small mirror in her hands, nodded briskly. 'Talk to *us.* You'll find us quite intelligent.'

The Freiherr's slow smile of embarrassment was irresistible. 'A thousand apologies, ladies. You are quite right.'

Lindemann got up. 'Who's ready for a drink?'

At that moment a high-pitched lacerating sound, a satanic forge worked by frenzied hammerers, shattered the silence outside. Rohrbach's heart jumped. The riveting! It was 22.11—at long last. He thought a prayer of gratitude.

The conversation started again, but Herr Kuhn and Mariotta Pereira were not much interested. 'They're tight,' giggled Hester. Mariotta heard her, yawned, and smiled weakly. 'I'm so *tired.*'

With an effort Kuhn pulled himself upright in his chair and passed his hand across his eyes. Then, smiling apologetically at his Captain, he picked up the stein, drained it compulsively and looked round the room with sleepy eyes. The tension in the cabin dissipated slowly and the party got into some sort of stride again until, perhaps ten minutes later, von Falkenhausen looked at his watch and spoke to Lindemann. 'Kapitän, please excuse me, I must be going. I came only to bring you the news of the repairs. There is much to do tomorrow. An early start is essential.'

Lindemann stood up. 'I am sorry you cannot stay, Herr Baron. The night is still young. But I understand, of course. Let me see you to the launch.'

The Freiherr shook his head. 'No. *Please!* Herr Schäffer will see me off. I insist that you remain with your guests.'

Heinrich Schäffer got up and joined von Falkenhausen. They stood together, clicking their heels and bowing this way and that.

'*Auf wiedersehen,* ladies and gentlemen!' said the Freiherr gallantly.

153

The men stood up, the women remained seated. Von Falkenhausen and Schäffer moved to the door—as they reached it they spun round, in their hands Luger pistols pointing directly at Rohrbach, the Newt and Johan. Schäffer was scowling, but the Freiherr's smile was as elegant as ever.

'Hands up, gentlemen!' The voice was hard, implacable, in spite of the smile. 'Quickly, please! No nonsense.'

Rohrbach remembered thinking: 'For Christ's sake, what's gone wrong?'

The Newt said: *'Quel drame!'* But their hands went up all the same.

Other than for Cleo and Di Brett's little shrieks of surprise, there was not a sound in the cabin. Moewe had picked up a revolver from somewhere while the Freiherr was talking, and now he moved over behind Rohrbach, Johan and the Newt, who were acutely aware of his presence. Lindemann, too, had produced a gun—he sat upright in the arm-chair in the corner, his weather-beaten face unusually drawn. He disliked violence and though he knew the Freiherr was bluffing, trying to frighten these Britishers into talking, he feared the situation might get out of control.

With his free hand the Freiherr pointed to the settee behind them. 'Keep your hands above your heads and sit down, please. I have something to say to you.'

They sat down and von Falkenhausen spoke again—the smile had gone now and there was an edge to his voice. 'You gentlemen are playing a dangerous game. This ship is German territory. There are penalties for spies in wartime and they are not pleasant——' While he allowed the significance of what he'd said to sink in, the brown eyes took on a new hardness and the strong mouth set implacably.

There was a long, frightening pause—no one moved, and but for the continuous metallic rattle of riveting which came from outside the only sound in the cabin was the subdued whirr of the electric fan.

But suddenly, dramatically, this tableau changed to violent movement with the explosive crackle of five shots fired in quick succession through a porthole on the starboard side.

The women screamed as the bullets ripped into the bulkhead behind Günther Moewe's head.

Chapter Fifteen

The firing was followed by the utmost confusion in the Captain's cabin.

The women screamed high shrieks of terror as von Falkenhausen and Schäffer, who'd been facing Rohrbach, Johan and the Newt, swung round firing at the porthole from which the shots had come.

When the second shot whistled past his head, Moewe threw himself down behind the settee on which the Britishers were sitting. After the initial shock, confused thoughts raced through his mind: there was an attack of some kind on the ship—of what sort and why he had no idea, but it had something to do with the presence on board of the three British naval officers. Somehow he must get out of the cabin—to the radio telephone—alert the shore authorities—this was a neutral port—whatever the British were up to was illegal—they couldn't get away with it!

Another good reason for getting out of the cabin was his desire to survive; there were armed men at the portholes, the chances of getting shot seemed pretty high, and Moewe had no desire to be shot. Within the brief moment of these thoughts he translated them into action, rolling sideways towards the pantry door, the revolver still in his hand. The noise was unbelievable, the screams of the women, more firing—it seemed *in* the cabin now—the hoarse shouts of Lindemann and the Freiherr and, above it all, the unceasing clamour of riveting coming over the water. Reaching the pantry door he slid through it feet first, propelling himself forward on his elbows, buttocks and heels. Behind him an English voice shouted. He shut the pantry door and ran through into the alleyway. A lot had happened in the cabin in the five seconds it had taken Moewe to reach the pantry. As von Falkenhausen and Schäffer swung round and fired at the portholes on the starboard side, the screen-door behind them opened and McFadden, Hans and Mike Kent, faces blackened, hair tousled, burst in with their automatics in their hands. McFadden's shout sounded above the general clamour. 'Hands up!'

Suddenly there was a superfluity of guns, for as von Falkenhausen and Schäffer turned away, Rohrbach, Johan and the Newt jumped to their feet, automatics drawn. Rohrbach covered Lindemann, for whom the pace of events was too much—he stood open-mouthed, gaping into the barrel of Rohrbach's gun, his own at his feet, his hands above his head. Kuhn remained in the arm-chair, alarmed, blinking in bewilderment, half-way across the threshold of sleep.

But the Newt wasn't taking any chances and he stood over the little man with the barrel of his automatic a foot from the close-cropped head.

On hearing McFadden's shout the two Germans had spun round to find themselves looking into the barrels of six guns—their guests' and the new arrivals'. The Freiherr smiled wanly, dropped his Luger and put up his hands. For a moment Schäffer looked as if he might make a fight of it, but he saw Johan's gun pointing at him and didn't like the look in the big man's eyes, or the broken nose and cauliflower ears, so he dropped his gun and put up his hands. He knew a tough man when he saw one. Schäffer was tough, too, but it was no good now. Maybe later.

Mike Kent picked up the guns the Germans had dropped, and McFadden said: 'Chuck 'em over the side, Mike boy.'

It was all over in the cabin.

They pushed the four Germans into a corner, made them sit with their hands clasped on their heads, and asked the women to go into the Captain's sleeping cabin and stay there until further notice. Mariotta was too tired to be really interested in what was happening—she kept yawning and mumbling 'Holy Mother!' Hester and Cleo helped her through the door and with Dì Brett they went into Lindemann's cabin. Di Brett sat on the bunk, Mariotta lay on it, and the others sat on small chairs.

The effect of these events on the women was variously catastrophic: Cleo Melanides was shattered by it all— the guns produced by the Freiherr and Schäffer, the firing through the portholes, the return fire from the Germans, the three thug-like men bursting into the cabin, arms and faces blackened, the whites of their eyes and their pink lips theatrically bright under the crude make-up, their faces grim, their guns menacing.

And then the final shock when Johan, Rohrbach and the mild-looking Mr Newton had produced their automatics—these so-called strangers whom it now seemed all knew each other—the whole thing was obviously prearranged. Whatever it was, it was like a bad dream. Terrifying! Unbelievable! What on earth was it all about? One thing seemed certain—the British, whoever they were, were getting the best of it and because she was Greek and had only done what she had for the sake of Mariotta whom she adored and who couldn't keep away from Lindemann, she was glad.

It served the Germans right. They deserved this after what they'd done to Greece! Yes, I'm glad, she thought. I'm very glad, but I'm frightened, too. Mixed with these emotions, was resentment that Rohrbach and Johan should have got her and Mariotta involved. She could see now how the women had been made use of.

Hester Smit, after an initial bout of terror notwithstanding Günther Moewe's warning that morning, was beginning to adjust herself to the pace of events. She liked excitement and had plenty of courage, but she was glad that the firing had stopped and she was glad, too, that Johan and his men had come out on top. She'd fallen heavily for Johan—he was her countryman—he was big and strong—kind, too, anyone could see that—and he had a sense of humour although he had seemed very fierce standing there with his gun aimed at Schäffer, looking as though he'd like to use it. But it had happened that, at that moment, her eyes had met Johan's and he had winked. She had wanted to laugh but somehow couldn't.

Mariotta was too heavily drugged to have much idea of what was going on. She heard and saw it all dimly, as through a mist. It was disturbing and yet funny, too, in a way—cowboys and crooks—that was what it was—they were acting—charades—not dumb ones though—the noise was fabulous!

Holy Mother! she thought, I'm drunk. Mariotta Manuell do Nascimento Pereira—daughter of a great plantation owner who wore the *Comendador da Ardem do Christo*—and I'm drunk. Holy Mother! What would the family say. Such degradation, such goings on. And me a Portuguese girl. Portuguese girls of good family didn't visit

157

ships for parties with officers; Portuguese girls of good family didn't go about without chaperons—and they certainly didn't have affairs with married sea captains.

Di Brett was frightened and confused. Her relief when von Falkenhausen and Schäffer had arrived and taken charge—her pride in the knowledge of the part she had played—had been dashed by what, incredibly, had followed. Where had all these men come from? Where were the rest of the *Hagenfels*'s crew? Why had no alarm been given? How could the British do this in a neutral port? What would happen next? Whatever she did, she must keep up the pretence of being Di Brett—that was vital! The Germans would never give her away but—her heart beat faster—if she were found out?

She shivered.

Although Widmark's five shots through the starboard porthole were fired to create a diversion, he had intended them for the man standing, gun in hand, behind Rohrbach and his companions. It was the German he'd identified as second officer by the two gold stripes on his sleeves. But Widmark had had to shoot fast and aim high so that he didn't hit his own men. When he saw Moewe fall, he experienced the same morbid satisfaction he'd had when looking at the unconscious German whom Hans had coshed: a curious surge of exultation, a racing of the blood, a desire to shout his approval. He had been waiting for this moment a long time, and it had assumed vast importance. But in spite of these emotions he remained cool and analytical and as he fired the last of the five shots he ran back along the side of the deck-house, opened the door, made sure the alleyway outside the Captain's cabin was clear, and stepped into it. Just then he heard McFadden's shout—'Hands up!'—and he smiled grimly at the success of the diversion. He was about to enter the cabin, when a door at the far end of the alleyway opened and a man came out, back towards him, and ran through the port door on to the deck outside. In the brief span of time this took, Widmark did three things: noted with a shock the two gold stripes, realised that he hadn't killed the second officer, and took a snap shot at him—that is to say, he pressed the trigger of his automatic but nothing happened. Cursing, he snapped back the breech, saw the cartridge jammed at the top of the
158

magazine, whipped it out, slipped in a full clip, and ran down the alleyway out on to the boat deck. The attempt to capture the *Hagenfels*, going so well until then, was suddenly threatened. There was the ship's siren on which the alarm could be sounded—there was the radio telephone which could be used to call the Port Captain's office—there were other dangerous possibilities.

Standing on the boat deck, temporarily blinded by the blackness of the night, Widmark estimated that the German had a five-second start. As his eyes grew accustomed to the dark, he looked forward first. It was fortunate that he did so for, silhouetted against the rain-blurred anchor light, he saw a man disappear up the port bridge ladder.

Silently, Widmark followed him. He reached the bridge and saw a glow of light as the chart-house door was opened and the man stepped in. The door shut and the light disappeared. Widmark made for the door.

As he reached it, he heard the rising note of a transmitting generator just switched on. Swinging the door open, he saw the German at the chart-table holding the telephone hand-set of the radio-telephone. It would have been easy to shoot him in the back, to smash his head in with the cosh; but Widmark did neither of these things. Throwing his automatic on to the chart-room settee, he leapt at Moewe, swung him round by the shoulder with one hand and with the other brushed the German's Luger from where it lay on the chart-table on to the deck—then, Moewe facing him, eyes wide with sudden fear, Widmark hit him across the side of his face with an open hand. The blow sounded like the bursting of a paper bag.

Widmark saw the gleam of fear in the German's eyes, and hit him again, full in the face this time and with a clenched fist—that made Moewe fight back. He got an arm round Widmark's neck in an attempt at a stranglehold, but Widmark's knee caught him a massive upward blow, thudding into his groin. Moewe screamed and dropped his arms. Widmark's hands went round the German's throat and he pushed him back against the chart-table. Moewe saw the mad glare in Widmark's eyes and tried to fight him off, but was helpless—the edge of the chart-table caught him below the buttocks, and as his shoulders went back, Widmark's knee smashed into his groin again. Moewe's second scream was muffled and choked as Widmark's fingers tightened on his windpipe. The second officer was bent over backwards now, with the South African on top of him. With a frenzied burst of strength, Widmark smashed the German's head into the R/T cabinet —once, twice, thrice. There were tinkling screeching sounds of broken glass and metal, and Moewe's eyes glazed as he slid to the deck, Widmark falling with him, his fingers tight on his adversary's throat, gasping with exertion, his eyes close to the German's.

When Moewe went limp, Widmark let go and staggered to his feet. Then he stood over him, leaning on the chart-table, looking down on the blood-stained face, the absurdly staring eyes.

'You poor bastard——' he muttered, breathing heavily, wiping the sweat from his forehead with the back of his hand. 'You poor miserable bastard—I've been wanting to do this to one of you for a long time.'

He pulled himself up on to the chart-table and sat there panting, cleaning his hands on a handkerchief which was soon mussed with blood and stove-black. Then he put a foot on Moewe's chest, and with dull eyes watched the dead man.

'Listen you, whoever you are,' he mumbled, rolling the face sideways with his foot. 'It was too easy for you—just a longish minute of fright and it was all over——' He shook his head. 'Not like Olafsen—he had an hour of it— with his guts shot out. And mother—*my* mother! What d'you think she went through?' He moved the German's face with his foot again, and the swollen tongue lolled out. 'What d'you think she felt? I mean, drowning like that —an old woman—alone in the water—in a gale in the middle of the night.'

Widmark shook his head again and then he sat on the settee, chin in hand, brooding. Later, he looked at his watch. It was 22.27. He got up, frowned at the smashed valves and broken metal in the radio cabinet, at Günther Moewe's dead, sightless eyes staring at the deckhead, and then, taking his automatic from the settee, he picked up the German's Luger and went out on to the bridge where he threw it into the sea. The riveting was as loud as ever as he went down the ladder, into the deck-house and along the alleyway to the Captain's cabin to find the four Germans sitting in a corner, hands clasped on their heads, the Newt and Rohrbach covering them with automatics.

'Where are the others?' Widmark was breathing heavily, still feeling the effects of his struggle with Moewe.

'You all right, Steve?' Rohrbach looked with dismay at Widmark's face, streaked with blood where the stove-polish had rubbed off.

Widmark did not appear to hear the question. 'Where're the others?' he repeated.

'McFadden and Hans went down to the engine-room a few minutes ago, Mike Kent's up for'ard on guard outside the fo'c'sle. Johan's hunting for the second officer and the steward.'

Widmark was visibly shaken. 'My *God*! I'd forgotten about the steward——!'

'We're worried about the second officer. He's much more dangerous.'

Widmark's face did something then—it wasn't a smile—it couldn't really be described. Afterwards Rohrbach said: 'For a moment I thought Steve had gone round the bend—I mean, his eyes, and the way he showed his teeth when he grinned and said: "He's dead." Then he stared at his hands and said: "Get these Jerries into the chain-locker with the others. Where are the women?"'

Rohrbach pointed to the Captain's sleeping cabin—the key was on the outside. 'We've locked them in. Told them it's for their own good and not for long.'

Widmark looked at the door. 'Any of them hurt?'

'No, Steve. All okay.'

The Germans had been watching them, but for Kuhn who, breathing deeply, slept. Then von Falkenhausen said: 'As one naval officer to another, Lieutenant-Commander, may I ask what is the meaning of this in a neutral port?'

Widmark turned dark, sullen eyes upon him. 'Same meaning as your drawing guns on my men. There's a war on.'

'Yes, but Portugal's not in it.'

'You and I are, von Falkenhausen.'

Lindemann said: 'I suppose, Herr Commander, you realise the seriousness of what you are doing? You say you have killed my second officer? How do you imagine you are going to explain this to the authorities? I think you should stop this dangerous game before it goes any further. It is one thing to try to get information, but when you force your way on board and kill men on a German merchant ship in a neutral——'

Widmark held up his hand. 'Stop that! I'm not here to listen to your views on what's right and what's wrong. You're in no position to moralise.'

He beckoned to Rohrbach. 'Shove them into the chain-locker, David. Then get cracking on those shackles.' He looked at his watch: 'It's 22.30. We're astern of station. I'll take a *shufti* in the engine-room and see how McFadden and Hans are getting on. If these people give any trouble, shoot them.' He looked at von Falkenhausen. 'I mean that. By a happy coincidence somebody's doing a bit of riveting tonight. In case you're thinking of being brave, just remember that the shots that kill you won't be heard, and that I'm not very fussy about German lives anyway.'

Von Falkenhausen knew he meant it.

Angus Duncan knocked on the door of Captain McRobert's cabin, but with the riveting going on for'ard he knew it wouldn't be heard, so he opened the door and went in.

The captain and the pilot, absorbed in their game of chess, had not heard him. Duncan tapped the captain on the shoulder. 'It's a bigger job than we thought, Captain—it'll be the best part of thirty minutes before we get those plates tight.'

McRobert frowned, took his pipe out of his mouth and looked at it, then at the bulkhead clock, then at Angus Duncan, and finally at d'Almeida. '*Plates*, ye say? I thought it was only the one of them?'

'The base plate must ha' worked loose a time back—it's affected the four plates around it—there's a lot of loose rivets. Mighty slow job—should be done by the shore gang by rights, but we'll manage.'

McRobert looked thoughtful. 'What time d'ye reckon we can sail, Chief?'

Duncan scratched his chin and looked at the clock. 'Safe enough if ye say 23.30, Captain.'

'Guid, Chief. My compliments to the mate. Tell him to let the Port Captain's Office know it'll be 23.30.'

'Aye, aye, Captain.'

Angus Duncan left the cabin and McRobert looked at d'Almeida. 'Sorry about the delay, Pilot. It's one of those things we canna help.' He shrugged his shoulders. D'Almeida repeated the gesture, smiling, the even teeth white under the dark moustache. 'Perhaps you will need the time, Captain, if you are to keep your Queen.'

McRobert sighed, puffing at his pipe. 'Aye,' he said gloomily, 'she's in a rare fix.'

John Withers, chief officer of the *Clan McPhilly*, winked at Angus Duncan. 'Okay, Chief. I'll be letting the Port Captain's Office know right away—guid luck with that riveting. It's making a braw noise—hard to hear rightly what a man's saying.'

He went up the companion ladder to the chart-house, picked up the radio telephone and called the Port Captain's Office. The call was acknowledged and he passed his message: 'Confirming that *Clan McPhilly* will be sailing at 23.30, repeat, 23.30. Pilot d'Almeida on board. Over.'

The voice of the Portuguese operator, remote and disembodied, came back. '*Clan McPhilly* sailing at 23.30. Pilot d'Almeida on board. Okay. Good night. Over and out.'

Withers put down the hand-set and sighed. 'That's the biggest bluidy lie I've told in a long time.'

Things were moving fast on board the *Hagenfels*.

Down in the engine-room Widmark found McFadden and Hans at work on the main diesels; assisting them was the German greaser, a pale young man with crew-cut hair and a pinched-in face.

McFadden was checking the pressures on the starting compressors when Widmark reached him.

'How's it going, Chiefy?'

McFadden looked up, shocked at Widmark's appearance. 'Fine. They'll be ready to turn in ten minutes. But what's happened to you, Steve boy? You don't look too good.'

Widmark waved his hand irritably. 'I'm okay. We've got the ship. Everything's under control. Can't find the steward though——' He paused, looked over to where the German greaser was working on the fuel valves. 'Is that man okay? Aren't you taking a chance?'

McFadden shook his head. 'He's fine, laddie! His English's not too good but he understands well enough. Hans told him his pals are in the chain-locker, that we've taken over the ship, and that he'd better give us a hand or else——' McFadden tapped the cosh dangling from his

163

wrist.

'That'd give their Lordships a twinge, Chiefy. I'm sure it's a breach of some Geneva Convention or other——'

'Sure you're all right, Steve boy?' McFadden couldn't hide his concern.

Widmark nodded briefly and started towards the ladder. 'We'll be testing the telegraphs from the bridge soon. 'Bye now.'

Half-way along the fore well-deck, he saw a dark shape slide behind a ventilator ahead of him. He tightened his grip on the automatic and as he reached the ventilator called: 'Tally-Ho?'

Back came Mike Kent's voice. 'Break out, sir!'

They exchanged news and Widmark said: 'As soon as we've weighed, I'll get someone to relieve you here. Then go along to the wireless cabin and get to know the gear. The R/T on the bridge is badly smashed, I'm afraid. I had a set-to with the second officer there.'

'Aye, aye, sir.' The others had already told Kent that Widmark had killed Moewe, and in the dim light he looked at Widmark's face for signs of what they'd said. He could see now what they meant. It was odd. Maybe it was because the black stove-polish had streaked out, maybe the white rims to the eyes made them stare, gave Widmark that ferine look.

'We haven't found the steward,' Widmark's voice was hoarse. 'Keep a sharp lookout for him.'

It was still raining, a humid drizzle. On the fo'c'sle Widmark found Rohrbach and the Newt busy with the anchor cables. In the blue light of a torch Rohrbach was at work on the shackle immediately abaft the port gypsy, picking out the lead pellet and withdrawing the steel wedge.

'We can knock the lug out any time now, Steve.' Rohrbach moved across to the starboard gypsy and got busy there, the Newt holding the torch.

Johan was struggling with a nine-inch manilla, hauling it up from a bin under the fo'c'sle. Widmark lent him a hand. It was hard work on a hot night, but they got one up on the port side before Rohrbach and the Newt came over.

Rohrbach said: 'Starboard shackle's all set now.'

'Well done, David. Did you have to use the hack-saw?'

'No. These Jerries keep their gear in good condition.

Came free as sweet as a daisy.'

When both hawsers were laid out on the fo'c'sle ready for running, they secured the ends to the cables forward of the gypsies, taking their weight with the manilla hawsers turned up on the windlass drums; then they'd lower the cables on to the bottom of the river as the *Hagenfels* moved ahead under her own power. Slipping the cables this way would be quick and comparatively noiseless, and when the hawsers had been run out to their bare ends on the windlass drums, they would be cast off and the ship would be clear of her anchors and free to manoeuvre.

'Tested the windlass, David?'

'Yes. Juice is on.'

'Good. As soon as you've slipped the cables, get Johan to relieve Mike Kent. I'm off to the bridge now. Got the charts, Newt?'

In the darkness the Newt found the bathing bag where he'd put it near the windlass. 'Okay, Steve.'

Widmark looked at his watch. 'I wish we knew where that bloody steward was,' he grumbled. Then he and the Newt went down the fo'c'sle ladder on to the fore well-deck and made for the bridge.

Paul Müller, the officers' steward, had been in the pantry washing glasses and plates and generally cleaning up when the sudden burst of firing sounded in the Captain's cabin. Even with the noise of the riveting there was no mistaking what it was. A gentle, inoffensive young man, he got a severe fright as he glanced through the half-open door and heard a British voice say: 'Put those hands up, quick!'

That was enough for Paul. If he lacked the aggressive spirit, he did not lack imagination. There was a war on, there was shooting in the Captain's cabin, and the British seemed to have arrived and taken over the ship. What it all added up to he had no idea, but he was at that moment free and the most important thing seemed to be to remain so.

Before Moewe had had time to reach the pantry, Müller had slipped out of the door, through the alleyway and on to the boat-deck. Had he been ten seconds later he would have been seen by Widmark who would by then have been coming in through the starboard door. As it was, he was clear and safe—for the time being at any rate.

For a moment he stood on the boat-deck, uncertain,

wondering where he could hide; eventually he decided on the foremost lifeboat on the port side. It was opposite him, just abaft the bridge ladder, and once under the canvas cover he would not only be securely hidden but when the riveting stopped he'd have a good idea of what was going on—be able to hear much of what was said on the bridge. Slipping into the boat he lay on a bench-thwart, his eyes level with the gunwale, just able to see out if he lifted the edge of the cover which was held clear of his head by a wooden stretcher. His breath came in short gasps, and his heart pounded with excitement and from his exertions.

Breathlessly he waited—but not for long. Opposite him the port door of the deck-house opened and he saw Moewe come out, gun in hand. The second officer shut the door and went up the bridge ladder, passing within a few feet of him. Almost immediately afterwards the door opened again—this time Müller saw, outlined in the glow of light from the alleyway behind him, a man in plain clothes, his hair tousled, his face black. He looked tigerish, frightening, pistol in one hand, cosh in the other. For a moment he stood there undecided, then he, too, went up the bridge ladder. A few minutes later, Müller saw a shape coming down and held his breath. It was the man with the blackened face, who went back into the deck-house, still with a pistol in one hand and a cosh in the other.

Paul Müller lay there frightened, mystified, peeping from under the edge of the lifeboat cover. But nothing more happened and the noise of riveting drowned effectively any other sounds which might have come his way. In the dark he could not see the time, but later on, feeling cramped, he changed his position and sat crouching in the sternsheets. Now he could see nothing, but that did not stop him thinking.

It was slowly becoming apparent to him that he should be doing something more than just hiding: there was a war on, the *Hagenfels* was a German ship, and somehow or other the British were taking her by force of arms in a neutral port. If he were asked afterwards what he'd done, it wouldn't sound too good if he said that he'd hidden in a lifeboat. Paul Müller had no pretensions to bravery, but his duty was beginning to take shape clearly and rather embarrassingly. Reluctantly, he realised that he must *do* something. But what? He was unarmed.

Herr Moewe had gone on to the bridge, but he had been followed by the man with the black face and then a few minutes later it had been *that* man only who'd come down from the bridge. That gave Müller an idea.

He'd go up there and see what had happened. Taking off his shoes, his heart beating faster, he got out from under the boat cover and went up on to the bridge. The chart-room door was half open and the light inside shone out, spilling a bright pool of light on to the deck. Müller looked in through the door and saw Moewe's dead eyes staring at him, his face smeared with blood. The steward's insides knotted and he felt sick. He'd never seen such a terrible sight.

Whatever was happening was in deadly earnest. The Britishers were killing members of the crew—officers—he felt alone and frightened and unsure of himself; but his duty was plain, so he forced himself into the chart-house. There he saw the shattered radio-telephone and other signs of a struggle. There was nothing he could do, though; he couldn't even try the radio-telephone—which he didn't understand anyway—because it was obviously damaged beyond use. That made him think of the wireless cabin— if the Britishers were taking the ship, they would want to use the wireless once they got to sea. He knew nothing about wireless—but he had an idea. Then it occurred to him that there might be a Britisher in the wireless cabin already and that he would have to be careful—they were probably all over the ship—there was no means of hearing them because of the noise of the riveting, and on deck there was little light and much dark shadow and it was misty and wet.

Chapter Sixteen

Widmark got the Newt to help him move Moewe's body from the chart-house to the after end of the bridge where they covered it with flags from the signal locker. Nothing was said while this was being done. The Newt felt faintly sick. Günther Moewe's face was not a pleasant sight.

In the chart-house they took the charts and sailing directions out of the canvas bag and laid them on the table.

'They're a bit bent and scruffy, but they'll do,' said Widmark. Although at the Polana the Newt had pencilled on to the charts the courses to be steered and the distances from point to point, he was pleased to find parallel rulers and a pair of dividers on the chart-table, and in a drawer two recent British Admiralty charts of the Port of Lourenço Marques and its approaches. They were duplicates of those they'd taken out of the bag.

The Newt whistled through his teeth. 'Needn't have brought ours. They've got 'em already, Steve. Amended and up-to-date.'

'Like to know how they got them?'

'Probably wrote to the Admiralty Chart Depot and asked for them. You know how polite we always are to foreigners.'

On the port side of the chart-room they found the switches for the navigation lights, and in a bin recessed into the chart-table three chronometers keeping Greenwich Mean Time. Behind the chart-house door were two pairs of Zeiss night glasses which they took from their leather cases. Among the books above the chart-table were a nautical almanac and sets of navigational and azimuth tables.

Widmark looked at the radio-telephone. 'Hope the port authorities don't try and call us on that.'

'Had it in a big way, hasn't it?' The Newt poked at the broken valves, smashed coils and transformers, wincing at the still wet bloodstains.

Widmark lit a cigarette. 'Come on. Let's go.'

Out on the bridge the rain still fell in a light drizzle, warm and clinging. Reflections from the anchor light fell dimly upon two glistening shapes standing by the windlass on the fo'c'sle.

There was a teak wheelhouse amidships, well provided with windows, and with doors which gave on to the open wings of the bridge. The Newt hooked back the doors and with his torch found the switches for the magnetic and gyro compasses and engine telegraph lights. To his surprise the gyro compass was already working. This could only mean that the Germans had kept the master-gyro running. More evidence, he reflected, that they were standing-by to make a break for the sea. Calling the engine-room on the voice-pipe, he was reassured by Andrew McFadden's cheerful 'Hallo there, Newt!'

'Okay down below, Chiefy?'

'Everything's fine, laddie.'

'I'm going to test telegraphs. We're about to weigh.'

'Okay, son. Go ahead.'

The Newt tested the engine-room telegraphs and reported to Widmark: 'Telegraphs tested and okay, Steve.'

'Good! Ring stand-by.'

The bells of the telegraph rang, an evocative purposeful tinkle, and the Newt reported: 'Engines on stand-by.'

Widmark went across to the port side of the bridge, leant over the canvas screen and aimed his torch at the fo'c'sle, showing a steady blue light.

There was an answering blue flash. He went to the wheel-house door. 'Wheel amidships. Slow ahead.'

The Newt rang the telegraph and repeated: 'Wheel amidships, slow ahead, sir.' The tagged-on 'sir' was force of habit, inextricably tied to the patter of helm and engine orders.

The muffled explosive notes of the main diesels came from the funnel abaft the bridge as the machinery started to turn, and the *Hagenfels* trembled and came alive. Widmark watched the line of lights along the shore and when the ship began to move slowly ahead he went to the fore-side of the bridge and flashed his torch three times. Three answering flashes told him that the manilla hawsers on the windlass drums were manned, and above the noise of riveting he could hear faintly the clank of the cable links passing through the hawse-pipes.

'Stop engines!'

The Newt repeated the order, the engine-room telegraph

jangled, and the vibrations ceased. More flashes of blue light came from the fo'c'sle and Widmark answered them—the cables had been slipped and the *Hagenfels* was free to manœuvre.

He went into the wheelhouse and saw from the clock there that it was 22.53.

Rohrbach and Johan would now, he knew, be going round the ship switching off lights and securing dead-lights over portholes. Soon the ship would be darkened.

For the next few minutes, juggling with helm and engines, Widmark kept the *Hagenfels*'s bows to the tide, more or less in her anchor berth but dropping slowly stern on the *Clan McPhilly*.

He looked at his watch and saw that it was 22.59, so he switched off the anchor light, ordered 'Starboard thirty! Half speed ahead!' and went out on to the bridge.

Soon afterwards the ship's head was paying off to starboard and the lights along the Gorjao Quay moved up the starboard side until they were almost ahead.

At that moment the riveting stopped and the sudden cessation of sound was as remarkable as its beginning, for it had become a part of the night, a silence of its own. Now a strange new silence fell upon the Espirito Santo and slowly other sounds, small and commonplace, obtruded.

Widmark stopped the main engines, ordered the wheel amidships, and then put the engines half-astern; the *Hagenfels*'s rate of turn quickened and before long she was heading downstream, the lights of the *Clan McPhilly* close ahead on the port bow.

'Amidships. Slow ahead. Steady as you go.' Widmark's voice for the first time communicated some of the excitement he felt, and the Newt smiled. At least the Butcher was that much human. There was a chink in the imperturbability he had displayed since their arrival on the bridge. Widmark's next order broke into his thoughts.

'Steer one-one-o.'

'Steer one-one-o,' repeated the Newt and then, a few seconds later, 'Steady on one-one-o.'

Widmark went back into the wheelhouse and stood next to the Newt, watching the steering compass. The rain clung like fine muslin to the windows on the foreside of the bridge. Lifting them up to the horizontal, Widmark secured them with brass hooks hanging from the deck-head.

170

'That better?'

'Fine.'

The *Hagenfels* moved slowly, passing down the port side of the *Clan McPhilly*. As they came abreast of her, they saw a weak light flashing from under the bridge; it was spelling out a message in morse code, slowly and laboriously: 'G-O-O-D-L-U-C-K.'

Widmark dared not reply because his signal might be read from the Gorjao Quay, but under his breath he whispered 'Bless you, McRobert,' and he hoped that one day he'd see him again.

It was 23.05 by his wrist-watch.

He went into the wheelhouse and switched on the navigation lights.

Ahead of them lay more ships at anchor and as the *Hagenfels* drew away from the Clan ship, course was altered to pass to starboard of them, so that they would mask the German ship from the quay.

The second of the two ships ahead was the *Tactician* and when they got up to her they heard the sound of her cables coming in through the hawse-pipes, a cluster of dark shapes on her fo'c'sle busy at the windlass.

Widmark had just given new helm orders, when he heard someone running up the starboard bridge ladder; it was David Rohrbach, who reported: 'Everything's okay, Steve. We've darkened ship. Nothing showing except navigation lights. Johan's on the fo'c'sle door, and Mike's in the wireless cabin.'

'Good!' Widmark sounded curt and business-like but he was grinning in the darkness. 'The big torch is on the chart-table. Grab it. We'll be up with Ponta Vermelha soon.'

Rohrbach fetched the torch. The rain slackened and Widmark frowned—he would far rather it had come down heavily. But he was grateful for the clouded sky and the darkness which concealed everything but the lights of Lourenço Marques and the ships along the Gorjao Quay floodlit by the clusters on the crane gantries. Nearby the lights of the ships at anchor were so close that Widmark feared the *Hagenfels* might be identified in their reflection. But there were few lights on the Catembe side of the river, not enough to silhouette the German ship, and, as he had concluded on his reconnaissances, all that could be seen of the *Hagenfels* from the harbour were her navigation lights.

They had passed the fourth ship and were almost abeam of the flashing light marking the entrance to the boat harbour when Widmark, standing in the starboard wing of the bridge, heard Rohrbach's urgent 'My God!'

He turned quickly and against the diffused glow of the port navigation light, reflected on the thin screen of rain, he could just see Rohrbach leaning over the back of the bridge looking down on to the boat-deck.

Widmark ran across and joined him. From the foremost lifeboat on the port side a beam of light was flashing. It came from under the canvas boat cover and was aimed at the shore.

There might have been five seconds between Rohrbach's 'My God!' his jump from the bridge rail on to the boat and his slither to the sternsheets where he struck with a cosh at the signaller under the canvas. Not a sound came from this struggling shape and soon it lay still.

Rohrbach, panting for breath, called up to Widmark. 'Okay. I'll have him on deck in a second. He's out, I reckon.'

'It'll be that steward. Get Mike Kent to help you take him up to the chain-locker. I'll look after Ponta Vermelha, but get back quickly.'

Widmark moved over to the foreside of the bridge. On the port bow he could see the green light of number nine buoy, and well to starboard of it the light at Esparcelado. A lot had happened, he reflected, since they'd seen those lights earlier in the evening. Things might not have gone quite according to plan, but they'd gone pretty well. Taking a grip on himself he abandoned these self-congratulatory thoughts: the *Hagenfels* was not clear of the harbour yet; the steward had been signalling the shore; maybe those signals had been seen; perhaps the alarm had been given; the greater dangers certainly lay ahead. He looked in at the wheelhouse door. 'David's just laid out the steward.'

The Newt said: 'Splendid!'

'Keep number nine buoy fine on the port bow. There are four or five more ships in the anchorage. We should clear them on this course.'

'Aye, aye, Steve. She steers a bit sluggishly. Think we could go on to half-ahead?'

Widmark looked across to port where the shore lights were moving slowly aft.

'Okay. Ring down half-ahead.'

Soon after the telegraph bell had rung, they felt the vibrations quicken and the *Hagenfels* took on new life.

It was 23.13. In another three minutes they would reach number nine buoy, then would come the alteration of course to head up the Polana Channel. Three or four minutes later they would be challenged by the signal station at Ponta Vermelha.

Widmark's thoughts went briefly to the cabin below: to the women in there. He wondered what Cleo was doing, how she was looking, what she was thinking about? It must have been terrifying for her. In his mind's eye was the dead face of Günther Moewe. He was glad Cleo had not seen that.

For the first time he saw the lights of another ship moving towards the harbour mouth; it was on a parallel course, closer inshore, passing the lights along the sea wall below the Aterro do Machaquene; but it was travelling a good deal faster, drawing quickly ahead. He gave it a long look through the night glasses.

It was a warship. One of the Portuguese gunboats, and it was in a hurry.

Widmark was not conscious of it, but he had bitten his lip so deeply that a small trickle of blood flowed down his chin.

The women had been locked in the captain's sea cabin for forty-five minutes; in the dark, too, for Rohrbach had smashed all the lamp-globes there and in the toilet before locking the door on them. 'Sorry,' he'd said, 'but we can't take chances. You won't be here long, anyway, and there's nothing to worry about. We'll see that you come to no harm.'

They had gone into the cabin in a state of considerable fright and it had persisted, which was not surprising after what had happened. All of them, that is to say, except Mariotta who was sleeping on Lindemann's bunk.

The portholes were open but it was hot and stuffy and but for the thin reflection from a deck light it was dark. Of what was happening outside the cabin they had not the faintest idea, for not only could they see nothing but the unceasing noise of the riveting shut out all other sounds.

When Johan left them their conversation had verged on

173

the hysterical, and it was eventually Hester Smit who calmed them down. 'I don't know what it's all about,' she said, 'but it seems to be South Africa versus the rest, so I suppose we've got ourselves mixed up in the war somehow.'

'It was terrible of Johan and David to get us into this. I'll never forgive them.' Cleo was tearful: 'We might have been killed in all that shooting.'

Di Brett said: 'There's going to be one hell of a row about this. Fancy trying this sort of thing in a neutral port! What do they think's going to happen tomorrow morning when the story comes out. They can't hold these Germans prisoners in their own ship for long. A launch is bound to come off in the morning.' She thought of something. 'Not even tomorrow. The company launch is waiting in the boat harbour *now* to come and fetch us at midnight.'

Hester Smit sighed. 'I hope Johan doesn't get into trouble. He's such a sweety.'

'I wonder who the others were, Hester? The men who came in through the door with black faces? They looked awful people.'

'I don't know, Cleo. But they must all be the same lot. They knew each other.'

'Of *course* they did. The whole thing was planned and organised.' Di Brett checked herself, took the edge of animosity from her voice. She must be careful. One never knew what was coming next. 'Very *well* organised, too. *Our* side's pretty good, I must say.' She hoped she'd got that across.

Hester giggled. 'Your friend Newton was certainly a surprise, Di. He looked such a softy. How did you meet him?'

'Same way as Cleo and Mariotta met Johan and David. At the hotel where I was staying. He said he was anti-war. An Englishman who lived in Portugal and whose heart was not in it. And that reminds me of something, too——'

'What's that?'

'There's another man staying at the Polana. I met him early in the war at Cape Town. His name's Widmark—a lieutenant-commander. When I asked him what he was doing in LM he told me he'd been invalided out of the Navy. He's quite famous for what he did in the Mediterranean. Or notorious. He pretended not to know James

174

Newton. I had to introduce them to each other. I'm sure he's involved in this, too.'

'Not *Stephen* Widmark?' said Cleo faintly.

'Yes. That's him. Why?'

Cleo realised that her heart was beating a good deal faster than usual. 'I have met him,' she said, and hoped it sounded casual. 'D'you think he's on board now?'

'He might be, Cleo. There seem to be a *lot* of strange people on board. But he wasn't one of those who came into the cabin. I'd have recognised his voice.'

So would I, so would I, thought Cleo. So that was what Stephen Widmark was doing in Lourenço Marques. Perhaps that explained why he'd not kept the promise he'd made at Costa's. But why hadn't he just telephoned her? What harm could that have done? Now something strange was taking place in her mind: her fear was going, had gone; she *knew* now that Stephen was mixed up in this, that he was on board, and her heart really was getting out of control, thumping wildly; somewhere inside her there was a seething and a longing—she would be seeing him soon. At any moment he might come into the cabin. In her mind she could see his dark, handsome face: the high cheek-bones, slanted eyes, and thin nose—the dark hair and bushy eyebrows and, above all, that sardonic, half-amused smile. 'Oh God!' she said it to herself, fervently, 'I hope I see him again.'

Her thoughts were interrupted by vibrations which shook the ship. 'What's that?' she asked fearfully.

'It's—it's—it *must* be the engines.' Hester Smit's shrill laugh was near to being hysterical.

'My God!' said Di Brett. 'The fools are trying to steal the ship.'

'Why *fools*, Di?' Cleo's voice was disapproving—she was thinking of Stephen. 'After all, it's our side.'

'I mean it's such a mad risk to take.'

'I think it's very brave. I hope they succeed.' And though her voice had been firm enough while she said that, Cleo felt small tears run down her cheeks.

Hester laughed excitedly, still a little hysterical. 'Hooray! We're off! I'll be seeing more of Johan.'

As soon as Johan took over from him at the fo'c'sle, Mike Kent went along the fore well-deck and up the companion ladders to the boat-deck.

There he turned aft and made for the wireless cabin abaft the funnel. The door was closed but not locked. He went in, fumbled in the dark for the light switch, found it and turned on the lights.

Somebody had got there before him: somebody German, somebody who had battered the wireless equipment so that everywhere was confusion, a tangle of wires, broken valves, broken coils and condensers and transformers. Even the two transmission keys had been smashed.

Mike Kent was suddenly very frightened. The wireless was essential to their plans. They might get through without it, but the odds against them would be immeasurably increased. He had to get it going again, somehow. And he'd have to be quick. He took off the tweed jacket he was wearing, removed his spectacles, cleaned them deliberately, put them on again, and took from his pocket a screwdriver, a pair of long-nosed pliers, a circuit tester and some insulating tape.

With an enormous sense of urgency he got to work.

There was no light in the chain-locker and the smell of mud and decaying vegetation, fetched up from the seabed by the anchor cables over the years, was rank and fetid. What little air there was came down the spurling-pipes, but the atmosphere was oppressive and breathing was a laboured business. From above, through the spurling-pipes, came the sound of riveting; but when they had been in the locker for some minutes they could hear, faintly, other sounds, such as hammering and scraping on the fo'c'sle above them, and from time to time the cables leading down from the gypsies rattled in the spurling-pipes.

When von Falkenhausen, Lindemann and Schäffer were pushed into the chain-locker, dragging with them an almost unconscious Kuhn, they found others already there—Hugo Kolbe, the bosun, Adolph Heuser, the carpenter, Karl Wedel, a seaman, and Eric Francke, the mechanician, who'd come off in the boat with the Freiherr. Francke and Wedel had been attacked by the Britishers. Francke seemed all right though he was dazed, but Wedel was only now coming round, groaning feebly and muttering.

They did their best to make him comfortable but under those conditions little was possible. Still not accounted for were Moewe, the second officer, Ulrich Meyer, a greaser, Heinrich Weicht, the night watchman, and Paul Müller, the steward; it was these men they were discussing.

'I wonder what has happened to them?' said the Freiherr.

Lindemann's deep voice came out of the darkness. 'I expect Weicht was killed. He was probably the first man they encountered, Herr Baron. If he were alive they would have brought him here.'

'I wonder, Kapitän, how they got aboard without the alarm being given?'

Lindemann sighed wearily. 'I don't know. The gangway was hoisted. They could not have come up that way. Some of my men must have been about.'

'We've not put up a very distinguished performance.' The Freiherr's laugh was forced.

Schäffer spoke then. 'What chance did we have, Herr Baron?'

'Very little, my dear Schäffer. Very little. The element of surprise was complete. And in spite of Herr von Ribbentrop's comforting assurances to the Führer, the enemy do not seem soft.

'Tell me, Kapitän,' he went on. 'These men still not accounted for—Moewe, Meyer, Weicht and Müller. If they are still at large—are they tough, resourceful?'

'Moewe certainly is. Weicht is tough, too, but stupid, I fear. Meyer is an excellent technical man but not aggressive.'

'And Müller, the steward?'

Lindemann hesitated. 'A pleasant, gentle young man. Hard working, but his heart is not in the war. He enjoys life ashore too much.'

'What I cannot understand,' said the Freiherr, 'is what these people are up to? That they want information about the *Hagenfels*'s possible break out I can understand—that they are concerned about the sinkings on the coast and our system of passing information about Allied shipping—all this I can understand. But what can they hope to achieve by coming aboard a German merchant ship in a neutral port and using violence? That I cannot understand! That seems to be madness! As Canrobert said of the Charge of the Light Brigade: *"C'est magnifique mais ce n'est pas la guerre!"* What do you think, Kapitän?'

'It is beyond my understanding.'

'I wonder,' said the Freiherr softly. 'I wonder. Widmark commands the party—Stephen Widmark—*The Butcher*. He has the reputation of stopping at nothing. He is thoroughly unethical, un-British in his approach to war. I wonder what he's driving at? I would love to know.'

From his corner in the chain-locker, Karl Wedel groaned, and the Freiherr put out a hand to comfort him. The man clutched at it, pulling von Falkenhausen down towards him.

'*Wasser, bitte! Wasser, bitte*——' he pleaded, his voice a croak. Water, thought the Freiherr, you poor devil! How can we give you water here?

'Stand clear below!' It was a British voice that echoed down the spurling-pipes. They heard the windlass above them turning, felt its vibrations, and a few minutes later, with a metallic roar, the starboard cable slid back into the chain-locker and the stale air was filled with dust from the mud-caked links.

'*Gott im Himmel*!' shouted the Freiherr. 'They're letting go the cables.' So that was it. He'd not had long to wait for Widmark's plans. The *Hagenfels* had been captured by a British naval party. It was the grossest breach of neutrality. To seize a ship by force of arms under the nose of the Portuguese and take her to sea. It was unthinkable. But it was happening. Then the wider implications filtered through the Freiherr's mind; there were U-cruisers and raiders waiting outside for fuel and provisions, counting on the *Hagenfels*'s break out to get these urgently needed supplies. And what was his own position? He had admitted to Widmark that he had been a spy in Alexandria. It would be quite evident that he had been doing the same thing in Lourenço Marques. And now he was a prisoner of the British. He knew what he could expect. While a sobering fear took hold of him, he accepted the position with stoicism; this was a chance he had long been taking. He had always known that it might—probably *would*—end like this. It was for that reason, in a very special sense, that he had volunteered for the work after Gina's death. In the darkness he shrugged his shoulders. All right—if it had to be like that —well, it had to be. Then he thought of Di Brett. She must be protected. She was in great danger. Her life depended upon remaining Di Brett.

Quietly he explained the position to the others and there

178

in the musty darkness, pressing their bodies against the sides of the chain-locker, waiting for the port cable to slip back, breathing in the choking air, Karl Wedel in his corner still pleading for water, Siegfried Kuhn snoring in another, they undertook to protect Helga Bauer, while they wondered at von Falkenhausen's courage.

Chapter Seventeen

As Widmark watched the gunboat draw ahead, leaving behind it the lights along the Aterro do Machaquene, a signal lamp flashed peremptorily from her bridge and with a shock he realised that beyond any doubt she was calling the *Hagenfels*. He collected the torch from the wheelhouse, said to the Newt, 'Not too healthy—Portuguese gunboat's leaving the harbour in a hurry. Calling us on her lamp,' then he was out on the bridge giving the acknowledgment. There was a pause and the gunboat made: 'W-H-A-T S-H-I-P?'

Signalling slowly in the uneven fashion of a merchantman, Widmark replied: 'C-L-A-N M-C-P-H-I-L-L-Y.' With jangling nerves he waited, wondering what would come next. Then the gunboat's lamp was blinking again: 'G-O-O-D N-I-G-H-T.' There was nothing more. He felt a great weight lift from his shoulders, returned the 'Good night,' and went back to the wheelhouse.

'Relax, Newt. Our friend was being polite.'

'Bless him. Number nine buoy's getting close.'

The green light of the buoy came forward to meet them. Widmark ordered: 'Port twenty!' The *Hagenfels*'s bow came round and the buoy passed down the side and drew astern.

Course was set on 058 degrees and the ship made up the Polana Channel; ahead of her, winking in the darkness, shone the sternlight of the Portuguese gunboat.

It was 23.16.

Broad on the port bow, Widmark could see through the night glasses the signal station at Ponta Vermelha, perched high on the cliff, a dark, menacing blur, thin shafts of light showing through shuttered windows. He waited, torch in hand, his anxiety mixed with irritation that Rohrbach was not yet back; there had been time enough, he felt, for them to take the steward to the chain locker. Although he was expecting it, he started with surprise as the signal lamp on the cliff flashed into life with 'W-H-A-T S-H-I-P?'

At that moment, Rohrbach got back to the bridge and

Widmark handed him the torch. 'About time, me lad! Grab this and make our signal letters.'

Breathing heavily, Rohrbach took the torch and made the *Clan McPhilly*'s signal letters: 'G-B-A-J.' Someone at Ponta Vermelha was evidently digesting that, for the pause which followed seemed inordinately long. Then it winked again, 'R' for Roger, and tension on the bridge eased.

'Somehow,' said Widmark, 'I've been worrying a lot about Ponta Vermelha. I mean, we knew the drill but there was always the chance of someone in the harbour spotting that it was us and not the *Clan McPhilly* that left the anchorage—anyway, praise the Lord and pass the ammunition.'

'That bloke I clobbered in the lifeboat was the steward. Poor little sod. Afraid I rather battered him.'

'Don't waste your sympathy, David. They're not worth it.'

'I find it difficult to hate people. In the abstract it's all right. But when you're face to face with them—well, they're just ordinary people. You know what I mean. The animus isn't there any longer.'

Widmark was looking over the bridge screen, watching the sternlight of the gunboat, relieved that it was drawing ahead so fast. 'You're getting soft, David. Watch yourself! They're *not* ordinary people. If they were they wouldn't behave as they do.' His voice was harsh. 'You know—after I'd finished off Moewe—with my hands like that—I thought I'd feel some sort of remorse or disgust. But I didn't. I was glad, actually, that I'd done it. It was tremendously satisfying. When I was at school I used to think the Old Testament's "eye for an eye and tooth for a tooth" was the most savage thing I'd heard of—I had a horrible picture of it all happening. Now I know I was wrong. There's something about revenge. It's high in the scale of human emotions. The only logical end to hatred. A sort of sublimation——' His voice trailed off.

Rohrbach, embarrassed at this pulling aside of the curtain to another man's mind, said: 'I'm a German Jew, Steve. I suppose if anybody should be able to hate I should, but I can't. Perhaps there's something wrong with me. When I went for that steward under the lifeboat cover he was just an anonymous shape. I knew I had to stop him. I suppose I went berserk. Then when I saw him

181

in the light afterwards—he—well, he looked quite a decent chap. His face was dead white and there was blood on it. I felt pretty shabby——'

Widmark's voice was flat, toneless. 'I think there *is* something wrong with you, David. And frankly, I don't understand that berserk stuff. Isn't it just a cliché? Or an excuse? "She was standing in front of me, my lord, an' I blacked out, an' when I come to she was lyin' on the floor and—I seen the gun in me 'and——" Lot of cock, David, take it from me. I knew what I was doing—every second of the time. I didn't even lose my rag. Afterwards my only regret was that he'd died so quickly. I mean, it was too easy for him. To get away with it like that.'

There was a long silence.

'War's not exactly an ennobling thing, is it?' Once he'd said it Rohrbach was sorry. But it was too late.

'Oh, for God's sake!' said Widmark in sudden anger. 'Let's stop philosophising and get on with the job.' He went across to the other side of the bridge.

It was 23.20.

Full speed was rung down on the engine-room telegraph and the *Hagenfels*'s pace quickened, the lights along the Polana Beach dropped astern and on the starboard bow the red flashes of number eight buoy slid towards them.

Under the overcast sky the smell of rain hung in the air, and from Chefine Island came the aromatic odours of beach and decaying vegetation. Ahead of them the light at Ponta Garapao flashed white and red, white and red, every five seconds.

The only sounds were the wind in the rigging, the muffled roar of the main diesels, and the slap of small waves along the side as the bow sliced through the water. Rohrbach thought it was the moment to break the news, so he went over to where Widmark stood looking back at Lourenço Marques, waiting for the navigation lights of the *Tactician* to show round the corner.

'There's bad news about the W/T, Steve.'

Widmark lowered the night glasses. 'Why, what's up?' He tried to conceal his anxiety.

'That Jerry steward must have got into the W/T cabin before Mike Kent. Somebody's smashed about in there with a heavy hammer.'

'My God! What's the damage?'

'Mike says it's bad. He's got one voice receiver going which he's tuned in to the Port Captain's frequency. But the main set's pathetic. The generators are all right but both transmitters and receivers are unserviceable.'

'Why wasn't I told before?'

'What difference would it have made, Steve? You couldn't have done anything. Mike's working like a black trying to rig up something, but he's a bit pessimistic.'

Widmark was silent. In the dark he glowered, clenching and unclenching his fingers, hating the steward and wishing he'd been able to kill the little swine before he'd done the damage. But all he said was: 'Tell Mike that a lot depends on getting that gear going.'

He sounded tired and Rohrbach felt sorry for him. The operation had been so thoroughly planned, so well executed in spite of the unexpected situation which had arisen, and now—for reasons which none could have foreseen—the *Hagenfels* was without the means of communication upon which so much might depend.

Rohrbach left the bridge and Widmark called after him: 'When you've seen Mike, do the rounds. See how Johan, Chiefy and the women are getting on. Then double back here and take over from the Newt. We'll need him for pilotage soon.'

'Okay, Steve.'

When he'd gone, Widmark went across to the wheelhouse and told the news to the Newt. The Englishman's calm was reassuring.

A man stood in the darkness on the cliff no more than a hundred yards from the signal station. He wore a raincoat over his shirt and trousers, and a hat pulled well down on his head. From a leather strap about his neck hung a pair of night glasses. Where he stood, surrounded by bushes, the earth was well trampled for he had stood there many times before and he would, he knew, stand there many times in the future, for it was to be a long war. A few minutes before, a ship with all her lights burning had gone past at high speed and had not been challenged. He had watched her through the night glasses—one of the Portuguese gunboats, going out for survivors he supposed. He could still see her stern light as she made up the channel towards Chefine.

There's not long to wait now, he thought.

In the distance he could see the navigation lights of a ship making its turn to port around number nine buoy. He would have liked a smoke but knew he couldn't, so he began to hum 'Stille Nacht'; he often hummed it when he was waiting here. It seemed appropriate somehow to these hot silent nights, even though it was evocative of another time and place, of cold and snow and boyish voices singing in Gothic cathedrals.

The ship had rounded the buoy and was heading up the Polana Channel. To the man's right was the dark bulk of the signal station, chinks of light glowing through shuttered windows.

It would not be long now.

A little later he saw the beam of light as the signal station challenged and he waited, his eyes on the ship's port side-light, for he knew the answering signal would come from above it. There it was. Flashing now. Concentrating, he read the message: 'G-B-A-J.' In the darkness he scribbled the letters on to a small pad he'd taken from his raincoat pocket and noted the time—23.18. After that he stood waiting again, stamping occasionally so that his legs would not get stiff. They never sailed singly. There would be another soon and then perhaps another. If there were two or three they would be sailing independently; if there were more they would be joining a convoy outside.

The ship was close to him now, perhaps three hundred yards away, and to pass the time he examined it with the night glasses and what had just been darkness around the steaming lights took on distant anonymous shape so that he could see dimly the high fo'c'sle, the sampson posts, the mainmast, then the bridge superstructure with more sampson posts against it; aft of that the squat funnel and the big engine-room ventilators—he was a sailor and it was while he was looking at them that he realised this was a German ship. Only German ships used that sort of ventilator cowl. Every sailor knew that. This must be a ship the British had captured on the outbreak of war: she was not the first he had seen in their service. Idly he wondered what her German name had been and whether she had been registered in Bremen or Hamburg. That made him think of his wife and family in Augsburg and he hoped they were not getting much bombing—as the time passed many other things went through his mind before his thoughts were interrupted by the lights of another ship coming up to number nine buoy.

She rounded the buoy, came up the Polana Channel, Ponta Vermelha challenged, and she made 'G-F-S-K.' He wrote the letters into the notebook and the time—23.31.

And then in due course there was a third ship, and when he read the message she flashed to Ponta Vermelha he could not believe his eyes for it was 'G-B-A-J' again—the letters given by the first ship.

It was impossible!

Two ships could not have the same signal letters.

What had happened?

In the darkness he shook his head, and then he remembered something: that first ship—it had been German built!

Was it possible that the break out signal had come at last? It was just like Herr Stauch to give him no hint of what was in the wind. Why should he, anyway? Security was the main consideration. He felt a tingling sense of pride. The Germans understood security. Knew what lack of it meant. That was why the U-boats were having such a rich harvest outside.

It was 23.34.

Walking quickly he made his way in the darkness up the winding path to the tarred road, went along it, turned right at the corner, and came to the parked car. Driving fast he made for the Silva Pereira park, round the corner beyond the Cardoso. From there he would be able to see across to the anchorage. He stopped the car, got out and walked through the park to the cliff's edge. He knew the position of the German ships in the anchorage as well as he knew his own face. With the night glasses he checked from left to right. There was the *Dortmund*, to her right and beyond her the sailing ship; then the *Gerusalemme*, then—should be—should be—— Ah! He was right. She'd gone. The *Hagenfels* had gone.

The break out had taken place. The fuel and provisions were on their way. This time his pride was mixed with excitement. He must report at once to Herr Stauch.

At seventeen minutes after eleven o'clock that night a car skidded to a stop at the corner of Elias Garcia and Miguel

185

Bombarda and a man jumped out of the driving seat, slammed the door behind him and ran up the long path through the gardens of the British Consulate General. With his own key he let himself in through a side door in the big white building, ran up a flight of stairs, along a passage, stopped before a door at the far end, knocked and went in. The pale man with the tired face looked up from his desk. 'What's the trouble, McMasters? You look as though you've seen a ghost.'

The younger man was worried, preoccupied. '*Hagenfels* has sailed.' The words burst out of him. 'She weighed and proceeded at eleven o'clock. I watched her turn and go down river.'

The other man said: 'My God, Peter! Are you certain?' and reached in one movement for the signal pad and the door of the wall safe.

'Positive. I've been watching the bloody ship every night for nearly three months. I'm not likely to make a mistake. Besides, three extra launch trips went off to her tonight. One at eight-thirty, a very sneaky one without lights just before ten, and one soon after ten. That was the crew build up, I suppose.'

'So you're certain? We've had false alarms before.'

'Not from me you haven't, old cock.'

The older man unlocked the safe, took out the cipher books, went back to his desk, wrote a message on the signal pad, tore it off and passed it to McMasters. 'Check that before I encipher it, will you?'

Frowning, McMasters read it and passed it back. 'What time d'you reckon combined ops. will get it?'

'Within four hours. I'd say.'

'Seems awfully slow.'

'It is. It's telegraphed through civilian channels to a Cape Town commercial address. All things considered, it's not bad.'

'Four hours—four hours,' mused McMasters. 'She'll be sixty or seventy miles away by then. She could get away.'

The pale man was irritated. 'Of course she could! But a great many people will be going to a great deal of trouble tomorrow morning to see that she doesn't.'

'It'll be like the cock we made of the *Tannenfels*.' McMasters's shoulders lifted in a gesture of despair. 'We should have our own W/T outfit here.'

'In a consulate general—in a neutral country in wartime? —my dear Peter. You're obviously not a diplomat.' The older man talked slowly, mechanically, his mind on the message he was enciphering, yet aware of what he was saying.

McMasters sat down on the edge of the desk, took out a cigarette case, lit a cigarette and pulled at it. 'God! I wish I was at sea. Outside. In something that could go fast.'

'Perhaps they'll send you back to sea now, Peter. But I doubt it. You're too valuable here.'

'Valuable!' McMasters made a rude noise. 'Sneaking between coal trucks on the Gorjao Quay every ruddy night. And the local English thinking I'm dodging the battle. What a way to spend the war.'

'I know. Distressing, isn't it?' The man wrote steadily, his voice quiet, soothing, absent-minded.

McMasters got up and stared at the bent head. 'You're not listening to a word I'm saying, George. I can tell. And here am I, *passionately* upset.'

'Be a good chap, Peter, and shut up. I *must* concentrate.'

It was hot and stuffy in Herr Stauch's office, and wisps of smoke rose from the ash-tray on his desk which was heaped with half-smoked cigarettes. Stauch sat at the desk in his shirt sleeves, beads of perspiration looking like transparent warts on his face, his eyes, normally deep-set, protruding and the veins standing out on his forehead. Pulling himself to his feet, his face working with emotion, he came round the desk and glared at the man on the other side. In his hand Stauch held a black book with well-worn pages. When he spoke his voice was thick: 'G-B-A-J are the signal letters of the *Clan McPhilly*, and you—you stand there and tell me that *two* ships gave the same signals. So that means *two Clan McPhillys*, which is not possible. Even a dolt like you, Kleinschmidt, will agree that that is not possible! Then you tell me that the first ship looked like a German ship——'

'*Was* a German ship,' corrected the young man stolidly.

'*Of course* it was——!' Stauch's voice rose. 'You yourself say it was the *Hagenfels*, that she has left the anchorage—and a moment ago I had a message from the *Dortmund* saying that they had seen her go——' He stopped, short of breath, his small eyes flashing.

The young man shifted his feet. 'I do not understand, Herr Stauch, why you are so upset? Surely it is a good thing that the ship has gone. Soon she will be giving fuel and supplies to our U-boats and raiders—surely that is——'

'*Ruhe! Schweigen Sie!*—Silence! Shut up!' Stauch lifted his hand, glaring at Kleinschmidt. 'I am not here to listen to your babbling.' He came closer to the young man. 'You say you do not understand why I am upset—Well, I shall tell you.' He waved his forefinger in the young man's face. 'I am upset, Herr Kleinschmidt, because *no signal has come from the Wilhelmstrasse*—do you understand? Because that man!—that—that great aristocrat, the Freiherr von Falkenhausen, has decided for himself to take the *Hagenfels* to sea—*with half a crew. Er ist verrückt!* He's mad, I tell you!'

Stauch was shouting now, his face thrust into Kleinschmidt's, the big body trembling with rage. 'He is too *important* to confide in Otto Stauch—Oh, yes! Far too important. After all, Otto Stauch does only the dirty work, takes all the risks, but he is not sufficiently important to be entrusted with the Freiherr's secrets. He must have known all along that he was sailing tonight——' He stopped, frowning, panting for breath, the receding eyes full of bewilderment. 'But *how* can he go without the signal from the Wilhelmstrasse?' he pleaded. '*How* can the *Hagenfels* rendezvous with the ships outside if they do not know she has gone?'

'The *Hagenfels* has her own wireless, Herr Stauch.' The young man was diffident. 'She can always——'

The fat man spun round on him. 'So! So! You think so. You think a raider supply vessel can risk breaking wireless silence to tell every British warship off the coast where she is? Idiot!' He glared at the young man; then, still frowning and with that bewildered look in the deep-set eyes, he went back to his desk. 'All right,' he said gruffly, now resigned, penitent. 'You can go, Kleinschmidt. I am sorry. It was not *your* fault. Now I shall have to let the Wilhelmstrasse know. They will have to inform the U-boats and raiders.' He lifted a tired arm: '*Heil* Hitler!'

'*Heil* Hitler!' repeated the young man.

Turning on his heel he opened the door and was gone.

Chapter Eighteen

The *Hagenfels* reached the end of the Polana Channel at 23.35 and as she did so the Newt called out from the chart-house: 'Alter to o-seven-o now, Steve.'

Widmark passed the alteration of course to Rohrbach who was on the wheel, and the light at Ponta Garapao moved slowly from starboard to port as the ship's head came round on to 070 degrees.

Widmark went back to the bridge-screen and looked into the darkness. The stern light of the gunboat was no longer visible, but the blackness ahead was broken at regular intervals by tiny stabs of red and white light. 'See those, Newt?'

'Yes. They mark the passage between the Serra and Ribeiro shoals.'

'How's the tide?'

'Should be north going at two to three knots, but I think there's a good deal of easting in it judging by the way we're nipping along.'

'What've we been making good?'

'About sixteen. Pretty good for a seventeen knot ship with a foul bottom.'

'Not bad. What time's daylight?'

'About 05.15.'

'H'm. We'll have steamed the best part of a hundred miles by then.'

'Just about. I think——'

Widmark interrupted him. 'Run along to the W/T cabin, see how Mike's getting on and ask him if he's heard anything over the voice radio. *Clan McPhilly* should be making her number to Ponta Vermelha about now.'

A few minutes later the Newt was back on the bridge, short of breath, but calm as ever. 'There's fun and games in the harbour. I've been listening in on the Port Captain's frequency. *Quel drame!*' He paused for effect.

'Come on,' Widmark was nervy and tense. 'Let's have it!'

'One—they've stopped the *Clan McPhilly* off Ponta Vermelha. Told her that a boat's coming out to her and she's not to proceed until further notice. Two—they've alerted the pilot cutter and the *Bartolomeu Dias*. She's the gunboat ahead of us.'

'Poor old McRobert. But he'll be able to cope. I told him this would probably happen. They won't delay him long, but for our sake I hope they're not too quick. Wonder how long it'll be before they wake up to the fact that the *Hagenfels* has sailed.'

'Shouldn't think it'll be long now, Steve.'

'Anyway, there's nothing they can do about it.' In spite of what he said, Widmark's voice was strained; he was, though the Newt didn't know it, reassuring himself. 'A German ship's perfectly entitled to make a break for the sea if she's prepared to take the chance.'

The Newt was silent, thinking about something which was worrying them both. At last he voiced it: 'As long as they believe it *is* a German break out.'

'I think,' said Widmark slowly, 'that it's going to be a long time, if ever, before they can *prove* that it wasn't. We've got the only evidence they could use against us.'

'The Jerries, you mean?'

'Yes. And the women.'

It was about twenty minutes later, after they'd passed the Serra Shoal, that Widmark, fretting with anxiety about the wireless situation, again sent the Newt to see how Mike Kent was getting on. The last report had been a cheerless one.

The Newt went off and Widmark was left on the bridge with his thoughts. When Chefine Island was well astern he switched off the navigation lights and the black unlit bulk of the *Hagenfels* moved purposefully through the night. It was past midnight, they were fifteen miles from Lourenço Marques, and the sound of the engines, the tang of the sea air and the ship's slow lift to the swells coming in from seaward were sedatives to his tired nerves.

He began to whistle, quietly but confidently.

In the wireless cabin Mike Kent was working harder than he had ever worked in his life, stripping broken parts, testing, improvising, patching and repairing, but while he did this he felt hopeless and frustrated and full of doubt. It
190

was bad enough that the equipment was strange to him and that he had to learn the circuits as he worked; but there was no one to work with him, to pass things and to hold things and to do all sorts of odds and ends to speed up the work.

He had found in a cupboard a set of tools, a soldering outfit, more circuit testers, and many of the others things he needed; there were, too, some spare valves; but there were valves, on the transmitting side particularly, which had been destroyed, for which he could find no replacements.

When for the second time the Newt came down from the bridge to find out how he was getting on, Mike Kent said: 'I'm doing my best. There's so much that's smashed that I haven't a clue whether I'll ever get the thing to work.' There was a note of despair in his voice.

He didn't ask for help because he knew there wasn't any to be had; they were already down to the barest minimum, operating the ship and guarding prisoners with seven men where twice that number would not have been too many. But the Newt's sympathetic eye spotted the young man's difficulty; saw how he tried to do more things at once than two hands could cope with.

'Wouldn't it help things along if you had an assistant, Mike?'

The youngster was bent down, one hand holding a circuit tester at eye level while the other groped for something at the top of the transmitting panel. His hair was dishevelled, the stove-polish on his hands and face was moist and streaked with sweat, and at times he had to stop to clean his glasses. The magnitude of his task, the knowledge of its importance, his feelings of inadequacy, had brought him close to tears, and his voice trembled. 'Of course it would. But what a hope.'

'Would a woman do?' The Newt watched him curiously. 'A young one?'

Mike stopped working, looked at him and smiled forlornly, but with relief. The Newt had thought of something which had never occurred to him.

'Marvellous idea, sir. Try and get one who's keen on radio.'

Back on the bridge, the Newt reported the situation to Widmark who said: 'Of course. First-class idea. What's more, ask McFadden if he'd like one to help him in the engine-room.'

The Newt started off down the bridge ladder.

Widmark called after him: 'Tell the girls to make some coffee in the Captain's pantry and push it round. Sandwiches, too, if they're feeling energetic.'

Soon afterwards, Hester Smit, smiling cheerfully, went to the wireless cabin, saw Mike Kent's back and tapped him on the shoulder. 'I'm Hester Smit,' she said. 'They say I must help you.'

He turned round and saw a large, cheerful young woman. 'Know anything about radios?'

'I can switch them on and off.'

'Good! You'll be terrifically useful. My name's Mike Kent. I'm jolly glad you've come.'

She looked at the panels of equipment behind him and at the tangle of wires and the dismantled parts on the desk. 'Heavens! Somebody's been having a good time.'

'One of the Jerries. He tried to smash everything.'

'*Tried!* I'd say he succeeded, Mike. By the way, I suppose you know your hands and face are black.'

'Yes. You'll find some of us like that. They say it comes off.'

'I wonder what you really look like?'

'Terrible. Come on. Let's get cracking.'

Widmark, concentrating on the task of getting the *Hagenfels* safely out to sea through the shoals which lay scattered across the bay, took a bearing of the flashing light which marked the Ribeiro Shoal. Leaving the compass on the monkey island, he came down the ladder to the bridge deck and went into the wheel-house.

'Steer two degrees to starboard, David.'

Rohrbach repeated the order and then reported: 'Steering o-six-seven, sir.'

'We're being set to port,' explained Widmark before going back to the foreside of the bridge.

Peering ahead into the darkness he was nagged by doubts about the women, for the Newt's idea of getting them to work had reminded him forcibly of their existence; an existence which, but for an occasional thought for Cleo in the cabin below, he'd almost forgotten. In the long and careful planning which had gone into the operation, there had never been any question of women on board; and yet when he'd first heard of Lindemann's party, the advantages of using it to get his men into the Captain's cabin had seemed to outweigh enormously the disadvantages. Now he was not so sure. Now that the ship was at sea and the real hazards of the break out were at hand, increased immeasurably by the sabotaging of the wireless equipment, he had these nagging doubts. Hester Smit and Di Brett were all right because they were British. Cleo was all right—she was a Greek and, anyway, the least problem of them all because, though she might not know it, he was going to marry her. But Mariotta—she was the problem. She was Portuguese. How could he make sure that she wouldn't talk? Was there any hope that she wouldn't? Of course it would be her word against theirs, and all the paraphernalia of wartime censorship and security would hang over the affair and operate to the advantage of his side. But it was a nasty thought, all the same. If they could get the transmitter working and inform Simonstown of the break out, let them know that the *Hagenfels* was heading for Durban in the hands of a South African naval party, all would be well. It was the fear that they wouldn't that worried him. If things went wrong the situation with which he'd be confronted would be a disastrous one. He'd flatly disobeyed orders, breached Portuguese neutrality, and now he'd added the further complication of getting women involved and one of them a Portuguese. It was certain that he'd face a court-martial if the operation failed. And quite possibly if it succeeded.

The sound of steps on the bridge ladder, lighter and more subdued than those of Rohrbach and the Newt, alerted him and he turned to see a dark shape come on to the bridge and stop near him.

Instinctively his hand slid down to his shoulder-holster and on to the butt of the automatic. 'Tally-Ho!' he snapped.

From the darkness a woman's voice answered, querulous and frightened. 'Oh! I have the coffee.'

With a pleasant sense of shock Widmark recognised her voice but because he could not see her she seemed remote and unreal; the circumstances were so bizarre—he there in the darkness with blackened hands and face, so much recent violence still fresh in his mind, and twenty feet away the body of Günther Moewe.

Rather tamely, he said: 'Hallo, Cleo. This is jolly good

of you.'

'Is that *you*, Stephen?'

'Yes. Funny, isn't it? I mean, I didn't think this would be how we'd next meet.'

'Didn't you?' Her manner changed. 'I understood you planned all this. Surely it should not be a surprise.'

He went up to her then and in the darkness found the tray she was carrying and took from it the two cups of coffee. There was no answer, really, to what she'd said. Something in him, a mixture of disappointment and re-morse, made him say: 'Oh, well. It can't be helped.' And then after an awkward pause he added: 'Thanks for the coffee. I'll give this cup to Rohrbach. He's on the wheel.'

When he got back from the wheelhouse she'd gone.

A few minutes after Cleo had left the bridge, the Newt came back from the wireless cabin. He was breathless and excited. 'Steve, a few minutes ago the Port Captain ordered the *Bartolomeu Dias* to reverse her course and stop us because we left harbour without port authority and made a false report to Ponta Vermelha.'

'Why wasn't I told immediately?'

'Hester Smit's working in the W/T cabin—Mike has the voice receiver on the Port Captain's frequency—and she speaks Portuguese. When I got there she told me there'd been a lot of chatter a few minutes ago, and when I said what about, she said about the *Bartolomeu Dias* being told to return to harbour. She didn't realise it was important, and then while I was there—just a moment ago—the other message came through ordering the gunboat to stop us.'

'Chart-house, quick!' Widmark shot off in the dark-ness, the Newt following. They concentrated on the chart, their minds full of this new threat, their nerves jangling.

'How far ahead of us d'you put her, Newt?'

The Englishman set to work with dividers and wrist-watch, and after a short silence he said: 'At her full speed —say, twenty knots—she must have got ten or eleven miles ahead. But she was ordered to reverse her course five minutes ago. Allowing for a bit of argy-bargy on the bridge and time to turn, she's probably six or seven miles ahead of us now and closing fast. Our combined speeds must be about thirty-six knots.'

'Thank God they haven't got radar yet.' Widmark concentrated on the chart, looking at the outline of the Ribeiro Shoal, at the tortuous and narrow channel to the north of it, bounded on the landward side by the complex of shoals off the mouth of the Incomati River, its thin neck no more than a few hundred yards across. Quickly he made his decision.

'We're going *inside* the Ribeiro Shoal. That'll put the *Bartolomeu Dias* on the one side of it and us on the other. It's five miles long, so even if she sees us she can't do anything about it. But on a dark night like this they'll never see a blacked-out ship to the north of the shoal.'

The Newt looked at the chart with renewed intensity, absorbing what he saw. Then his eyebrows went up and he looked at Widmark. 'It's taking one hell of a chance, Steve. There's not much water there. Only twenty-four feet at mean low water springs, and it's bloody narrow.'

'You'll be able to get bearings on the Garapao and Ribeiro lights. We won't be going it blind, and we know what the set's doing. Anyway we've no option. If we keep to this buoyed channel we'll run slap into the *Bartolomeu Dias*. Switch on the echo-sounder, pronto, and let me know if the water shoals below twenty-six feet. We've had two hours of ebb, so there'll be two to three feet on top of the charted depths. There's not much swell. We're only drawing about twenty-two feet. But first give me the course to clear the southern tip of the shoal. Make it snappy!'

The Newt knew from Widmark's voice that there was no point in arguing—the decision had been made. Quickly he laid the parallel rulers on the chart, marked the course line to clear the southern tip of the shoal, rolled the ruler across to the compass rose and read off the course.

'Course o-one-four, Steve.'

'O-one-four.' Widmark's calm had returned. 'Let me have the times to turn and new courses to steer, quick as you can.'

He went into the wheelhouse and gave Rohrbach the new course. The wheel was put over and the *Hagenfels*'s bow swung to port until she was steaming almost at right angles to her former course. He noted the time—two minutes to midnight.

We won't be long on this course, he thought, and hoped that the Newt would be quick.

From the starboard side of the bridge he looked beyond

the Ribeiro light for the gunboat and there sure enough, rather closer than he'd expected, were the lights of a ship. She was about four miles away and from her steaming lights he could see that she was inward bound. Because she was a neutral the gunboat had not darkened ship, and Widmark was soon able to confirm that it was her and not a neutral merchantman. He knew that on her bridge there would be men scanning the darkness ahead, seeking the large bulk of a ship without lights. But they would, he also knew, be looking *ahead* along the buoyed channel and not inside the Ribeiro Shoal where no ship of that size ever went, nor ever would go: not even by day, let alone by night.

The Newt called out: 'At three minutes past midnight, alter course to o-seven-two, Steve. I'll give you a shout from the monkey island when the time comes. We must turn when the Ribeiro light bears one-one-o. Echo-sounder's showing round about twenty-eight, twenty-nine feet.'

The Newt's cheerfulness was infectious. 'Okay!' shouted Widmark, repeating the course. 'The gunboat's about three miles away, bearing green four-five, heading down the channel.'

'Bravo,' shouted the Newt. 'Please God, keep us off the shoals!'

He went up to the monkey island and Widmark stood by the wheelhouse door watching the gunboat's lights and searching the darkness with the Zeiss glasses, in his mind's eye a picture of the Ribeiro Shoal on one bow and the line of shoals off the Incomati River on the other, expecting at any moment to feel the ship shudder as she grounded.

The main diesels thumped and grumbled as she drove ahead into the night, the wind murmured in the rigging, the seas slopped and gurgled along her sides, and the bows dipped to the ground swell. Astern, the flurried water in the *Hagenfels*'s wake twisted and bubbled in whorls of phosphorescence.

Chapter Nineteen

The bearing of the gunboat's lights opened steadily as she came down the channel past the Ribeiro Shoal and when the Newt called from the monkey island, 'Steer o-seven-two now,' she was almost astern.

Widmark ordered the wheel to starboard and steadied the ship's head on 072 degrees; now the *Hagenfels* and the gunboat were on parallel courses, but past each other and steaming in opposite directions, the distance between them opening at their combined speeds of about thirty-six knots. The passage between the shoals was narrowest at the entrance into which the *Hagenfels* had just turned, and while Widmark stood at the bridge screen peering ahead through night glasses, ears straining for the sound of breakers where the water shoaled to port, the Newt was in the chart-house, eyes on the stylograph needle scratching the sound-trace on to a strip of moving paper. The water which should have been getting deeper was shoaling and from the chart-house door he called to Widmark: 'Steer fifteen degrees to starboard,' then he was back at the trace, staring at it with smarting eyes; the water got deeper, he breathed freely once again, corrected the course to port and steadied the ship's head on 076 degrees.

Soon the trace showed eight and nine fathoms, and he knew that the channel was widening. At twelve minutes past midnight, course was altered to 037 degrees, and ten minutes later they had cleared the Ribeiro Shoal.

The lights of the gunboat were no longer visible and they estimated she must now be nearing Ponta Garapao. It was almost certain, Widmark reflected, that the gunboat's captain would assume that the *Hagenfels* had gone to the south of the buoyed channel where there was ample water and room to manœuvre. It would never occur to a seaman that she had gone to the north.

Ahead of them, running north and south, lay the long line of the Cutfield, Paivo Manso and Domette Shoals, but the *Hagenfels* had no lack of sea room now. Turning on to a northerly course she steamed parallel to the coast, the

197

shoals to starboard, the land to port. Soon after one o'clock in the morning she was past the Cutfield Shoal and course was altered to seaward. By daylight she would be well out in the shipping lanes—she would then turn on to a southerly course, and should other ships sight her they would conclude that this was a steamer from the north, inward bound for Lourenço Marques. No one, felt Widmark, would credit the captain of the *Hagenfels* with the stupidity, once he had broken out, of steering a course directly back to the port.

But he chafed at the delay in getting the W/T transmitter to work and at the dilemma in which they had been landed through the absence of any means of communication with the outside world.

In the early hours of the morning the Newt took over the bridge and Widmark went off to do the rounds. His first call was at the wireless cabin where—while insisting that they continue their work—he asked Mike Kent to explain briefly what the trouble was. It was not pleasant hearing.

Apart from the fact that much complex repair work had to be done, the necessary valves to get the transmitter going could not be found; but the young telegraphist was trying to rig up a simple emergency transmitting circuit, though he was far from certain that it would function, and somewhat in the dark as to what frequency it would be on if it did. There was, however, one cheering item of news. He had found an ordinary radio broadcast receiver in the dining saloon and had set it up in the wireless cabin, where he tuned it to 500 kcs, the waveband used by merchant shipping. He had found that that channel was carrying most traffic and he had thought they might glean something useful from it. The ship was now out of range of the Port Captain's radio telephone, so they had no means of telling whether the disappearance of *Hagenfels* had yet been established by the port authorities.

With a quiet word of encouragement, Widmark left the wireless cabin and went down to the engine-room where he was heartened by his chat with McFadden. The little Scot assured him that everything was under control, including the greaser whom they'd named Fritz because they couldn't pronounce his real name.

Widmark's next call was on Johan, whom he found sitting

on the coaming of number one hatch, bored and feeling out of things.

'Sorry we had to do this to you, Johan,' he said, 'but we've no guarantee that we've rounded up all the crew. There's always the danger that an odd Jerry may pitch up in the dark, go down to the chain-locker and let his chums out. Seen or heard anything?'

'Not a sausage,' said Johan. 'My problem's been to keep awake.'

'We'll issue a round of Benzedrine soon. Did the girls bring you some coffee?'

'Yes, Cleo did. The Greek girl you met at Costa's. She's been the only bright spot in the last three hours.'

'At daylight you can pack this up, Johan. Come up to the bridge then and join us.'

'What about those poor sods in the chain-locker? It must be pretty grim down there.'

'We'll see about that once it's daylight.' Widmark was unsympathetic. 'Won't do them any harm to stay there for a bit.'

Leaving Johan, he went up to the Captain's cabin. As he opened the door he heard women laughing. That's better, he thought. They stopped talking when he came in—Cleo and Di Brett.

He looked at Di Brett. 'Where's Mariotta?'

She inclined her head towards the captain's sleeping cabin. 'In there. She's drugged. Somebody must have put something in her food or drink. She can't wake up.'

Widmark smiled. 'Poor girl. Too bad. It was intended for her hosts. She'll wake up in due course.'

There was a long silence, Cleo looking away from him, Di Brett doing her lips. Stopping for a moment, she watched him, lipstick in hand, her head on one side.

'You look *too awful* with a black face, Stephen. Why don't you clean that muck off?'

'It's quite a business. It'll have to wait.' He rubbed his eyes with the back of his hand, looking at Cleo. 'I just want to say this. I'm sorry we had to involve you girls. But there's a war on and we have to do all sorts of things we don't like. Within twenty-four hours we expect to land you safely in Durban. What happens to you then will be for the naval authorities to decide, but as three of you are on the Allied side and Mariotta's a neutral, you'll come to no harm.'

'D'you think it was fair? To get us mixed up in this?'
Di Brett's eyebrows arched above cold, calculating eyes.

'*We* didn't invite you on board, Di. The Germans did.
You may not know it, but they planned to break out tonight. The party was simply cover. So that the shore
authorities wouldn't know what was on the go. Our job
was to nip their plan in the bud.'

The subjective part of Widmark's mind observed dryly
with what fluency he was putting this across; but it's all in a
good cause, he reflected. The explanation had been devised
when he'd made the decision to launch the operation on the
night of the party, and each of his men was familiar with it.

The story was thin in places, he knew, but it would be
their word against any who chose to contest it and the key
witnesses, the German prisoners, would be available only
to the British.

Di Brett's face gave no indication of her thoughts; she
was acutely aware that if she were to say what she knew,
she would incriminate herself. Cleo was beginning to soften
for she believed Widmark, and though outwardly she main-
tained her aloofness her heart warmed to him as he spoke.
Odd though he looked with his grimy face, she was excited
by his closeness and felt once again the strange attraction
of that night at Costa's.

Sitting on the edge of the desk, one knee over the other,
Widmark ran his fingers through his tousled hair, took out
his cigarette case and lit a cigarette. 'What's more,' he went
on, blowing the smoke away from them, 'this ship was
taken out of Lourenço Marques by Lindemann and his
crew. Not by us.' His eyes narrowed as he watched them.

Di Brett laughed. 'You're an awful liar, Stephen! The
last we saw of poor Lindemann and his officers they were
being marched away under the guns of your men.'

Cleo eyed him curiously, wondering what he would say
to that. But he didn't bat an eyelid. 'Out on deck—in the
dark—we were overpowered by other members of the crew.
They locked us up and took the ship to sea. Later on,
Johan, who'd hidden in a lifeboat, released us and we took
charge again. Now the Germans are our prisoners. In
other words, we captured this ship on the high seas.'

'It's a fascinating story, Stephen.' Di Brett smiled. 'Make
a wonderful film.'

'Wouldn't it?' he agreed. 'But it happens to be true.

You know—truth's stranger than fiction sort of thing.'

Di Brett's laugh was thin, but he was unconcerned and puffed away at the cigarette.

Cleo was thinking, well it could be true. Stephen wouldn't lie, and then because she wasn't really quite sure she consoled herself with the thought that there was a war on. Anyway, she decided, I'll back his story if it comes to the pinch.

'Another thing,' said Widmark, eyeing the end of his cigarette and feeling rather pleased with himself because what he was about to say was partly true.

'We're not an *official* naval party. We were in Lourenço Marques on leave, enjoying ourselves quite innocently, when we learnt from the local grape-vine that the Germans were planning a break out for the *Hagenfels*. So we thought we'd combine business with pleasure and spike their guns as a sort of private lark.'

Di Brett held out her hand. 'Cigarette, please. Your manners aren't what they used to be, Stephen.'

He gave her the cigarette case. 'Sorry. It's been a busy night and I'm tired. You, Cleo?'

She shook her head. 'I don't, thanks.' But she smiled and he realised he was forgiven. His spirits rose, 'I must go back to the bridge.' He stood up. 'See you later.'

Cleo followed him into the alleyway. 'Stephen,' she called.

He turned round. 'Hallo, Cleo. What's up?'

'Stephen——' she hesitated. 'Is everything going to be all right?'

He moved close to her, touching her cheek with his hand. 'Yes. Everything's going to be all right. And when we get to Durban you and I are going to dance again.'

She put her hand on his. 'I'm so glad.'

Widmark wanted to kiss her then, but he felt he couldn't with all that stuff on his face. He patted her shoulder. 'I know a marvellous place. The Silver Slipper. We'll go there on Saturday night. Is that a date?'

'I've got no clothes,' she said. 'But it's a date.'

At three o'clock that morning Widmark issued Benzedrine tablets to the men—and to Hester Smit, on the insistence of Mike Kent.

He had worked like a beaver in the wireless cabin, sometimes explaining to Hester what he was trying to do but mostly in silence; at moments, when he felt he was making progress, his spirits rose; at others, when he tested some newly fixed component and found it was not functioning, they sank. While he worked, his mind was a jumble of thoughts; snatches of involved philosophical argument mixed with scraps from text-books on the theory of electronics, mixed again with mental pictures of his room at home, his books, his mother, and shadowy glimpses of a girl at university with whom he'd embarked on a slightly erotic friendship just before the war, whereafter they'd gone their separate ways.

Then, quite inconsequentially, he would find himself thinking of Austin Robert's bird book, of the Drakensberg, of the Lammergeier and the Nerina Trogon, and he would have to discipline himself and think: Keep your mind on the job, it requires all your concentration.

Down in the captain's cabin Di Brett and Cleo were resting, their bodies exhausted but their minds active. Cleo lay on one settee in the day-cabin and Di Brett on the other; both of them silent, the swish of electric fans, the occasional creaking of the superstructure, and the sound of the sea outside, the only accompaniment to their thoughts.

On the bridge, Rohrbach was at the wheel, and the Newt was in the chart-house busy with the ship's navigational tables and nautical almanac, getting ready for the star sights he planned to take at dawn. They were not essential so soon after leaving harbour, but it kept him occupied and an early morning position might be useful. Widmark was pacing the bridge, alert, watchful, evaluating the dangers threatening the *Hagenfels*, above all those from submarines; they were not so much to be feared now—the night was too dark—but once daylight came the risk would be a real one, though he hoped the closeness of the coast would give them some protection. At dawn the *Hagenfels* would start zigzagging and with the ship steaming at fifteen knots, and U-boats keeping down because of the danger of air patrols, she should not be too easy a target. But if only the W/T transmitter had been serviceable he would long since have arranged for air cover and a surface escort at daylight.

No use bellyaching about that, he thought. Nobody

could be trying harder than Mike, and if anything could be done he'd do it. For the rest his mind was occupied with a patchwork of thoughts: pictures of Cleo and a future together with her, confused with nagging snatches of imagined dialogue and tortuous explanation when he told the Chief of Staff why he had embarked on the operation after the Commander-in-Chief's categorical 'No.' The answers had long been prepared and he was banking upon the knowledge that a successful operation, even if orders had been disobeyed, was to some extent its own explanation. But he was troubled by feelings of doubt and insecurity.

At about four o'clock in the morning, these thoughts were interrupted by Hester Smit's arrival on the bridge with a message scrawled on a German signal pad by Mike Kent.

It read: '*Have just picked up a QQQQ message from Havana City on 500 kcs in position 26 20′S: 34 30′E. Immediately followed by "Am being shelled by . . ." whereafter message ends.*'

Widmark went into the chart-house and with the Newt plotted the position: it was approximately seventy miles to the south-east of the *Hagenfels*. He looked at the Newt, tapping his teeth with the metal top of the pencil.

They both knew that QQQQ meant 'armed merchantman wishes to stop me' and that in turn meant a raider; but it was a dark night and it might just as well have been a surfaced submarine using its gun.

'Pity the poor devil couldn't get off the last word of his message,' said Widmark. 'Must have been "raider" or "submarine"—but which?'

The Newt shrugged his shoulders. 'Nothing we can do about it either way, Steve.'

Widmark's thoughts were in the combined operations room in Cape Town. 'No. But it makes a hell of a difference to the chaps who *have* got to do something about it.'

'What raiders are operating round here these days?'

'Three weeks ago, when I was last in combined ops, there were two out which could be here now: the *Köln* and the *Speewald*. *Köln*'s a big chap of about eight thousand tons, and *Speewald*'s about four thousand. Both formidable.'

'And U-boats?'

'Three or four large U-cruisers for certain and possibly some others.'

'I hope somebody'll pick up the *Havana City*'s survivors

in due course.'

'I expect help will be around during the day. That position's only about a hundred and twenty miles from LM.'

With the coming of daylight their spirits rose. Although it was the beginning of a more dangerous time, the cover of darkness having gone, daylight had a powerful psychological effect, and with the cares of the night behind them their thoughts turned to the promise of the day. Johan came up from the fore-deck, course was altered to 247 degrees so that they were steering for Cabo Inhaca, the normal landfall for a vessel making for Lourenço Marques. They would continue on that course until the Venturas from 22 Squadron had completed their morning reconnaissance, then when the *Hagenfels* was past Inhaca they would alter course to the south, enter Portuguese territorial waters and make for Durban which they expected to reach by two o'clock the following morning. Widmark hoped soon to get off a message, for Mike Kent, working with renewed energy, the Benzedrine having taken effect, had sent Hester Smit to report that he might get the emergency transmitter going within the next hour or so.

In the distance, to the south-east, they could see the smoke of a steamer; but for that, there was nothing in sight. Wisps of cirrus in the eastern sky reflected the glow of the hidden sun; a light breeze played on the sea, and an occasional flying fish broke surface and whirred in brief flight before splashing back into the water. The bridge was moist with dew, the morning air limpid and good to breathe.

Black-backed gulls flew round the ship and far away on the starboard quarter Widmark saw the smoke-like wisp of a whale spouting. These simple things pleased him and he felt it was good to be alive. That made him think of Moewe and the dead night watchman. Something would have to be done about them before the women arrived on deck.

He and Johan carried and dragged Moewe's body down to the after well-deck and bundled it over the side, following it closely with the body of the night watchman. For the first time, in a remote way, Widmark felt sorry for these men. The high emotional peak of the night had gone. But he was not conscious of any remorse and still glad of what

204

he'd done. Indeed, the thought of the *Havana City*'s survivors away to the south-east, struggling for their lives, stiffened his resolve and he soon forgot the dead men.

When he got back to the bridge he told Johan to bring Lindemann and von Falkenhausen to him.

Minutes later they arrived, hair dishevelled, hands and faces streaked with mud, and eyes bloodshot from the long period in darkness. Lindemann's white uniform and the Freiherr's tropical suit were crumpled and dirty.

"Morning,' said Widmark stiffly.

Lindemann said nothing, but von Falkenhausen clicked his heels and bowed, the trace of a smile in his eyes.

Widmark looked away from them. 'Captain Lindemann. I'm going to release you and your men and place you on parole. Your party must remain for'ard of number one hold. That gives you the fo'c'sle and some deck space to move about in. Lieutenant le Roux will see that you are given bread and coffee. There's water in the fo'c'sle and later in the day we'll give you more food. You and your party will be watched from the bridge. If any man comes aft of number one hatch without my permission, he'll be fired on.

'Tonight you'll be locked in the fo'c'sle. My men are all armed, so I advise you to accept the position that you are prisoners of war. Is that quite clear?'

Lindemann said: 'Yes.'

Von Falkenhausen bowed. 'Quite clear, Commander. We accept the position. But we have two men who require medical attention. They have head injuries. Wedel and Müller. Wedel is bad.'

Widmark's forehead puckered into little furrows of irritation. 'What sort of medical attention d'you think they can get here?'

'Some first-aid will be better than nothing.'

'We'll give you what material we can from the ship's medical locker, but I've no one to spare to give first-aid.'

'One of the women, perhaps?' suggested the Freiherr.

Widmark looked at him sharply. 'You will have no contact with the women. You must look after yourselves.'

Von Falkenhausen knew that that was that.

He and Lindemann left the bridge with Johan and not long afterwards some of the prisoners appeared on deck forward; at first a crumpled sorry-looking lot, but later,

205

when they had breathed the fresh air and enjoyed the crispness of the morning, they became gayer, talking and laughing among themselves.

The sun came clear of the horizon and what was for Widmark a promising morning became a radiant one when, soon after six, Cleo arrived on the bridge with coffee and buttered toast.

Chapter Twenty

The first hour of the morning watch in the combined operations room in Cape Town was a busy one: just after 4 a.m. the *Havana City*'s QQQQ message came in, followed immediately by her report that she was being shelled, and while the officers on duty were puzzling about that, a message arrived from the British Consulate General in Lourenço Marques announcing the break out of the *Hagenfels*. That was followed by a report that a Greek cargo steamer had been torpedoed by a U-boat off Port Elizabeth, where a corvette and a destroyer had picked up survivors and were searching the area.

There was a buzz of excitement as all this information was transferred to the plot, while fresh messages kept coming in from HM ships at sea which were reacting quickly to these events. The cruiser *Northampton* reported that she was eighty-five miles north-west of the position given by the *Havana City*, and that she was closing it at twenty-five knots. She added that at first light she proposed flying off her Walrus aircraft and that she was assuming that the attack might have been by raider or submarine.

The destroyers *Cullington* and *Carisbrooke* reported that they were carrying out an A/S sweep one hundred and twenty miles south-south-east of the position and asked for instructions.

Three armed whalers of the SA Naval Forces, escorting a slow convoy from Durban to Lourenço Marques, gave their position as ninety-eight miles to the south-west of the *Havana City*.

Messages soon started to go out from the combined operations room: the last known positions of the raiders *Köln* and *Speewald* were given, together with a brief assessment of their possible movements since; 22 Squadron in Durban was ordered to fly off aircraft to carry out a search at daylight, not only for the raider which might have sunk the *Havana City*, but for the *Hagenfels* now presumed to be operating as a supply vessel. Combined operations suggested that she was most likely to be making for the open sea on an easterly course which would get her farthest from land in the shortest time.

The *Cullington* and *Carisbrooke* were ordered to search for the *Havana City*'s survivors and for the U-boat which might have sunk her; the *Northampton* was informed that the action she proposed taking was approved. These signals were repeated to all HM ships in the vicinity and to all naval and air authorities concerned.

The probable disposition of German U-boats in and near the danger area was re-broadcast; merchant ships were warned of the possibility of a raider operating off Lourenço Marques, and the slow north-bound convoy was diverted.

By the time all this had been done it was 05.17 and the duty staff then settled down to wait; they had done all they could, everybody was now in the picture, and it was over to the ships at sea and to the aircraft which were already leaving the runways outside Durban. At 05.30, Commodore Carrington, Chief of the Naval Staff, arrived in the combined operations room to look at the plot and discuss the latest developments. When he was satisfied that everything possible had been done he decided to bath and shave. At that stage he remarked to Commander Bensford, the naval officer on duty: 'Pity Widmark's not here. He had a bee in his bonnet about the *Hagenfels* breaking out.'

Bensford smiled. 'I know, sir. Almost an obsession.'

'He was right, of course.' The Commodore nodded forlornly. 'These bright young men so often are.'

At 05.19 the *Northampton* flew off two Walrus aircraft, one to investigate the area of the *Havana City*'s sinking, the other to search along the *Hagenfels*'s probable track from Lourenço Marques eastwards, since it was in this area that combined operations had suggested she was most likely to be found.

On the bridge of the cruiser, Captain Gillies was thinking of a number of things: of the danger of taking his ship into the waters off Lourenço Marques where there were known to be a number of U-boats operating; of the exciting possibility of intercepting either the *Köln* or *Speewald*, for never before had the *Northampton* been so close to a raider sinking, assuming always that it was a raider and not a U-boat. Nothing, reflected Gillies, would give him greater satisfaction than to meet and destroy a raider. These ships, apart from the havoc they wrought among merchant shipping, tied down large numbers of British warships—of which the *Northampton* was but one—which were urgently required for other duties. He was thinking, too, of the *Hagenfels* and how important it was that she should be intercepted before she lost herself in the empty spaces of the Indian Ocean, from which she could rendezvous at will with raiders and U-boats.

Earlier he had sent for silhouettes and other particulars of the *Köln*, *Speewald* and *Hagenfels*; he had paid special attention to the *Köln* for not only was she one of the most successful raiders of the war, but she was commanded with skill and daring by Korvettenkäpitan von Lüdecke, who had commanded the raider *Geier* in the North Atlantic two years earlier and who was believed to have with him many of his former crew. Gillies had known von Lüdecke before the war and liked him.

Now he noted that the *Köln* had a main armament equivalent to six six-inch guns, a useful secondary armament and six torpedo tubes. She carried two Arado seaplanes, and a motor launch with fourteen-inch torpedoes and two 20 mm. guns. The *Köln* was known to have radar and, one way and another, she would be able to give an excellent account of herself.

It was known, too, that she could change her appearance overnight by means of movable masts and a dummy funnel and that her speed was about eighteen knots. Gillies had already warned the crews of his slow Walrus aircraft not to make a close approach to any suspected raider because of the considerable anti-aircraft armament which these ships mounted.

It was while he was examining the silhouettes of the German ships that Gillies first became aware of the resemblance between the *Köln* and the *Hagenfels*. Though they had been built by different shipyards for different owners, they were both of eight thousand tons, and their hulls and superstructure were much alike. The differences were mainly in the positions of the sampson posts and the size of the funnels—the *Hagenfels*'s being rather larger than the *Köln*'s—but since the latter was able to alter the appearance of her funnel and masts, these differences could not be relied upon.

At 06.28 the signals officer reported that the Walrus

which had flown to the south-west—that is to say towards Lourenço Marques—had sighted a merchant ship of about eight thousand tons; the aircraft had approached to within three miles and had called the ship by Aldis lamp and by R/T but could elicit no reply. The aircraft's observer had added that he assumed she was an allied merchantman as she appeared to be inward bound for Lourenço Marques.

On board the *Northampton*, the navigating officer examined the plot and reported that there was no Allied merchant ship in the position reported by the Walrus. Captain Gillies's suspicions were now aroused and he instructed the Walrus to continue to shadow the ship while he checked her position with the combined operations room at Cape Town.

Combined operations confirmed at once that there should be no Allied ship in that position at that time and that the *Northampton* should assume it was the *Köln* or the *Hagenfels* until the contrary had been established.

The *Northampton* increased speed to thirty knots and altered course for the position given by the Walrus, at the same time informing the aircraft that the ship was probably the *Köln* and repeating the instruction to keep at least three miles from her.

It was the Newt who first sighted the Walrus. He had come out of the chart-house to give Widmark the *Hagenfels*'s position when he heard the distant sound of an aircraft coming down to them in the light easterly wind.

'Hear that?' He was tense and alert.

Widmark listened, then, looking astern, said: 'It's somewhere down there. Bit early for the morning Ventura.'

They tried to pick up the aircraft with binoculars but failed; eventually Widmark saw it with his naked eye. Training his glasses on it, he said: 'Good show! It's a Walrus. That means one of our cruisers is somewhere in the offing.'

Johan was near them and Widmark ordered him to hoist the white ensign. This he did, but once hoisted on the triatic stay which stretched from funnel to foremast it looked ridiculously small. It was for this reason that Widmark had decided to fly it from the bridge rather than from the stern where he was pretty certain it wouldn't be seen at all, particularly with a following wind.

In spite of a thorough search they'd not been able to find an Aldis lamp on the bridge, and when Johan asked Lindemann where it was kept the Captain said that the ship hadn't got one; they relied on the all-round signal lamp above the monkey island. Widmark knew that such a lamp, while serviceable enough in the dark, could not be read in daylight, least of all in bright sunlight.

He realised then that they would have to rely on the signal torch which could be aimed, and he was glad that they had brought it.

Until the Walrus came up to the ship, however, there was no means of making contact with it. They couldn't hoist the ship's signal letters because Widmark knew only too well that, in the absence of a wireless message from him, neither combined operations nor the cruiser had any reason to believe that the *Hagenfels* was not under German command.

The Walrus had been about three miles away when it was first sighted; a few minutes later it was no closer, although its bearing was drawing rapidly ahead.

'She *must* have seen us,' Widmark complained to the Newt.

'Of course. Couldn't miss us at this range. Perhaps she's got other fish to fry.'

As he spoke the Walrus turned to the south-west and flew ahead of the *Hagenfels* taking station on her starboard bow, still a good three miles away. At that moment Rohr-bach, who was in the wheelhouse keeping the ship to a zigzag diagram, put the wheel to starboard so that the *Hagenfels* turned in the direction of the Walrus; they noticed that the aircraft at once turned away and regained her position on the bow.

'My God!' said Widmark, shocked at the discovery, 'she's shadowing us. She's keeping out of range.'

'Wonder why?' said the Newt, but he was already beginning to suspect that he knew the answer.

Widmark didn't hear him, he was too absorbed in his thoughts. The Walrus was keeping three miles away because she feared the *Hagenfels* might shoot her down—that could mean only one thing: the *Hagenfels* was being treated with the respect accorded an armed German raider. The Walrus was shadowing, reporting back to the cruiser from which she had come, and the cruiser would be closing the position at high speed. Widmark remembered the *Havana City*'s

QQQQ message.

With a shock which caused him to draw in his breath he became aware of the approaching climacteric. The Newt reported: 'Walrus is calling us by lamp.'

They read the signal as it was slowly winked to them from the aircraft: a series of 'N-N-J.' They knew that meant: 'Make your signal letters.' But they dared not. To do so would be to invite destruction.

With the torch the Newt made R—'Message received.'

The Walrus kept repeating N-N-J and eventually spelt out. 'Make your signal letters' in plain language. On the *Hagenfels*'s bridge they went on making R R Rs, then tried 'Roger' and eventually spelt out 'We are British. Please close us,' but to no avail. Slowly the ugliness of the situation became apparent: at three miles, in bright sunlight, the signal torch could not be read.

The Newt admired Widmark's understatement: 'They can't read us. I'm afraid this may be rather serious.'

Then, at Widmark's request, he went to the wireless cabin with the inevitable inquiry. Mike Kent, white-faced, eyes bloodshot, shook his head. 'Sorry. Tell him we're doing our best. No joy yet.'

'Jesus!' breathed the Newt as he ran back to the bridge.

When the Newt gave him the news from the wireless cabin, Widmark panicked for a frightening moment, but this was not apparent to the Newt. Then he pulled himself together and faced the situation which could not have been more frustrating: they were in visual touch with an aircraft of the Royal Navy but could not communicate with it, nor with the ship from which it came. Widmark now accepted that the range of the signal torch in bright daylight was probably no more than a mile; they had neither R/T nor W/T. There remained four possibilities: semaphore flags, flag hoists, a signal on the ship's siren, or using the sun to signal with a mirror.

But semaphore flags couldn't be read from an aircraft three miles away. Nor would it be able to hear a ship's siren above the sound of its own engines. The use of flag hoists was another possibility, but they could only be read up to a mile or so with the aid of a telescope. From a circling Walrus, shuddering with engine vibrations, they would never be read. If the cruiser, when she arrived on the scene, came reasonably close there was just a chance that flag hoists might work. Sound signals wouldn't if such wind as there was, was the wrong way. The Walrus was down sun from the *Hagenfels*. A mirror could not be used unless the aircraft went up sun by flying over to the port side of the ship.

While he was contemplating these problems, the sun rose higher above the horizon, the easterly wind dropped, the surface ruffle disappeared and the sea became a flat calm. The *Hagenfels* was still steaming at full speed and the crisp swish of water at the bow and down the side, the muted rumble of the diesels, and the noise of the aircraft's engine combined in a single pattern of sound.

Widmark called the Newt into the wheelhouse where they discussed the signal problem with Rohrbach who plumped for flag hoists. Later, as the full implications of their dilemma became apparent, they were thoughtful and preoccupied.

A number of alternatives were considered before they decided that the most effective signal would be: 'British prize—manned South African Navy.' A shorter message would have been better, but they saw no way of achieving it with reasonable safety. As it was, the signal would require five hoists amounting in all to sixteen flags, and five sets of halyards would have to be used. There were only three on the triatic stay and two on the fore yard-arm. They decided to use both the stay and the yard-arm.

In the chart-house they found the German edition of the International Code and the Newt took over the wheel so that Rohrbach could work on the signal; he took out the signal groups which made up the message and they pulled the flags from the signal lockers and bent them on to the halyards. From the fore yard-arm flew two hoists reading 'BRITISH-PRIZE' and from the triatic stay the three hoists making up the rest of the signal: 'MANNED-SOUTH-AFRICAN-NAVY.'

Some of the flags flew foul, but by hoisting and slackening the halyards in quick succession, and jerking on them, they got the flags clear. Seen from the bridge, they made a brave show. Widmark, however, was in no mood to deceive himself. Flag signals were all very well at close range: they were not when distances were measured in miles. But it was the best they could do. There was nothing for it now

213

but to wait.

It was 06.35. He wondered how far away the cruiser was.

Rohrbach pointed at the Walrus which had shifted her position from four points on the bow to the starboard beam.

But she was still down sun. No good for the shaving mirror which had been brought from the Captain's cabin.

'He's seen our hoists go up,' Widmark sounded weary, 'and he's wondering what the hell it's all about.' The only wind of any consequence now was that made by the ship and since the flags were flying fore-and-aft the signal could only be read from abeam.

Once more the Walrus blinked 'N-N-J'—again it followed up in plain language with 'Make your signal letters.' Had they been able to make them it would have been a hoist of only four flags so Widmark could well understand the aircraft's surprise at the *Hagenfels*'s lavish display of bunting.

'Must look like a make-and-mend,' he said sourly, but there was nothing funny about the situation and he could have shouted with frustration. Then he thought about the women and prisoners and the men in the engine-room. There might not be much time.

With a despairing glance at the circling Walrus, he turned to Johan. 'Ask the women, Lindemann and von Falkenhausen to come up here. Tell them to make it snappy.'

When Widmark had explained the situation he asked the Germans if they could think of any other means of communication, but they couldn't. Though they realised they were in danger, they made no secret of their admiration for what Paul Müller the steward had done.

The women, including Mariotta, who was still drowsy and making her first appearance of the day, were puzzled at first and then, as Widmark hinted at the dangers, they showed some apprehension, although he did his best to put a good face on things. When the position had been explained he said to Johan: 'Lieutenant le Roux, you are to be responsible for the safety of the women. Concentrate with them in the stern until further orders. You'll find a docking phone there through to the bridge.'

Johan was obviously not happy at the task given him, but he nodded and then looked at an exhausted Hester Smit whose face and hands were smudged with grease. 'What about her?'

Widmark had forgotten Hester. After a moment's pause he said: 'She can carry on with Mike Kent until I give the word. Then she must join you aft. That okay, Hester?'

She yawned, putting up her hand. 'Of course. I can't leave poor little Mike by himself. He'll never make it alone.'

Johan beckoned to the girls. 'Come along, please.' Cleo looked at Widmark for a moment as if she wished to say something, but she must have thought better of it for she turned and went after the others.

When they'd gone Widmark said to von Falkenhausen and Lindemann: 'You'll have to be responsible for your men. We may have to abandon ship. If so we'll use the disengaged side. Concentrate there and await orders if and when the time comes.' Purposely Widmark had not told the women this, but the Germans noted his use of the words 'disengaged side' and understood what he meant. There was no wind or sea so there would be no lee or weather side to worry about. But there were likely to be other and more pressing considerations.

At 06.58 they sighted the masts of a ship broad on the starboard quarter. Soon the upperworks and hull lifted above the horizon and by 07.05 there was no longer any doubt. It was a cruiser, coming up from astern at high speed.

Chapter Twenty-One

On the bridge of the *Northampton* the signals officer was making a report to the Captain.

'The Walrus says the ship has run up five hoists of about fifteen flags in all. The aircraft can't read them at three miles and the ship continues to ignore the request to make her signal letters.'

'Thank you, Ransome. I expect she's trying to brazen it out. Putting on the "I'm a stupid merchant ship and don't understand your signals act." It's a favourite raider technique.' Captain Gillies turned to the midshipman behind him. 'Ask the navigating officer at what time we should sight her.'

'Aye, aye, sir.' The midshipman saluted, went to the bridge phone, spoke into it and came back with his report. 'At approximately 06.55 if the position given by the Walrus is correct, sir.'

'I expect it isn't,' said the Captain who was a salt horse and mistrusted flying sailors, though he conceded their usefulness.

'Yeoman,' he said, 'can you think what she's up to with all those flag hoists?'

'Must have a message to pass, sir.' The yeoman-of-signals was not easily shaken.

The Captain had a great respect for his yeoman. The man abounded in common sense. 'Yes, yeoman. But what message?'

The yeoman stroked his chin. 'Sounds like delaying tactics, sir. There's seamen on that bridge. They know hoists can't be read that far, sir. Why don't they use an Aldis, or W/T, or R/T?'

'That, yeoman, is exactly what I feel.'

Captain Gillies looked at his watch. It was 06.42. He beckoned the midshipman. 'Let Benshaw know I won't be having my bath for some time, Higgins.'

Midshipman Higgins saluted, said 'Aye, aye, sir,' and spoke to the bridge messenger, who doubled off to pass the word to the Captain's steward.

The Captain spoke next to the officer-of-the-watch. 'Radar picked up anything yet, Simmonds?' He knew it was an unnecessary question—the instant the radar operators obtained a contact they would report to the bridge—but it was force of habit; it helped to pass the time and it reminded the operators that the Captain relied on them for the first report of the ship ahead. They would see the blip on their screens long before the bridge lookouts sighted the masts.

While he waited on the bridge, searching the horizon every few minutes with his binoculars, Gillies was thinking of the Confidential Admiralty Fleet Order which had been issued to all HM ships after the loss of the cruiser *Sydney* in November, 1941. The British warship had sighted a merchantman two hundred miles off the Australian coast and had steamed towards it, repeatedly making the signal 'N-N-J.' At about six miles range the *Sydney* again made the signal but this time in plain language; the merchant vessel then hoisted signal letters on the triatic stay in such a way that they were obscured and could not be read by the *Sydney*.

Eventually, when the *Sydney* had closed to within 1500 yards, the merchant ship had dropped her gun screens and opened fire at point blank range with four 15 cm. guns.

The first salvo had wrecked the *Sydney*'s bridge, destroyed her aircraft, and a torpedo from the raider had put the cruiser's forward turrets out of action.

The *Sydney* put her guns into local control and fought a bitter action with the raider at short range, eventually leaving the German ship on fire and sinking. The cruiser, heavily damaged and down by the bow, steamed slowly to the south-east and was never seen again.

Some three hundred survivors from the raider—which turned out to be the *Kormoran*—were picked up but there were none from the *Sydney*.

The Confidential Fleet Order issued as a result of this action enjoined commanding officers of HM ships to exercise the utmost care when interrogating suspect merchant ships and in particular to remain at long range and to manœuvre at high speed until identity had been established.

It was with these thoughts very much in the forefront of his mind that Captain Gillies heard the officer-of-the-watch report: 'Radar contact bearing one-four-eight, forty thousand yards. Classified "ship," sir.'

The Captain immediately ordered action stations, and the alarm rattlers sounded throughout the cruiser. From every compartment men streamed to their stations and reports began to flow through to the bridge from the gunnery and torpedo directors, the gun turrets, the action information centre, damage control stations, and the plot. Speed was increased to thirty-two knots and the *Northampton*'s stern settled deeper in the water, the spray under her forefoot rising high.

At 06.56, the Captain was first to sight the masts of a ship almost directly ahead. Seven minutes later her upperworks were plainly visible. The *Northampton* altered course to starboard to bring the merchantman broad on the port bow, so making it possible for all turrets to bear on the stranger.

At sixteen thousand yards, by which time the merchant ship was bearing six points on the cruiser's starboard bow, the *Northampton*, using a fourteen-inch signal lamp, made 'N-N-J' and repeated it in plain language.

This was done three times, but there was no reply from the merchant ship. The yeoman-of-signals struggled with his telescope but could make nothing of the various flag hoists the ship was flying.

At 07.08, the *Northampton* fired two warning shots and shell splashes were seen to port and starboard of the merchantman's bows.

It was now possible to see the ship's hull and superstructure clearly, and it was beyond all doubt that she was not only a German ship, but certainly either the *Köln* or the *Hagenfels*. It was clear to Captain Gillies that whether she was the one or the other he had to sink her; a raider supply vessel was no more desirable afloat than a raider, but with the fate of the *Sydney* in mind prudence demanded that he should assume that this was the *Köln*.

After the two warning shots, the German ship was seen to slow down and begin to turn to starboard but she continued to ignore all signals from the cruiser. It was at this stage that the yeoman remarked to the Captain: 'Those hoists could only be read by a ship a mile or so away on her beam. I think they're a decoy, sir, to get us into that position.'

Captain Gillies agreed with the yeoman's observation.

He had himself already assumed that the German ship was turning to starboard to bring her guns and torpedo tubes to bear. With the *Northampton* still zigzagging at high speed, he gave the order to open fire.

The first salvo straddled the German ship and thereafter she was hit repeatedly. When it was seen that her bridge and superstructure were on fire and that she had begun to settle by the bows, Captain Gillies ordered the cease fire. The fact that the German ship had not returned the cruiser's fire suggested that it was the *Hagenfels* and not the *Köln* but, deciding to take no chances, he turned away from the sinking ship and left the scene at high speed.

Before she was out of sight, Captain Gillies had the satisfaction of seeing the German vessel list over to starboard and sink, but it was not possible at that range to see whether any boats had got away.

Soon afterwards the Walrus reported that a lifeboat and some rafts had left the ship and that flying low over them the observer had counted sixteen survivors.

Captain Gillies spoke afterwards of his shock on learning that so few men had survived out of a ship's company which he estimated at not less than sixty if she were a supply vessel, and many times more if she were a raider. It was for this reason that he took the unusual step of ordering the Walrus to land on the water and interrogate the survivors. The sea was calm and no danger was involved. While this was being done, the *Northampton*, mindful of U-boats, carried on to the eastward at high speed.

Chapter Twenty-Two

As the cruiser approached, Widmark got the Newt to make a final inquiry from the wireless cabin but when the answer came it disposed of their last hope: the emergency transmitter was not yet working, though Mike Kent hoped to have it going fairly soon.

'Fairly soon,' echoed Widmark hopelessly. That was likely to be too late. With his binoculars on the approaching ship he thought grimly of the course of events which, starting so promisingly, threatened now to end in disaster. The utterly unforeseen had occurred. Never in their most pessimistic moments had they assumed in their planning that they might be without means of communicating with a British warship with which they were in visual touch. They had been incredibly unlucky. The damage to the R/T in the fight with Moewe; the German steward's sabotaging of the ship's main W/T installation; the absence of an Aldis lamp; the sinking of the *Havana City* and the consequent hue and cry which had brought the Walrus and the cruiser on to the scene and, finally, the refusal of the aircraft to close to a range from which she could read either the signal torch or the flag hoists, or to go up sun when the mirror could have been used.

The pressing question was, what would the cruiser do?

Would she come sufficiently close to read the *Hagenfels*'s signals or alter course to port so that she could read a mirror signal?

Widmark, too, knew about the *Sydney-Kormoran* action; he, too, had read the Confidential Admiralty Fleet Order, and he had few illusions about what was likely to happen.

It was a macabre situation, standing there waiting, powerless to alter the course of events, yet hoping against hope that the worst would not happen and that somehow the flag hoists would be read.

Immediately after sighting the cruiser, Widmark had passed the word that it might be necessary to abandon ship but he could not yet indicate which side. Johan, with the help of the Newt and the Germans, had turned out lifeboats on either side and cut away the lashings from life-rafts so that they would float clear if the ship sank.

Thereafter, Johan went back to the women in the stern and the Germans gathered in front of number one hatch. Kuhn, the chief engineer, had come out of his drugged sleep, and Müller the steward was up and about with a bandaged head.

Wedel, still unconscious, was laid on a mattress under the break of the fo'c'sle, so that he could be carried to a boat or raft if necessary.

When the cruiser was about eight miles away a powerful signal lamp blinked from her bridge. It was the inevitable 'N-N-J,' followed in plain language by the equally inevitable 'Make your signal letters.' These signals were repeated several times. Widmark clenched his fists in angry frustration.

At 07.08 they heard gunfire and shortly afterwards there were shell splashes to port and starboard of the *Hagenfels*'s bow, about two cables distant from the ship.

Widmark knew that the *Hagenfels* was being called on to stop, but he knew also that if he stopped on that course with the cruiser on his starboard quarter—and with no wind —the flag hoists would droop and it would be impossible for them to be read at any range.

For these reasons he ordered speed to be reduced to 'slow' and course altered to starboard, so that the wind made by the movement of the ship would be sufficient to fly the flags, and so that the *Hagenfels* would be beam-on to the cruiser, thus making it possible for the hoists to be read if the warship closed the range. It was a desperate measure, but it was all he could do.

Less than two minutes after the turn to starboard began, he saw the bright flash of a salvo ripple along the cruiser's side—it was the last thing he was to see for shortly afterwards he lost consciousness as the shells exploded on the superstructure, destroying the bridge and blinding him.

During the next few minutes the *Hagenfels* was hit repeatedly and holed below the waterline in several places forward of the bridge; the funnel collapsed and a fire blazed amidships. In the wrecked wireless cabin, Mike Kent was dying—pinned down by wreckage, he was still conscious and through a mist of pain and delirium he knew that he had somehow failed though he could not remember in what way.

When the ship took on a list to starboard and began to sink slowly by the head, the shelling ceased. Down below, water was pouring into the engine-room and McFadden, unable to get a reply from the bridge, stopped the engines and went on deck, taking with him Hans le Roux and Fritz the greaser.

On the port side they found the German prisoners with Rohrbach, Mariotta and Di Brett sheltering under the awning deck. Above them there was the crackle of fire, smoke billowed and they were assailed by the acrid smell of burning paintwork. Cleo and Johan were nowhere to be seen. Rohrbach, dazed by the explosion on the bridge and partially blinded, thought they had gone to look for the others. The only prisoner missing was von Falkenhausen. Lindemann said he had been with them after the firing had ceased, but had since disappeared.

McFadden told Hans and the greaser to take the Germans round to the starboard side to get a lifeboat ready for lowering. After a moment of indecision, he went in search of the rest of the party, making for what was left of the bridge. Amid the smoking wreckage there he saw the remains of the starboard bridge ladder. Pulling himself up on to the deck outside the chart-house he came upon the body of the Newt. The Englishman lay on his back, spread-eagled, a small smile on his lips as if he were quietly amused at something. Inside the wrecked wheel-house McFadden found the others. Cleo was sitting on the deck near the wheel, with Widmark's head in her lap. There was an uneven wound across his forehead and his eyes were covered with blood, the face still black with stove-polish. McFadden heard him groan and Cleo, ashen and dry-eyed, stared at Johan. 'He's dying,' she said unsteadily.

McFadden saw that there was more than the face wound: Widmark's trousers were ripped about the thigh where torn flesh showed from a jagged wound, the blood pumping out, the pool on the deck steadily widening.

'Come on,' the Scot spoke roughly, checking his emotion. 'Fire's coming this way. Boat on the starboard side's ready for lowering. We won't be afloat much longer.'

Johan stooped and gathered Widmark in his arms. McFadden shook his head. 'It's no good, laddie.'

'I'm not leaving him,' the big man said. He moved off

222

through the wreckage towards the port bridge ladder, staggering under the weight of his burden. They followed him down to the boat-deck and round to the lifeboat on the starboard side. With the help of his brother, Johan laid Widmark in the sternsheets. Then he gave Cleo a grubby handkerchief and told her to make a ball of it and try to plug the thigh wound. One of the German sailors came back and reported that he could not find the Freiherr. Hester asked Johan about Mike Kent. He looked away, shaking his head. 'He's had it,' he said gruffly, and the tears ran down her cheeks.

The bows were deeper in the sea and the list to starboard was increasing. There was the sound of water rushing into the foremost holds, and the sharp hiss of escaping air.

Di Brett was pale. Mariotta, still thick-headed from the drugs, looked round owlishly, and Karl Wedel, his life trickling away, lay in the bows of the lifeboat where the prisoners had put him.

Johan ordered them into the boat. The women went first: Di Brett, Cleo and Hester. Then the Germans: Müller, Schäffer, Fritz the greaser, Heuser and Francke, Kuhn and Lindemann. After them Rohrbach, McFadden and Johan. The German bosun, Kolbe, and Hans le Roux stayed on the boat-deck to man the falls. Johan gave the order to lower away. The falls squeaked through the running blocks and the lifeboat went down slowly, the list keeping it clear of the side. When it touched the water the falls were cast off and Hans and Kolbe slid down into the boat.

Paul Müller, his pale face agitated under his bandaged head, said: 'What about the Freiherr?'

Lindemann touched his arm. 'Be quiet, Müller,' he spoke gently.

'But we can't leave him behind,' the steward pleaded.

Di Brett's eyes were unnaturally bright. 'Why not?' she said. 'He's probably dead, anyway.'

On Johan's orders they bore off and rowed away from the *Hagenfels*. When they had gone about a hundred yards, they rested on their oars and sat watching her. Clouds of black smoke climbed into the air, twisting and turning, and fire glowed through the portholes in the deck-house amidships. Slowly at first, but with increasing speed, the ship listed over to starboard and with a vast hissing and sucking began to slide, bows first, beneath the sea. The stern remained, perched at a curious angle, as if unwilling to make the final plunge; then it, too, had gone and where the ship had been there was turbulent water and great bubbles came from the vortex and blew obscenely into the heat of the day. Two life-rafts floated clear, and for some time afterwards grating and other pieces of wreckage came to the surface. Diesel fuel, dark and oleaginous, formed in pools and spread, its pungent odour hanging in the air.

The survivors were silent, all feelings of race, of friend and enemy, put aside as they watched the ship go. Absorbed in this, they scarcely noticed the aircraft flying low over them, so low that Johan saw the face of the pilot through the perspex windshield. Twice the Walrus circled before it landed on the sea and taxied towards them.

Cleo was sitting in the sternsheets with Widmark's head in her lap. Her lace handkerchief was over his eyes. It had been white, but now it shone carmine and limpid, glistening in the sun like a jewel. She bent her head over his as if she were listening.

Hope rose in Johan. 'How is he?'

Cleo shook her head. 'He died—a few minutes ago.' Her voice was flat, toneless. 'He tried to say something—then he just died.'

The Walrus was close to them now. The engine stopped. The roof over the cockpit slid back and two heads appeared. One of the men put a small megaphone to his lips. 'Any of you speak English?'

There was a pause. Johan stood up in the sternsheets. His lungs were as powerful as the rest of him and he didn't need a megaphone. 'Yes!' he shouted, his deep voice rolling across the water. 'We do.' He hesitated. 'I suppose you silly bastards know you've sunk a British prize and——'

There was a lot more he wanted to say, but he shook his head and stopped.

After all, he thought, what's the use?